ALGIS BUDRYS

"Science fiction"—or SF, as I learned to call it from Judith Merril—takes up where unreality leaves off. It is a superb tool for exploring what is real about people and about the universe in general. Most fiction is devoted to perpetuating easy, comforting ideas. Some science fiction does the same, but in some cases it has at least no deliberate flaws of that sort . . .

Why do I, for instance, choose to write stories—not all of them "science fiction" but obviously all from the same world-view—which can be aptly collected under the descriptive title BLOOD AND BURNING? People have said I write about maniacs. Why do I like maniacs so much?

Well, few of them are *maniacs* to me . . .

from the author's *Introduction*

BLOOD & BURNING
ALGIS BUDRYS

A BERKLEY BOOK
published by
BERKLEY PUBLISHING CORPORATION

Copyright © 1978, by Algis Budrys

All rights reserved

Published by arrangement with the author

All rights reserved which includes the right
to reproduce this book or portions thereof in
any form whatsoever. For information address

Berkley Publishing Corporation
200 Madison Avenue
New York, New York 10016

SBN 425-03861-0

*BERKLEY MEDALLION BOOKS are published by
Berkley Pub ishing Corporation
200 Madison Avenue
New York, N. Y. 10016*

BERKLEY MEDALLION BOOK ® TM 757,375

Printed in the United States of America

Berkley Edition, SEPTEMBER, 1978

ACKNOWLEDGEMENTS

Be Merry Copyright © 1966, Galaxy Publishing Corporation

Wall of Crystal, Eye of Night Copyright © 1961, Galaxy Publishing Corporation

All for Love Copyright © 1962, Galaxy Publishing Corporation

A Scraping at the Bones Copyright © 1975, Conde Nast Publications, Inc.

The Price Copyright © 1960, Mercury Press, Inc.

The Ridge Around the World Copyright © 1957, Algis Budrys

The Girl in the Bottle Copyright © 1959, Great American Publications, Inc.

The Last Brunette Copyright © 1965, HMH Publishing Co., Inc.

Scream at Sea Copyright © 1954, Ziff-Davis Publishing Company, Inc.

The Master of the Hounds Copyright © 1966, Curtis Publishing Co., Inc.

The Nuptial Flight of Warbirds Copyright © 1978, Conde Nast Publications, Inc.

For Roland Meyer. Thank you.

Contents

BE MERRY	4
WALL OF CRYSTAL, EYE OF NIGHT	51
ALL FOR LOVE	74
A SCRAPING AT THE BONES	93
THE PRICE	110
THE RIDGE AROUND THE WORLD	114
THE GIRL IN THE BOTTLE	124
THE LAST BRUNETTE	131
SCREAM AT SEA	146
THE MASTER OF THE HOUNDS	155
THE NUPTIAL FLIGHT OF WARBIRDS	184

INTRODUCTION

I HAVE BEEN a professional writer some twenty-five years, now. This fact sometimes comes as a bit of a shock to the rather naive face that peers back at me from my shaving mirror. So does the thought that, after years as an editor, a print production consultant, an advertising and public relations man, a bicycle hobbyist with one repair manual to his credit and an anecdotal book on bicycles due to be published, a political speechwriter and campaign advisor, a biographer of Harry S Truman, a motor vehicle tester and columnist, a soccer organizer, a complexly middle-class householder and retired poultry farmer, I am nevertheless always introduced as "a science fiction writer." And rightly so. The nonwriting is done for the liking of it, or the occasional need of a paycheck. The writing is done because I cannot help but do it. And it is usually in some of the many forms recognized as "science fiction," though far from always.

"Science fiction"—or SF, as I learned to call it from Judith Merril—takes up where unreality leaves off. It is a superb tool for exploring what is real about people and about the nature of the universe in general. Most fiction is devoted to perpetuating easy, comforting ideas that make life softer for us. Some science fiction does the same, sometimes with more ingenuity. All science fiction, like any other human expression, is full of hidden flaws of self-delusion. But in some cases it has at least no deliberate flaws of that sort. I leave it to you to decide how well I hew to that ideal. But I can tell you I try, very hard.

The publishers of this volume have asked me to tell you something about each of the stories here. I have done so, in a shortish blurb preceding each one. I hope you do not find me immodest, and I hope you are not dismayed by some of my motivations and the sources of my inspiration. To the best of m ability to determine, they are different only in detail from those of any other writer I know, or have reliably learned about. But any given story springs from my general background as a human being who is unreservedly bound to express reactions to what he notes around him . . . that is, who is an artist.

It so happens I write more successfully than I draw, sculp, sing, or act. And so I tell stories, within which it is usually not too difficult to see what has been of particular interest to me this time. But what is of general interest, and why? It's a big world, with much happiness and charm to be found in it. Why do I, for instance, choose to write stories—not all of them "science fiction," or even "SF," but obviously all from the same worldview—which can be aptly collected under the descriptive title, *Blood and Burning*? People have said I write about maniacs. Why do I like maniacs so much?

Well, few of them are maniacs to me. They are people whose motivations are focussed on some single object, so that I can show them to you better. In real life, such people would give the impression of mania. But many of my characters have other thoughts, and do other deeds at other times; it's that they're not doing them right this minute. Some of them are only just entering upon whatever singleminded activity confronts their consciousness as the story opens. Others are going to abandon their immediate drama as soon as the story ends, though they will certainly not be the same as they once were.

None of them does anything I don't believe is possible to a driven but logical person. Although, of course, some of them are doomed by their actions in the story. I like them. None of them—certainly not the crippled ex-officer with his Dobermans, or the overwrought architect in Panorama Towers, or the man who called his neighbors chicken punks—is villainous to me. I love them. I do not love Dusty Haverman, but, then, where is he to be found, that someone might love him? I feel for him as much as he could feel for you or me. I love Austin Gelvarry.

Nevertheless, I am a writer because when I was very young I laid eyes on the great maniac. I stood in the window of an apartment in what was then Königsberg, East Prussia, and watched Adolf Hitler go by in the back of his open black ~~car~~. I watched the onlookers—my neighbors, their ~~k~~indergarten playmates, the adolescent boys and girls who lived in that city where Immanuel Kant lies buried in a cathedral, the impeccable *poliziers* who directed traffic and were always so helpful—lose all control of themselves. They ran for the bushes in the park and on our front lawn, tugging at their clothes, clutching at each other, fainting, soiling themselves, and making an indescribable sound. For someone who has just been given his first book of instructive Doré-illustrated tales from the New Testament, who has just emerged from a fascination with matters of the toilet, and who at other times had been coddled and fawned over by some of those same confident and knowledgeable inhabitants of a rational and essentially conformable world, this sort of thing comes as a revelation. In short, when I was four, the thunderclap fell upon me that I was come to consciousness in a world of werewolves.

I would not put it so strongly now. And it wasn't all that much longer before I discovered that I had no business holding myself out to myself as an aloof—and blameless—observer who need have no fear of the full moon. You give me the right reason, and I will be as hairy as the next lycanthrope, in an instant. Or something as close to it—as foolish, as hopeful, as essentially optimistic. They really thought he was making them better, you know. He could do it to them not because he promised conquest and material comfort—those were means and products. What he promised them, I really think, was that they would no longer be constrained by circumstance from being able to do the noble and right thing every time. No matter what.

And that is hope. All my people have hope.

—Algis Budrys
Evanston, Illinois
1978

Some of my story scenarios assemble themselves over the years. This is one of them. First—when I was just beginning to list ideas I might write as SF professionally—I noted that eating an intelligent alien might not, under some circumstances, fall under the taboo of cannibalism. Then, years later, my family and I lived in a coastal Atlantic community—among good people, who were kind to us—which serves as the physical model for the locale of this story. Finally, one day in Illinois I had a need to think about immunology, and I thought about all this, instead.

You might say this story is a hell of a way to repay hospitality, and you might be right. But none of the people in this story is drawn from among our many friends in New Jersey, although they are equally human. The operatic scene is from my aunt, Vladislava Grigaitiene, prima donna of the Lithuanian State Opera, and from Delilah, *a neglected novel by Noah Goodrich.*

Be Merry

OUR OLD MAN is a good Old Man. His name is Colston McCall, and I don't know what he used to do before. Now he's Chief of Policing for the Western District of Greater New York, and he knows what's important and what isn't.

I was sitting under a big pine tree, feeling weak and dizzy. I had taken a load of aspirin, and my stomach wasn't feeling right. But it was a nice sunny day. I could feel the soft, lumpy bark giving in to the weight of my back. The branches made a sweet, shady canopy.

The ground was soft under the spongey pine needles, too, and it felt good sitting there, looking out over the meadows. There were wild flowers growing.

We might have had that ground plowed up, and people planting things. But there weren't enough people to plow up everything, and we had as many fields going as we had machinery for. We were doing our best. It still took a lot of people who had to go into the warehouses for packaged food that hadn't spoiled. There just wasn't any way we could have been organized better. We all had something useful to do, all of us who weren't in beds. I shouldn't have been sitting under any tree.

But it was a beautiful day, and I had been hurting bad all night and morning. The doctors in the hospital had given me a piece of paper saying I only had to work when I wanted to. I guess that means I only had to work when I could stand it, but if they had written it out that way it would have made a sadist out of anybody who asked me if I would do something for him. We've gotten very careful. Very considerate, in nice practical ways. Our manners are lousy, because there's no time to be polite, but it's true what people used to say—the fewer people are, the more important people become. I remember what it was like back before the Klarri had their accident, but I can't believe how mean people used to be to each other. I remember specific things they did to each other, and it gets me boiling mad because that's how I'd feel if somebody tried to do that kind of thing to me these days. It's how we'd all feel.

I think some of the things that used to make us sick, before, came from living like that. I think that if I was fifteen years younger and just coming to make my own way in the world we have now, I wouldn't have my trouble, and I wouldn't have to sit here thinking. I mean, a man like me who had come so well through the Klarri sicknesses should have had a lot to do in this world, and instead I was shutting off because of something the old world had done to me.

I wished I wasn't sitting under the tree. I wished I wasn't trying to soak it all in. I knew that if I could, I would soak in all the sun and pine trees and wild flowers in the world, just for me.

I had thrown away the note the doctor had given me on the back of a page torn off a calendar pad. Well, you don't keep a note like that. Not when it's been written with a pencil stub by the light of a gasoline lantern in a big tent. Not when the doctor's so tired, and the people in the tent are so bad off from sicknesses nobody knows. I mean you don't walk around with something like that in your pocket. I would rather just sit here for a while and feel guilty.

But, you know, you can't keep that up very long. You know all you're doing is playing with yourself, because any time you feel guilty for having something simple and clearcut like cancer, you're really just pretending you can afford luxuries. I didn't have to feel guilty about anything, not one blessed thing. But it's human to feel guilty, and the thing about any kind of pain isn't the pain. It's that it turns you back to that wet, helpless thing you were when you were born. You know the sky and the earth have gone soft and could smother you or swallow you any time. You know it's not that way for anybody else. Other people are still doing things in a world that will still be there and be dependable tomorrow. But you're not. You've poled your raft to a one-man island of jelly. So you enjoy the chance to put splinters into yourself. And that's playing.

I was just starting to get up when Artel, my partner, came walking to me from the Old Man's house. "Ed," he said. "Mr. McCall wants to talk to us."

"Right," I said, and the two of us walked back. Facing this way, I could see all the tents, and the houses that had been turned into offices, and the tracks of trucks and people cutting back and forth across what used to be the front and back lawns of the development. The whole thing was turning into a plain of mud, but at least there was a decent amount of space between the houses and a decent amount of open ground to put up tents and prefabs on, instead of everything jammed together the way it was in the cities and towns.

It was rotten in the cities and towns. Not just the fires, or the other kinds of trouble you get when a bunch of close-packed people get awfully sick and lose their heads. We were over that, but still when you went into some place where the buildings were like walls along the street and everything should have been alive and working, selling shoes and groceries, the feeling of death would come over you and you couldn't do anything useful. They used to talk about how people were all moving out of the cities, before. Maybe because they already had something like that kind of feeling. Anyway, this place where the Old Man had set up was a development out along Route 46, and back in there up in the hills, there were lakes and wild animals, and you had a better feeling. You had better contact with the permanent things of the world.

"Is he sending us out on something?" I asked Artel.

"Yes."

Artel didn't ever talk much. The Old Man had teamed us up about a year ago, and it worked well. Klarri are a lot like us. Their arms and legs are longer in proportion to their bodies, and their shoulders are wider. They have long, narrow skulls, with all the cerebral cortex formed over what would be the back of the brain in a human, so if you're a highbrow among the Klarri, you're a bigdome. When they haven't washed for a few hours, there's a light, rusty deposit that forms on their skins and turns them that color. And nobody likes the way their teeth look. If a human being had teeth like that, he had some bad vitamin deficiency when he was a kid. But they're decent people. When they look at a hospital, I think they feel exactly the way we would if spaceships of ours had brought pestilence to a whole world of theirs.

There's one other thing about Klarri. Their kids all walk bent forward, and so do some of their adults, because that's the way their spines are. But they have a lot of trouble with that. It's like appendicitis with humans, and there isn't a Klarr who isn't aware that he could have severe back trouble almost any time. So there's a lot of them have had a fusing operation on the lower spinal column, either because they became crippled, or they started to feel little twinges and they got worried and had it done right away. It's just like people. Only instead of appendicitis scars, the ones who've had the fusing operation have this funny way of walking and standing as if they were about to fall over backwards. Artel was like that, but he also had to wear a back brace because he'd been hurt in the lifeboat crash that killed his wife and children. Back braces are faster than re-fusing operations.

You see, there can't be any doubt about it any longer. You do the best you can. We don't much believe in theory any more. You can be as civilized as the Klarri, and know you shouldn't go around contaminating other people's worlds, but when your faster-than-light ship breaks down and you've got to ditch, you pile into the lifeboats and you ditch. If you're really lucky you've had your FTL breakdown within reaching-distance of a solar system, and the solar system's got a planet you can live on; you come down any way you can, and you don't put decontamination high on your priority list. Life is hard; it's hard for Klarri, it's hard for humans. You spend each day living with whatever happened the day before, and that's it—that's how it is in all Creation, for everything with brains enough.

II

Colston McCall was a big man—there must have been a time when he weighed close to two hundred fifty pounds. He was way over six feet tall, and now he was all muscle and bones except for a little bit of a belly. He was about fifty or fifty-five, I guess, and he would lean back in his chair and look at a problem and solve it in a voice that must have been hell on his help in the days when he was running some kind of company. Whenever he raised his voice and called out a man's name, that man would get there quickly.

We went through into his office, and he looked up and waved us toward a couple of folding metal chairs. "Sit down, men." We did, with Artel straddling his chair backwards the way cowboys did in movie saloons.

"How are you feeling, Ed?"

"All right."

The Old Man looked straight at me for just a second. "Can you go twenty miles to someplace where there might not be any doctors?"

Well, the only other answer to that is, "No sir, I'm ready to lie down and die," so I didn't say that.

"All right. There's a town down the coast where nobody's sick."

Artel sat up straight. "I beg your pardon?"

The Old Man laid his hand down flat on a small stack of papers. "These people have never asked for any medicines. Now, I don't know what that means. We first contacted them about two and a half years ago. One of our scouts found a party from their town foraging through the highway discount houses down along Route 35, there."

I nodded. That was the usual pattern in those days. The towns were all gutted on the inside, and any survivors had to start spreading out and looking for supplies outside. But that was a mug's game. You burned up what fuel you had, running emptier and emptier trucks farther and farther, coming back with less and less. What happened after that was they'd pool their remaining fuel, load everybody into the trucks and come busting up north, because everybody had the idea the big city had to be different.

The Old Man went on: "Well, it turned out that, for once in a great while, these were the kind of people who'd stay put if we'd promise to send food down. So that's how it's been ever since."

And pretty grateful we were, too, I thought.

"Well, that was all right," the Old Man said, "but it's getting to be too much of a good thing, maybe. They're not complaining at all. You've got to figure any medical supplies they might have had left would be pretty much down to basics by now. Your antibiotics and your other fancy drugs either don't exist any more or have turned to mush. Well, hell, you know that."

We knew. It was the biggest problem we had; things were tightening up pretty badly. And it wasn't any use being able to grow penicillin or any of those fermentation drugs you don't need much of a plant for. All that stuff was just so much extra peanut butter on the sandwich for the strains of bug we had now.

"But these people don't seem to have noticed that. They don't even complain about their food; they take whatever the trucks bring, they never ask for more, they never ask for anything different from what they get. I don't like it when people don't gripe about what we can deliver. And these people just take it and go away with it and never say a word."

"How many people?" I asked.

"A hundred and eighty-odd. I cut down their ration by three per cent just to see what would happen. They haven't reacted at all. About the medicine, I had one of the drivers ask them if they needed a doctor, and they said no. They didn't say they had a doctor, and they didn't say they were all healthy. They just said 'No' and walked away."

"They're either very lucky or very generous," Artel said.

The Old Man gave him a quick look. "I'm always ready to believe in those things up to a point. But now I'd like to know if maybe there's something they haven't told anybody about."

Artel nodded.

I wanted to know about the food part. "What kind of a town is it?" I asked. "What kind of people are they? Could they be fishing or farming?"

"Not in that country," the Old Man said. "They're just property owners—squatters, some of them, but it's a community. All friends and relatives, all townies. Real estate agents, storekeepers, tree surgeons—all they know is how to sell cars and salt water taffy to each other." He sounded angry. The same thing angered us all: it had turned out farming was more than scratching the ground and dropping seeds into it. And it's slow, besides being hard to learn. He'd tell you just the opposite, but your hungry townsman would rather die than farm.

It sounds good, to just wave a hand and say, "Let there be light again." But *that's* the kind of thing that drives you wild. The Four Horsemen of the Apocalypse are ducks, and they nibble you to death.

"No, I don't believe it," the Old Man said, slapping the inventory control forms again. "Go down there and find out about it. Come back and tell me about it. Quietly."

"Of course," Artel said. "It wouldn't do to raise false hopes."

"Or even real ones." That was what made him a leader and me and Artel troopers. Our Old Man likes to go softly. He might not have been a top man before, when you had to move bing, bing, bing because the competition was clicking along right behind you. But he was good for us now.

You want to keep it soft. You want to take it slow and easy, and you have to know what to let slide. Cancer, they say, used to hit twenty-five per cent of the population in one of its forms or another. They had been pretty close to cures, before. They weren't any closer now, because you can afford to ignore something like that when you've had diseases that each kill sixty, seventy per cent in one summer.

You don't even care whether it was all the Klarri's fault or not. They were in awful trouble, too, cast away on an uncharted shoal, with our diseases beating the hell out of their survivors, and them with fewer biochemists than we had. I mean—what are you going to do? You could have some kind of lurching war and string them all up to lampposts, but there were better things to do with the energy, especially now that the first impact had passed and most of us that were going to die of each other were pretty much dead. If somebody was to put me in a time machine and send me back, the people then ought to shoot me down like a mad dog in the streets; I was carrying more kinds of death in me than anybody ever dreamed of, before. And if it wasn't for this home-grown thing of my own, I'd count as a healthy man by today's way of judging. So you don't worry about yesterday. You take what you have, and you work with it today.

"All right," the Old Man said. "Go down there, the two of you. Maybe we've got a miracle." That was as close as any one of the three of us got to laughing and clapping each other on the back and crying hallelujah.

I went down to the hospital while Artel waited for me. I walked through to the back, to where the dispensary was. The idea was, if you were well enough to walk in and ask for medicine, you had better be sick enough to walk by all those beds and still want medicine. I saw them all; the ones with the sores, and the ones with the twisted limbs, the ones with the blind eyes, and the ones with the hemorrhages. I heard them and I smelled them, human and Klarri.

These were survivors. The losers were dead. These were the ones you could expect still had a chance to live, if they could be kept strong enough to avoid things like pneumonia and the other killers of the weakened. I still had some kind of low-grade lymph node trouble. My arms would go to sleep, and I couldn't squeeze anything very hard without having my fingers go numb for hours afterward. While they were trying to do something about whatever bug it was that made my lymphatic system react, they found this other thing that had been living in me for quite some time already.

It didn't matter. I was around yet to walk down between the beds. Now, my Mary had drowned in her own blood. And I'd had this kid, about six, with his own little two-wheeler. A sidewalk bike, with solid rubber wheels, that was supposed to be for just diddling around in front of the house. Kind of a first step after graduating from a trike. There was an ice cream store that was open on Sundays fourteen blocks away from where we lived, and about ten days before the Klarri lifeboats came showering in from the sky, this kid and I had gone to that ice cream store, with me on my Sears, Roebuck three-speed and him on that boneshaker of his. Six years old, and pumping away like mad with just a little four-inch crank sprocket that gave him no speed at all, and me reminding him to slow down and pace himself, and him grinning over at me as he went bouncing over the potholes in the alleys. Good little kid.

The dispenser nodded when he saw me coming. He was a young Klarr, usually with his head bent over a medical dictionary; the wall had human and Klarr anatomical charts, and there was a human clerk putting together the mimeographed pages of a new medical text. We were beginning to shape up. For a long time, now, the Old Man hadn't been letting them put Klarr and human patients at separate ends of the tents. The idea was, if you were a doctor in the ward, by now you ought to be able to work most of the problems you saw no matter who had them. You'd have maybe one or two Klarr patients in the hospital at any time. It meant something that you'd always have more Klarr than that on the staff, or studying to join it.

Anyway, I showed the dispenser my Special Branch requisition permit, and he punched another notch on the edge of it and gave me a plastic bottle with twenty-five aspirins, and I said thank you and went back out through the tent. There was a supply truck running down to Trenton that would come within twenty or twenty-five miles of this place we were going to. Artel had drawn a couple of bikes from the transport pool for us on his permit and was just lashing them on to the side of the truck. We got in and we rode in the back, on top of a bunch of cases and bags. Artel made a kind of a hump-back pad out of bean sacks for himself and lay down on his stomach. I wedged myself into a nice tight fit where I wouldn't be bounced around too much, and after a while we took off.

III

The name of the town was Ocean Heights. After the truck dropped us, we moved toward it through some very pretty country, using the Garden State Parkway for a while. We had good gear; Artel's bike was a Peugeot and mine was a Raleigh, both of them fifteen-speed lightweights with high pressure tires and strapped pedals; they weren't specially comfortable, but they were very fast on any kind of decent surface, and with all that gearing to choose from, hill-and-dale touring was a snap.

We each had a .22 hunting rifle—the Old Man would have had our hearts if we'd carried anything to kill more people with—and some food, some tools and a water bottle apiece. We looked very technological, and you feel pretty good when you've got good gear. So we were both pretty well off in our own minds as we went zipping along, through the pine woods and along that smooth asphalt track. When we cut off and got onto Route 35, of course, we started running into signs of taffy salesman life—lots of roadside stands and one saloon painted DaGlo orange, and a lot of garden tool and outboard motor shops, along with great big discount centers. All of it looked shabby, beat up, and just a shell. There was nothing left in the discount houses but phonograph records, and little plastic pots to raise rubber plants in, and games made by the Wham-O Manufacturing Company. The wind was in off the ocean, and that was all right too.

It started to get dark while we were still five miles away from Ocean Heights. That was the way we wanted it.

We took ourselves a couple of miles farther, and then we cut out up a side road, into the woods. We found a good place to leave the bikes and made a little bit of a camp. It was good getting off the bike. Artel was walking very slowly, and he was leaning farther over backwards than ever. I didn't remark on it; I guess I've already said that in our own eyes from ten or fifteen years before, we'd all seemed like very rude people. Artel sighed when we were finally able to sit down and lean against something. So did I, I guess.

We sat down close together. Artel had one of those squeeze type flashlights that generates its own power. We put my windbreaker over our heads to muffle the light and we studied the map, laying out a heading for Ocean Heights from where we were. We'd be able to walk it in not much more than a couple of hours. We got our compass headings straight in our heads, and then we were able to come out from under the windbreaker, which was all right with me. One of the reasons Artel and I could work as a team was because I didn't mind his smell. (That was what I said; actually, I liked it). But not in big doses like this. It was like eating a pound of milk chocolate.

We'd done this kind of thing before; we knew what we were doing. A couple of hours from now, when it was still dark and we could expect most people to be thinking of sleep, we'd get moving, so that by the time we hit the place it would be tight-fast in dreamland. We'd ghost around and find out what we could. Get the lay of the land, figure an escape route and boltholes if we needed them. It sounds like playing Indians, but it's the kind of technique you work out when you're dealing with unknown people these days. You can't even tell in advance sometimes whether they're humans or Klarri; that was originally why a Special Branch team had to have at least one of each.

We sat in the woods and waited until it was time to move. We didn't talk much as a rule. For one thing what had happened to Artel's respiratory system gave him a lot of trouble with breath control. For another thing, life's too simple to need a lot of conversation. But it was lonely out there, and nightfall bothers me. "Listen," I asked Artel, "do you think your people will ever find you?"

"Pretty unlikely," he said after a while. "The volume they'd have to search is mighty big." After a while he added: "It'd be better if they didn't. We'd be as deadly now to our home as we were to you." I could see him smile a little. "We Klarri here have traded too much back and forth with Earth. We've become much more like you than like our people."

He folded his arms with his hands over his shoulders, the way they do. "I don't see much difference between us, in anything, really. Our machinery may be a little better. But most of us don't understand it any better than you understand yours. We lose ships, once in a while. We don't find them any more often than you'd expect. We have to pretend this isn't so, because otherwise we couldn't sell tickets to each other."

"Travel agents about the same any place, I guess," I said.

He shrugged. "Civilization's about the same any place. You take a ship from one star to another, and you say to yourself,

'Here's something my father couldn't do.' It's true. My father couldn't infect a world with a population of three billion, either. Nor lose an interstellar passenger ship. And end with only a few thousand survivors from it. And have a whole future to solve."

He pushed himself down and lay on his back for a minute, with his hands behind his head, looking up. "I'm glad I don't have to imagine how they're going to do it." He didn't sound particularly worried; well, it wasn't our problem. I'd heard humans and Klarri talk about things like what'll happen when we build spaceships again. It's a cinch they won't be rockets; they'll be a lot like the Klarr ships, I guess. But where will they go? Looking for planets where Klarri and humans from Earth could start the same business of living together, or contacting the Klarr worlds, or what? What would happen if we met Klarri from some political faction that didn't like our Klarri? Well, there are damn fools everywhere, I guess. When the real problems really came, they'd more than likely have some shape of their own, and they'd either be solved or flubbed in some way that was possible to their own time.

"You heard about this new idea?" Artel said cautiously. "There's some biochemist with a hypothesis. He says that with two or three generations of gene-manipulation, it might be possible to have Klarr- and human-descended compromise people who could breed true with each other. Think there's anything to that?"

"I've heard that. What do I know?" It shouldn't have, but the idea made my stomach turn. I guess Artel felt the same way.

"It's an idea," Artel said, and I could see he didn't like it any better than I did. But that was one of those things the two of us didn't have to worry about. And I appreciated what he was trying to do. You try to make as much contact as you can. Probably the Old Man had put us together originally because we were both lonely in the same way. Everybody wants to see a team as good as possible. Just for its own sake; not just because so many of the Klarr ships had happened to hit the Western Hemisphere. Other places, there'd been so few Klarr, I think they killed them all during the pestilence feelings. There were people who talked about national pride being involved; they said a lot of things like that, maybe getting ready to hand the next generation something they could go to war about.

Talk's all right in its place. Now we'd done some, Artel and I just waited in the woods.

IV

At about ten o'clock we started to slide into the outskirts of Ocean Heights. These Jersey coast towns are all a lot alike. There's always a highway paralleling the ocean, leaving a strip maybe three miles wide with feeder roads running down to the Atlantic. Follow the feeder road and you find you're on the main street of some town that was in its heyday in 1880. Right up near the water there'll be a strip of big Steamboat Gothic summer homes; frame and shingle construction, three, four storeys high, with lots of cupolas, and gingerbread, and maybe even an imitation widow's walk. Big verandas, hollow wooden columns and lots of etched glass in the ground-floor windows. Some people think that's a sign of gracious living. I think it just proves how much we wanted mass production.

Closer in toward town there'll be a lot of stores. Some of them will have bright new cast stone or aluminum fronts, but the buildings are all fifty years old behind them. There'll be a couple of yellow fire-brick structures, with almost anything in on their ground floors now, that used to be the A & P and the Woolworth's. Those moved out to the shopping center back in the 1950's. There'll be a couple of movie theaters, and one of them was closed long before the trouble hit the town itself. There's a Masonic Temple, churches of various Christian denominations, a hotel for little old ladies and salesmen. Used car lots full of stuff carrying ten dollars worth of paint over the salt rust. A railroad track. A couple of television repair stores, and a weekly four-page newspaper dedicated to getting people to shop at home.

On the ocean there are some seafood restaurants, a miniature golf course and a building that looks like a horse barn but in the summertime houses a wheel of fortune and a couple of dart-toss games, with most of the stalls standing empty even in the height of the season. The parking lot for the oceanfront amusements is where the dog track used to be. The boardwalk is falling down everywhere. There are piles and sheets of rusty iron sticking up out of the beaches farther along, where the boardwalk used to reach. The people say it's the Republican legislators from the inland counties, with their blue laws, that killed these towns. If you approach from the beach, the first thing you notice is the plastic-coated paper from the frozen custard stands. It doesn't mash up and wash into the ground at all; it just turns gray.

We slid on in through the outskirts. Artel said: "It was bad here."

Looked like it. There were a lot of burnt pits full of bricks and pieces of charred timber, with dead trees standing around them, where there had been fires. There was all sorts of trash in the gutters, swept in from the fires and the general scraps that blow around and pile up when nobody collects them. The gutters were clogged with odd pieces of wood, tarpaper, sand and gravel. The sewer grates were all choked, and the streets were broken down. Rain water and frost had broken up the asphalt and undermined the cement. Some of the streets had been laid in brick, and they now looked as if long walls had collapsed onto the ground. It wasn't unless you looked hard, toward the ocean, that you could see the occasional lantern burning and could believe that anyone lived on beyond this mess.

We found only one street that was really open. It had truck ruts in it, with trash smashed down into them, and unmarked sand washed into pools in other places. The last supply run had been a couple of weeks ago, and it looked as if our trucks were the only things that came and went. Once we had found the main drag this way, we moved off away from it and worked our way along the back streets. We came across dead cars, and the weathered tumble-down of barricades. Once I tripped over a shotgun with a broken stock; the wood grainy from rainwater and sunlight, the barrels just tubes of rust. "You'd think they'd have cleaned up the useful things," Artel said.

"It's broken."

"But it could have been fixed."

"No, not here," I said. The soil was sand, just one great big bar that the Atlantic had raised over thousands of years of pounding itself up against the rock coast of what were now the northern counties, and you couldn't raise anything on it but scrub pine. West of the line running from New York down to

Camden you were off the interstate highways and main railroads. The only thing you could do with this part of the world was sleep in it and play in it, and sell taffy to each other. We'd passed a horse-racing track coming in. Big looming plant, standing dirty in the darkness. Its parking lots had been full of cars, and there was a smell, originally trapped in all that wet upholstery, that hung in the air. That was as far as they'd gotten—the people trying to get out of the city. They were turned back by the local cops, cursing and sweating, and thanking God there was some place to point to where all those people could go to die.

Farther in toward the town we passed the Women's Club building—a big place with a phony Grecian front, that the local people had probably tried to make into a supplementary hospital at this end of town. We padded on up the steps, and there were three-year-old bodies right up against the doors, inside. We backed off.

"We won't find anyone living right around here," Artel said. Twenty years from now, the Women's Club building and the cinderblock walls of the bowling alley down the street would be all that stuck up out of the second growth. There'd be trees growing out of the sewers.

We crossed the railroad tracks, and we stood there as if we'd just sat straight up in bed in the middle of the night. The first thing I noticed was the smell of fresh paint. But there was plenty of other stuff to hit you, all at once.

It must have been one of the best parts of the town to begin with. The houses were brick, two and three storeys high. They were all set in the middle of very nice lots, and most of them had those Georgian fronts that spell class. In daylight, we might have seen soot and patches in some of the brickwork, but we didn't see it now. All the outlines were crisp and sharp; there wasn't a warped board or a sagging roof anywhere here. There were neat, well located privies in the backyards, we found as we started to move around. The fronts of them were made out of brick and had shrubs planted around them.

It was all like that. The hedges were trimmed. The lawns were like velvet. There wasn't a chipped place in any sidewalk, nor litter on the grass, or anything.

There were lanterns burning upstairs in two or three of the

houses. "What the hell?" I said. There were eight or ten solid blocks of this stuff. All it needed was a wall around it.

"This is 'way off the supply route," Artel said. "To see this part, you'd have to do what we did. You notice the trees—how thick they are? I think they even had airplanes in mind when they picked this spot."

"Listen," I said. From one of the houses, through a window open to the soft night air, you could hear it: *"Bella figlia del amore . . ."*

"What is that?" Artel asked.

"Opera. Somebody's got a windup phonograph."

"Or a generator."

"But no bulldozer to bury his dead with."

Artel looked back over his shoulder toward the other side of the railroad tracks. "That is different."

We kept moving, with faint music. There was no other living sound. No night birds, no cats in love, no dogs. There wasn't any sound of people sneaking through yards. This town didn't have teenagers who liked to visit each other. All these people were locked up tight in their little clean town-within-a-town, most of them sleeping the sleep of the innocent. The innocent and the healthy.

We worked our way closer toward the ocean. We were only a block away from it. The waves were rolling in to the shore regularly and gently, making the only steady sound we could hear, now that we were out of range of the phonograph. I looked back over my shoulder, and I could see nothing but those few upstairs lights, some of which had been put out since we had gone by. Solid citizens turning in. I thought they were lantern lights. They might have been lightbulbs on low voltage. We were getting more questions than answers out of this town.

We got down to the beach, and we found another dirty fringe—a motel with its windows broken out, a playground with scrub bushes growing up among the teeter-totters and the monkey bars, a flight of wooden steps tumbled down the stone jumble of the sea wall. If you had been going by in a boat you would have never known about that neat little clean patch with its edged flower beds and its unlittered streets.

There was a big, dark building just inland of the playground.

Flat-sided and square, it was two storeys high, and the ground floor windows were well over the height of a man's head, long and very narrow. If this was a war, and the building was at a crossroads, I would have reported it for a bunker. The sign over the doorway said "Ocean Heights Professional Bldg." The double doors were at the head of a flight of stairs set back and flanked by solid masonry. I could have defended it from the inside with one machine-gun. There was a padlock hanging on the doors, closing a chain looped through the handles.

"There was a gambling casino in Ocean Heights during World War II," Artel said. He was the one who'd gone through the Old Man's background file on the town. "It was closed by state investigators in 1947."

"We've found it." Going by the delicately scalloped, once white-painted directory board bolted to the wall beside the stairs, an architect and a real estate agent had set up offices in it after the space became available. There was no sound in it now, and no lights. But I noticed something, and it made me wonder. I pulled in a deep breath through my nose.

"It's not empty." I said.

"I agree," Artel said. "I have that feeling. And yet I can't say why." In the starlight, I could see him shake his head quickly. "It bothers me. It was built to be a hiding place. They might be doing almost anything in there."

"Let's look around some more," I said.

"If you say so," Artel said hesitantly.

The other thing we found was down at the beach. It was something looming, most of it under the water, the waves phosphorescing weakly against the one side that we could see. It stretched away into the darkness, and its curved sides went up like the biggest dead whale in the world. I could see a long strut extending out over the water at a shallow angle, and the round circle of a landing pad hanging at a crazy angle from the end of it. It was a crashed Klarri lifeboat.

"What happened to the people in it, I wonder," Artel said.

"They're in that building back there. Locked up and kept out of sight," I said. I had smelled them, the scent seeping out weakly through the double doors and God knew how many other barriers inside. "What do you want to do about it?"

It was up to him. They were his people. If he wanted us to go in there and break them out now, I didn't see any way for me not to help him. Maybe we could get away with it; I wasn't crazy about the idea of trying to do all that without making any noise, but it was up to him. "Anything you say."

"Come off it, Ed. We don't know anywhere near enough about the situation in this place. We haven't found what we were sent for." Artel sounded a little mad. He had a right to be. I'd as good as said he wasn't a team man. I felt bad about having been rude. "Come on—let's go back to camp," he said. "We had a plan and let's follow it." Artel slipped off into the darkness.

I followed him. We didn't say anything more to each other that night. We got back to our camp and sacked out.

A team is a little bit like a marriage. I don't care what anybody says, sometimes it's better not to talk it out. It makes you feel like hell for a while, but you've got an even chance the next morning one or the other of you will say some thing in a friendly way and then the other one will feel relieved and it will be all over.

V

In the morning we went in straight. There's no point to horsing around. If we'd had things like phone taps, snooper microphones and truth serum to work with, we might have decided on something different. But life's too simple these days for any of that kind of stuff to be worth a damn. We'd just ask them questions, and then see what their lies added up to.

Coming down the main drag on our bikes, we went through the dead shopping district of the town and then cut right on a concrete street a couple of blocks in from the ocean. I figured we'd be coming up to signs of life soon.

What we heard first was the sound of a ball bat from some field two or three blocks away and off to our right, somewhere near where the clean patch of houses was. We couldn't see anything, but we could hear kids yell; it was the kind of noise you get from a schoolyard at recess time.

We made another half a block, still going by houses that were all abandoned, and then we heard some little kid yelling "Daddy! Daddy! Daddy!" The sound of fast little feet on the floor of a veranda went clattering in echoes along the street, and then a screen door slammed shut. We'd finally been spotted. We stopped and began walking our bikes up the middle of the street.

About a hundred fifty yards ahead there was a traffic light hanging from guy wires over an intersection. There were a couple of gas stations there, and the drive-in apron of an ice cream stand. It made a kind of open place where you might expect people to gather when you unloaded your supply truck. Between there and us there were a couple of houses that might be lived in. They didn't have any broken glass in their windows, and there were light-colored streaks of unpainted putty in places along the sash. They didn't look neat, but they looked livable. They looked about the way you might expect houses to look in a town, if it wasn't a town on its feet enough to have that nice little residential section tucked away back there.

A screen door slammed again, and this time we caught the direction of the sound. It was coming from a couple of houses down and to our right. It was a big green three-story house, and we could see faces at the windows, but the glass was dirty, and we couldn't tell much about them. What we could see was the man coming out from the veranda and walking down the front steps. He stood there for a minute as we came closer.

He was a tall, thin, oldish-looking man with a checked shirt and suit pants, wearing glasses and carrying a pipe in his hand. He looked seedy and comfortable, with the pants hanging down flat and butt-sprung behind, and the knees baggy in front. He waved a hand at us in a nice neighborly way, and then he walked around the side of the house. There was a sudden hammering of metal on metal—a wild, carrying sound—and all the other noises we'd been hearing stopped. The only things to listen to were the steady wash of the ocean off to our left and the grit of our tires on the street. The man came back from around the house just as we reached his front walk. He had bushy salt-and-pepper hair growing out of the sides and back of his head, and a streak of it growing back from his forehead; his hairline was shaped like a thick-tined pitchfork, and he reminded me of all the retired men who might come around to your place in the summertime and help you build a rose arbor for a few dollars.

"Howdy!" he said. "Didn't hear you coming." He was looking closely at Artel. I had the feeling he was having trouble making up his mind whether Artel could possibly be a Klarr.

"Howdy," I said. "My name's Ed Dorsey. This is my partner, Loovan Artel. Artel's his first name. What was all that racket?"

The man came forward and stuck out his hand. "My name's Walter Sherman. Got one of those iron fire-alarm rings set up next to the house. I kinda let people know when we've got company. Pleased to meet you." He shook my hand, and then he gave Artel another look, very fast. He thought it over and shook Artel's hand. "Pleased to meet *you*."

"My pleasure," Artel said, grinning a little.

Sherman blinked once. He was trying to act right. He was doing pretty well, I thought, considering he hadn't ever before seen a Klarr wearing human clothes and riding a bicycle. Sherman looked all right, too. He was getting old, but there was a nice glint in his eye and good color in his face. His hair wasn't dead and dull, and the whites of his eyes were clear. He didn't move or talk like a man who was anywhere near sitting down and waiting to get older. He looked like an upstanding gent, and you don't get to see very many of those any more.

I took a quick look around.

There were people beginning to show up. One or two of them were coming out of nearby houses, but most of them were beginning to gather down at the intersection under the traffic light, coming up side streets and back from where the clean houses were. Just looking down that way, if you were a supply truck driver, say, you'd guess that they had all come out of the houses down there. "We're from Philadelphia," I said to Sherman. "Survey team." Artel and I got cards out of our shirt pockets and showed them to him. They were signed "F. X. Daley, United States Commissioner, Philadelphia District."

"We're just starting to check this part of the country," I said as Sherman took the cards in his hand and studied them, peering and blinking with the pipe in his mouth. The pipe was cold and empty—had been for years, probably. "We'd just like to find out a little bit about this community—how many people, what kind of social organization . . . that kind of thing."

"That's right, sir," Artel said. "We'd appreciate your cooperation. Or if you'd rather direct us right away to your mayor or whoever's in charge, why, we'll get out of your front yard and let you go back to what you were doing."

"Oh, no—that's all right," Sherman said, handing us back the cards. "I imagine there'll be some people from our Town Council here in a minute. Glad to help."

There wasn't any doubt we were bothering him. He was talking off the top of his head and thinking very hard about something else. I wondered for a minute if these people had some way of knowing there wasn't anything in Philadelphia—not a blessed thing—but it didn't seem likely. One of the hardest things to be sure of in this world is nothing.

"Well, come in and—" He waved with his pipe toward the steps of his veranda. "Ah, why don't you sit down?" He was looking at the touring saddles on our bikes. "I imagine it might be nice to rest yourselves on something flat."

He tried to chuckle. He was trying to be pleasant, he really was. But we had caught him off base very bad by not coming into town with a truck engine roaring ahead of us, and by not both of us being human.

We sat down on his front steps. We left our bikes up on their kick-stands, with the .22's strapped down to the carriers, just like any survey team would have.

"You—ah—people look bushed," Sherman said. "You come all the way from Philadelphia on those bikes?"

I nodded. "Easy stages, yeah," I told him. "There's a lot to check out." He looked a lot healthier than either one of us, that was for sure.

"We ought to explain," Artel said. "It's the people who can't do a regular day's work they can spare for things like surveys." Like me, he was watching the bunch of people coming toward us. They were walking fast. Not running; just coming on at a good pace. There were young and old, and a few kids, a good mixed human crowd coming to the railroad station to watch the streamliner go by. A good, healthy crowd. Even not running, they were moving faster than any bunch of people I'd seen in years. They looked good; clean, eager. They looked the way people ought to look when something exciting is happening. You could see the front ones slow down and frown as they made out what Artel was.

A freckled man in suntans and a rainhat, with squint-wrinkles around his blue eyes, came through them as they began to gather into a clump on Sherman's front lawn. "Hi, Walt!" he said as he came up to us. "I see you got company."

"Couple of government men from Philadelphia," Sherman said.

"Philadelphia, eh?" he said, shaking hands with us as we stood up. "My name's Luther Koning. Pleased to meet you both."

"Luther's sort of like our mayor," Sherman explained.

Whatever he was, he was the man we'd come to see. I guessed he was about fifty; all long, flat muscle under that weather-tight skin, and able to act as if it was nothing unusual to see a Klarr walking around instead of being in that big, silent building out behind the abandoned playground. He had fast reactions, Koning did, and where other people had slowed to a walk and stopped, he had come on forward.

"Glad to meet you," I said. I told him my name, and I told him: "This is Artel, my partner."

"Mm-hmm," Koning said. "Well, I can see that," he said in an agreeable enough voice, looking over at the bicycles and the two rifles. "Two equally intelligent races in the same jam, after all. They waste their strength in fighting, there's no hope at all. So they work together. It makes sense." He looked at me and then at Artel. "You look tired—both of you. Things still aren't so good in the big city, huh?"

"Things aren't so good anywhere, Mr. Koning," Artel said. "But we're trying to make them better. That's why we're here."

"Why *are* you here?" Koning grinned again. "We're standing here talking, and for all I know you two are anxious to get something done right away."

"They've got I.D. cards here from Philadelphia," Walter Sherman said. He had gotten a chance to settle down some, and his voice was easier. But he was really fast in getting that across to Koning, even though he said it in a careless voice. "Gave me a turn, coming in that way. On bicycles." He chuckled: "Real fancy machines, those are. Smart idea. Saves on gasoline." I think the point he was trying to make was that we were dissimilar from the people who came in trucks, and that we might not even know about any other organization.

"We're just trying to find out if you people need anything," I said harmlessly to Koning. I was watching the crowd. There were thirty or forty of them, and it seemed to me that any time you can collect twenty per cent of the total population at the drop of a hat, you're dealing with an excitable population. But they didn't look jumpy the way a crowd of sick-nervous people might. You don't see the kind of shuffling and fevery face-jerking you get sometimes. These people weren't looking for excitement. Sick people need excitement because it interrupts their misery. When they get it, they lose their dignity; it's a dose of the stuff they crave, and when you pour it out in front of them they can't hide how much they need it. These people weren't like that. They didn't need to be a mob. But they were very, very interested. Like members of the same club, and a famous guest-lecturer. There wasn't a Klarr among them. That would have struck me even if I hadn't known about the special building.

I couldn't make this crowd out. I kept looking at them; men of all ages, housewife-types in cotton print dresses, some of them with water-spotted aprons around their middles where they'd been washing up the breakfast dishes. There were young men in T-shirts, who looked as if they'd been working around the yard, and older men who were like Sherman and Koning in looking like they'd lived useful, cheerful lives, and had a lot of useful time in them. It was the kind of crowd that gives you the feeling life is comfortable and pleasant all the time. There wasn't another one like it in the whole world.

It bothered the hell out of me. Some of the kids had brought their gloves and started a game of catch out beyond the fringes of the crowd. Other kids were circulating back and forth; you couldn't get their attention with a conversation on a veranda, but they were either going to be where the attraction was, whatever it was, or they were going to spread the news. Some of them had been up to Sherman's house and back down to the intersection several times already. Now one of them on the edges of the crowd yelled: "Here comes Tully!" Koning turned around as if he'd been shot, but he recovered nicely.

"Hey! Let's keep it down; we're trying to talk here," he said.

But he kept looking sideways over at a man ambling along the sidewalk, so Artel and I did too.

VI

Tully was like one of those men you'll see sitting on a beachfront bench staring out over the water. Nobody can do anything for or to them. They're past the big tussle. He had given up trying to look as if God never made pot bellies, and was wearing loose-weave light pants with a big, comfortable waistline and baggy legs. He had rubber-soled cloth shoes on and bright socks that you could see showing under the flipping cuffs of his pants. He had broad-strap suspenders holding up his pants, and he was wearing a short-sleeved, bright shirt. His bare arms were thin and knobby, tanned an even darker and shinier brown than Koning's face was under his freckles. He was wearing a headband with a transparent green eyeshade. There was a fringe of white hair around his stuck-out ears, and the top of his skull was tanned and glistening. He had a big, amiable grin. He walked along as if he had all the time in the world, knowing that he was a center of interest, too, and the rest of the show would wait for him.

Neither Koning nor Sherman said a word. People will do that. People think that if they stop, time stops.

Tully ambled into the crowd, still grinning, and the crowd drifted out of his way. There wasn't anything obtrusive about it; it wasn't like the Red Sea parting for Moses into two straight-edged and shiny walls. It was just that they drifted out of his way, easily and naturally as if everybody in town knew from a baby that you didn't stand close to Tully. Tully walked forward, still grinning.

He cocked his undersized, round-chinned, round face up at the veranda. He looked at Artel, and then he looked past Koning and me at Sherman. When he spoke, his voice was high, like the cackle of a chicken with the biggest egg in the yard. "Ah-heh, Doc. Heard you had one of them Hammerheads visiting on your porch." He looked Artel up and down. "Looks like a prime example, considerin' how puny critters are these days."

He looked at me now. His eyes under the shade were small and black, and smart. "His partner don't look so good either, does he?" He stood there with his little squirrel-paw hands hooked into the front of his trousers, and when he began to laugh, first his cheeks quivered, and then the loose skin in his neck, and then his belly under the shirt, and then he was bouncing on the balls of his feet. But he didn't make any noise. He flapped with laughter as he ran his eyes around from Sherman and quickly across Artel and me to Koning, and then he began to turn very slowly and his glance didn't miss one of the people around him. And then he walked away. He went back down the sidewalk the way he'd come, his hands still hooked in the waistband of his pants, his back shaking a little bit, the suspenders tight across his wizened shoulders, and a reflection of sunlight bouncing off the curved sheen of his eyeshade.

"Well," Artel said in an amused and careless voice, "I see every town has its character."

Koning rubbed his hand across the back of his neck, where the skin was seamed and granulated from years of exposure to sunlight. His jaw was out; I could see his lower teeth. They were wet and brown, and snaggled by oncoming age. The breath was pushing out steadily through his nostrils, making a very thin whistle. He took off his khaki rain hat and ran his hand over his scalp. He put the hat back on, all without taking his eyes off Tully. The crowd was looking up at us expectantly, and I believe half of them were holding their breaths.

"I didn't know you were a doctor," I said to Sherman, as if this were interesting but not vital. Of all the things that had been happening to us since Sherman had given the alarm, this was the one that I couldn't make out to have not noticed. "Want to make a note of that, Artel?" I went on. "It's good news. It means we won't have to send one of our own in." Artel nodded and took a pad of mimeographed form sheets out of his pocket. He got out a pencil, licked the tip and made an X-mark in a box.

"Doctor present. Right," he mumbled boredly.

"By the way, Doctor, congratulations," I said to Sherman. "You must be doing a fine job here. These people look fine."

Sherman said quickly: "Now, wait—you're getting the wrong idea. I'm no doctor. We don't have any doctor. That's just something that crazy old coot calls everybody." His glance flickered over to Koning.

"I ought to lock—no, God damn it, I . . . can't . . ." Koning wasn't talking to me. He was talking directly to Sherman.

Whatever it was, it had them completely shaken up. I can imagine how they must have planned for snoopers in advance, sitting around a kitchen table and nerving each other. *"Well, listen, Luther—what'll we do if somebody comes around asking questions?" "We'll handle it, Walt. After all, it's our town, we live here. The important things are all kept out of sight, and how would they know what questions to ask? Don't you worry about it, Walt. You just always let me do most of the talking, and I'll make sure they don't find out anything but what we want them to know."* That was exactly how it had gone between them; it's the kind of conversation smart, decent men with a secret have held between themselves since time knows when. And it had worked, back when things were looser.

They were looking at each other like two men tied to opposite ends of a rope, and the middle of the rope hooked over a spur of rock on the side of a twenty thousand foot mountain.

"Oh. Sorry, Mr. Sherman," I said. "Artel, looks like you're going to have to start a new form."

"Yeah. Before I do that—Mr. Sherman, do you have very many seniles in your population? Will you require any special supplies—tranquilizers or that sort of thing?" Artel asked.

"Well, I wouldn't know," Sherman, said doggedly. "And Tully don't seem to do any harm, as long as you don't pay him any mind."

"We've been very lucky here," Koning said. He was beginning to get back to himself. He was talking a little fast, and the wrinkles at the corners of his eyes weren't completely relaxed. But he was doing a good job of recovering. "We're all healthy people here. Oh, once in a while somebody mashes his thumb with a hammer or something. But that's not anything that can't be taken care of. We live nice and quiet. It's good. When I look back on how it was in the old days, I've got to say we live better. That's a terrible thing, when you think of how this town used to have twenty-five thousand people in it and mighty few of them ready to be dead. But now we've got through the bad time, things are pretty good. For the live ones. Meaning no insult, maybe a lot better than they are for you outside."

He was looking steadily at Sherman. And he had come to something in his mind. He wasn't back on his heels any more. He was nervous, and he didn't like to trust his own improvisations any better than anybody else would. But he was going to go with it, whatever it was. He wasn't looking to Artel and me for his cues any longer. You could see that happening in him; you could hear it in his voice. "Look, gentlemen," he said, stepping back and smiling. "I got taken up here in a hurry, and there's a couple of little things that I'd like to finish up, if that's all right with the two of you. I mean, this isn't any kind of an emergency. It's a surprise, but it isn't an emergency. So if you could excuse me for about a half hour, I could come back then and I'd have the rest of the day clear to talk to you. I'm sure Mr. Sherman can keep you entertained, and maybe fill you in on some of the background. Just the general stuff; I'll be back in time to give you the specifics. How would that be?" He grinned at Sherman with everything but his eyes. "Why don't you take them inside, Walt? Millie could maybe give them a little refreshment."

"Well, I don't know—" Sherman looked at Koning as if he had gone just as wild as Tully. "I mean, the house is a mess . . ."

It was sad, watching a man turn into a nervous housewife right in front of my eyes.

"No, you go ahead and take them inside," Koning said. "Don't worry about the house." He grinned again. "Relax, Walt! You're just not used to company," he chuckled.

Sherman nodded slowly. "All right," he said, "take your word on that."

His face went through a spasm; I think he started to grin back, and then realized immediately he couldn't make it stick. I didn't dare look over at Artel myself, for fear we'd lay ourselves open in the same way.

The crowd was livening up again; Koning's starting some kind of action was taking the dismay of Tully out of them. The kids, of course, hadn't stayed quiet for more than a minute. Some of them were back to playing catch, and some of the others had drifted on down the street after Tully—I didn't know whether on purpose after Tully or just happening to be headed in the same direction. I noticed nobody had tried giving Tully any catcalls or joshing, not even the kids.

It was a nice town; they were polite to their sick ones.

"It sounds like a practical idea," I said. "And I sure could use a cool drink, Mr. Sherman. How about you, Artel?"

Artel nodded. "Yes."

"Oh, well, sure," Sherman said. "No problem about that. Got a good well down by where the Nike site used to be. Deep, Government-dug well. Lucky that way, too, we were. Lots of good water."

"Well, that would be fine!" I said.

I could hear Koning sigh just a little bit. "Okay! So it's all settled—Doc here'll take care of you two fellows 'til I get back, and everything'll work out just fine." Koning turned and trotted down the steps. "Be seeing you!"

I waved a hand cheerfully after him. So did Artel. "Well," Sherman said. "Let's—let's go inside." So we did.

VII

A blonde young woman of maybe twenty-five was waiting in the hall, carrying a baby over her shoulder, one arm around it and the spread fingers of her other hand supporting it over the fresh, clean diaper. There were a couple of other kids clustered around her; a girl maybe a year older than the baby, and a boy in a T-shirt and corduroy rompers who was just under school age. He had little leather shoes on, scuffed up around the toes since the time this morning his mother had coated them with some of that polish that comes in a bottle with a dabber. The little girl had her arms around her mother's knee and her face buried in the side of her skirt. Sherman said: "This is my wife, Millie. And my kids. That's LaVonne, and Walt, and the baby's name is Lucille. Millie, this is Mr.—" He looked over at me.

"Dorsey. I'm very pleased to meet you. This is my partner—"

"Loovan Artel. Loovan's his family name," Sherman said.

Millie Sherman nodded, looking at Artel. Her eyes were very big, and the corners of her mouth kept twitching. Finally she said, "Oh."

"It's all *right*, Millie," Sherman soothed.

"We just need a place to sit, Mrs. Sherman," Artel said gently. "Until Mr. Koning gets back."

"That's right, honey," Sherman said, throwing Artel a grateful glance. "Luther just asked me to give these men some refreshment until he gets back. He asked me to bring 'em in."

Putting the seal of authority on it seemed to buck her up, some. "Oh." She wet her lips. "Well, won't you come in?" She pulled the boy Walter out of the way and stood back against the wall. We were in one of those narrow foyer things, that runs through toward the back of the house and has doors opening off it into the main rooms, and a flight of stairs going up.

"Let's go straight on through to the kitchen. I'm sure you fellows don't mind," Sherman said.

"Not at all," Artel said, and we followed him toward the back of the house. I threw a glance into the living room as we went by. There were couches and a lot of chairs up against the walls, with a coffee table in front of each couch. There were books on the tables, bound in bright-colored cheap cloth. Novels.

The kitchen was big, with a chrome-legged table, wooden cabinets and a lot of chrome-legged chairs with padded plastic seats and backs. Next to the capped stub of a gaspipe coming up through the floor was a cast iron wood range, and in the sink was a big, galvanized iron pan with the washing water in it. The drinking water was in a regular office-type water cooler with a big glass bottle held upside-down in it. And in one corner, standing spindly legged, was a kerosene refrigerator. "Well, now, that's something," I said, nodding toward it. "You people are really starting to get straightened around here." Sherman's eyes followed mine. He looked at the refrigerator as if all hope were lost.

"I have to have it," he said.

"Oh? Are you a diabetic?" I said.

What happened to his face now was like nothing I could recognize, but if he had been made out of strings, I could have heard them snap. The look he gave me was damn near unbearable; I might have been a cobra.

Without taking his eyes off me, he said to his wife: "Millie,

I'm sure you and the kids have things to do elsewhere. I can take care of these gentlemen by myself. You go on, Millie. You go on, now."

Millie nodded and backed out of the room, taking the kids with her. The kitchen had a swinging door on it, and it swung shut.

"What do you mean, am I a diabetic? All the diabetics are dead."

"It's just that refrigerators and insulin go together in this house, Doctor," I said. "And before you tell me again you're not a doctor, any fool can see Koning doesn't care any more whether we find out or not. Artel, you figure his office is across the hall from that waiting room?"

"Uh-huh. I could smell the antiseptics."

"Look, Dr. Sherman, why don't you relax?" I said. "Koning told you that, and I'm telling you that. So you're getting it from both sides, and you might as well believe it. Let's sit down and just wait. We can talk if you like. Koning's obviously gone to do something."

"Town Council meeting, I guess," Sherman said desperately.

"I figured something like that. Take it easy. Doc—it's us that may have our heads in a noose. Artel, drift out there and see what his office looks like, will you?" Artel nodded and went out. I could hear Millie Sherman gasping out in the hall and Artel murmuring something reassuring that ended in " 'scuse me, Ma'am, kids . . ."

Sherman sank down in one of the kitchen chairs. He held his head in his hands with his elbows on his knees. "You had to bring one of them in with you," he mumbled.

I pulled another chair away from the kitchen table and sat down. "Well sure, Doctor. He's a United States citizen. At least where we come from he is, and he's got just as much right to walk these streets as I have."

"You don't realize what you're doing to us."

"No, I don't, except I know guilt when I see it. But it's a pretty good question who's doing what to whom."

Sherman's head came up fast. "What do you mean? What do you know?"

"Whatever we know, we'll know a lot more, and if we never

go back to tell our Old Man about it, why that'll tell him something, too."

I started to talk very fast. I had him on the ropes, and win, lose or even, I was going to press that as long as Koning would let me. "What do you people think you're doing here, Sherman? Living in some little world of your own? You may think so, all fenced off behind a bunch of skeletons and burnt-out houses, but there's a whole goddamned world out there, and in the middle of the night sometimes you know it. This is just one town. *One* town, in a whole country. On a continent. On a world. We're not just dying out there—we're living and breathing, too. You think it's *fun* for me and Artel to come down here and play patsy with you people? There's no time for that."

He was white and sweating. He was shaking his head back and forth. "No. No, this is a good town. You're not the only people we've seen. We've seen other people from outside. You're all sick—all of you. You're weak, and you're in pain. I've been watching the way you move, Dorsey. You treat your bones like glass. I can imagine what it's like out there. You lived through it—you were the lucky ones, and look at you! Your livers and your kidneys must be like old pieces of sponge. Your lungs are in rags. And maybe, maybe if you get halfway decent food, and enough rest, and enough time, you'll slowly get back toward what you were. But most of you will never make it. Your kids might—for those of you who've got the energy for parenthood, and those of you who can successfully transmit immunities to your offspring. What's your infant mortality rate, Dorsey? What's your live birth rate? Who takes care of your kids? Who educates them? Who keeps up the public sanitation? How many psychotics have you got?"

Artel came back into the kitchen. "All he's got in his layout is surgical stuff. He's a bonesetter. Just about the only medicines he has are aspirin, iodine and vaseline. Funniest doctor's office I've ever seen. Well, Koning told us. But it's no surprise they thought they ought to hide it." Artel got a chair for himself and sat down watching Dr. Sherman with a sleepy, unwavering expression. "I'm sorry your wife and children are so upset by me," he said. Sherman nodded blindly, not looking up from the floor.

"Boy's by my first wife," he said. "I married late. Always figured it would be too big a change in my life. Got older, changed my mind."

"You've been very fortunate," Artel said.

"I know it. There isn't another family in town with two survivors. You think I didn't know the odds, when I finally realized what we had on our hands? What do you think I wouldn't have done to save Mary and the boy both? It was hopeless in the hospital by then. I voted to dynamite the place, it was so bad. Didn't matter—if they'd all voted with me, there wasn't time nor sense or strength to do it. Man, you can know how to swim, but when the wave hits you the next thing you know you're smashed up against the shells on the shore. I came home and I barricaded this place. Had big pans full of carbolic acid, soaked rags in it and stuffed them in the windows. Had spray guns full of disinfectant. You could barely breathe in here. What good was it? I wasn't even thinking. We were all out of our heads. We were sick, and we were using it all up. When it started, we were using up the antibiotics as if we could always order another truckload in the morning. Had lab technicians—*technicians*—working up slides, and had all the doctors out on the floor. We did everything backwards. We couldn't believe—" Sherman held his head and laughed. "We couldn't believe what was going to happen. We couldn't act like we believed what was going to happen. I mean, if we'd let ourselves think about what was going to happen—"

He stood up quickly. "I never got you your water." He went to a cabinet over the sink and got out some glasses.

"We kept listening to the radios, telling ourselves somebody somewhere would announce treatments. I had a radio with me everywhere I went, in my shirt pocket. I listened to that radio night and day, had my pockets full of batteries. When I couldn't get stations any more, I kept it on anyhow—kept it on wanting to know if WRKO would get back on the air." He pushed the glasses clunking under the spigot of the water fountain.

"I wasn't listening for any announcement. I was just listening to the cities die. Every time a station went off the air, I'd say to myself 'There, you smart people at Massachusetts General. There, you fancy labs down at Johns Hopkins. There, Columbia Presbyterian Medical Center—you couldn't find it either.'

That's how we were—you remember how you were?" He came over to us and pushed the glasses into our hands. "Here. Here." Water slopped on my wrist.

VIII

Sherman went back to his chair. He sat there looking at us. His hands turned the pipe over and over, and the ferocity had taken hold of him. "Luther wanted me to give you the background. All right, I'll give you the background. What do you think happens to the organization of a place like this? The water mains lead from a reservoir that belongs to a town fifteen miles away. What happens when they close the valves up there because they're scared they'll need it all to themselves? What happens to your food storage when your refrigeration goes? How much do you think we had stored around here, when we could always bring everything down from Newark in a couple of hours? What happens when you realize that's all there is, hah, and you're not going to bring any more from any place else, 'cause nobody's producing any more, nobody's packing it, nobody's putting it on trains? By God, they fought for it in the dark! They broke into houses where fat people lived, sometimes before and sometimes after they set fire to a block on account of pestilence.

"It's dead, it's dead out there," he said, pointing. "You came in through it. You saw it. You lived through it where you were, but you were in a goddamned metropolis with the rivers to scoop water out of and the warehouses jammed up. Do you know what we had to do to clear the site for that well you're drinking from now? They were dead! They were all dead, and we'd come crawling through the gutters, we'd come through three hour journeys that took a block. We didn't clear them out. We—we as good as burrowed through them. We were twisted around them like snakes." He looked up. "Of course, it's all clean and neat now," he smiled. "Everything's clean and neat. This is a model community." He wiped out his eye sockets with the backs of his hands. There was sweat drenching his shirt under the arms.

"Drink your water," he said.

"Thank you," I said. I took a hearty swallow. "I gather you didn't save your Mary."

"No," he said bitterly, outraged at my manners. "I didn't save my Mary."

Well, I hadn't even intended for him to get some of my point. But it would have been nice if he'd been able to realize you couldn't buy anything with that story these days. They were always like that, when you contacted them. The loners—the ones we pick up in open countryside because they used to be farmers—would run around our town for days, telling their particular story over and over again.

It always took them a while to understand that nobody was listening. The communities we'd contact couldn't believe that the rest of the world was just like them. They all had this vision that theirs was the only town blighted, even though nothing that used power or fuel or the cooperation of large groups of people could be seen in the world any longer. We had all run screaming. We had all spent everything we had, trying to run, trying to learn an answer, trying to hide, trying to wipe out. You could only be glad the world's military was still shocked from what the air defense missiles had done to the incoming Klarr lifeboats, because if they'd been full of their usual spirit we would have found some excuse for unloading that stockpile on ourselves, too. The only special grief Ocean Heights might have would be from having that lifeboat land on their doorstep and provide them with five hundred-odd immediate centers of cross-infection instead of their having to wait their turn from the winds and the refugees. But I figured that silent building farther down canceled that excuse, too. And besides, Mary is a common name.

"Look, Doctor," I said, "we've got cards from the United States government. You remember the United States. We obviously represent the return of some kind of social organization to the world. You see us—you see what kind of shape we're in. You say you've seen other people. What's more, you can't tell me somebody in town doesn't know how to build a crystal set. There isn't much to pick up, but there's something. You're trying to tell me you're cut off, but you're not—you know what kind of shape the world's in, even if what you know is only little bits and pieces. We're sitting right here in your kitchen working on the little bits and pieces we know, and it adds up bad. It adds up real bad, Doctor, just from what you've given us. What's going on in this town?"

Sherman shook his head miserably. "I can't tell you," he whispered.

"You've been trying to," Artel said. "You're doing everything but putting it into words." Sherman's glance jerked over toward him and met pity. I don't know whether he could tell that's what it was on a Klarr face or not. "Doctor, you have a great secret in this town. But you are its only sentry. It's possible to get as far as your house without being detected. And then you call attention to yourself by hammering on a gong. When you and Koning talk to each other in front of us, you make sure we notice every lie. You think Tully told us about you? We didn't need Tully for that. But it was you and Koning who told us Tully is important—you and Koning, and all your other neighbors and friends. When you tell us how things were in this town, you're apologizing in advance for what we'll know when we put all the pieces together." Sherman was going whiter and whiter. The wood of the pipe was creaking in his hands as he squeezed them and the skin slipped damply over it. "You couldn't fool anybody who's the least bit interested," Artel finished up, still gently. "You know that. You've always known that."

I put down my water glass and walked over to the refrigerator. "He marched us by the waiting room because it was smart not to let us sit there and figure out he was a doctor, so we wouldn't ask him any medical questions. He walked us right in here into the kitchen. Where the refrigerator is." I opened it.

Sherman cried out: "We couldn't get two! We could only find one, and it made sense to keep it in the kitchen!"

I nodded. "And there was a fuel problem, too," I said. I could afford to be understanding. I didn't have the foggiest notion yet what the hell he meant. "It's a hard world; we've got to economize."

I was looking through the refrigerator, and it was dark enough in there so that I was having trouble. There were a couple of heads of lettuce, wrapped in cellophane with the New York seal on them, and some leftovers in plastic covered dishes, half a sausage . . . and, up close to the weak cooling coils, a half-pint cream bottle with a homemade rubber diaphragm stretched over its mouth.

I took it out and held it up to the light. It was three-quarters full of a just faintly yellow liquid with white clouds stirring around the bottom.

Sherman stared at it and me and Artel. Then he jumped up and made a lunge for it. He had his hand open, and he was trying to slap it away and smash it. His eyes were bulging. His face looked like it was a foot wide and made of chalk. "No, let me!" he panted as I ducked it out of his reach. "Please!"

First, I stepped back from him, so that he fell clumsily against the standing cabinet, and then as he put his hands down to catch his balance, I said: "All right," quietly, and held the bottle out. He straightened up, and I carefully put it into his hands. He stood looking down at it, and just as suddenly as he'd jumped up, tears began to fall on his shirtsleeves. Woebegone, he carefully put it back in the refrigerator and closed the door. He turned around and leaned his back against it. He took a long, gasping breath, and then he sniffed sharply. Well, anyone will when they're crying.

I looked over at Artel.

"That's the kind of setup they use when they want to measure out doses for injections."

Artel nodded. "He'd do his sterilization in here, on the stove." He began opening cabinet doors, and on the second try he found the leatherette-covered tin case with the syringes and the needles carefully nested. I turned to Sherman. "We've been in this town what—forty-five minutes? That's how long it took you folks to lead us straight to the wonder drug. Sure this is a good town." Sherman kept his eyes on the floor. He had shrunk inside his clothes. He was shuddering, and he was still weeping. I looked over at Artel. Artel shook his head—he couldn't tell what that stuff was either.

IX

"That's it, huh, Doctor?" I asked. "The stuff in that bottle replaces all other kinds of medicines. You come into Dr. Sherman's office with, say, liver flukes, a bad heart and a broken arm. He sets your arm, and he goes back into the kitchen and comes back with a syringe full of this stuff and squirts it into you, and you walk out smiling, all cured. You come in with spots in front of your eyes, a roaring in your ears and a swelling in your armpit. Doctor gives you the needle, and six hours later you're dancing with your best girl. Doc, is that the way it is?"

"Don't make fun of it," Sherman whispered.

He was down to that. It was all he had left. We had broken him—well, no; the three of us together, and this town, and this world had broken him. That'll happen, if you let it, every time. Sherman was saying: "It's specific against Klarr-transmitted infectious diseases and allergic reactions. And it has broad-spectrum applications in treating the older forms of infectious disease. It won't repair a damaged heart, no. But it reduces that heart's burden."

He looked at Artel and winced the way he would have if he were hit with a gust of windy rain. "It may be a panacea," he explained. "In a matter of hours after a three cubic centimeter injection, the subject is completely free of everything that can possibly be destroyed by an antibody. I'm—I'm trying to make myself clear to you. The human body reacts to the stuff by manufacturing counteragents which not only destroy it, but every other invading organism. At least, I've never seen the infectious disease that one dose isn't effective for. I—" He waved his hand in the air. "The population's too small for me to have seen examples of all the sicknesses that humans could get. But it's never failed me yet. And the reaction's nearly permanent. The only people we routinely need it for is the new babies. There's no disease in this town, Mr. Loovan." The tears were starting in his eyes again; not the big, steady running wetness on his face he'd shown before, but he had to keep blinking. "You see, the human body has its defense mechanisms. And this stuff stimulates them. Fantastically." He shook his head violently and turned to me, because Artel had kept looking at him deadpan.

"You can see it, Dorsey! You must know that the normal human being's body is constantly engaged in staving off all sorts of potential illnesses. At any time, a great deal of the human mechanism's functioning is directed toward the destruction of invading micro-organisms and the filtering and disposal of the resultant wastes. And I'm sure I don't have to tell you how vulnerable the organism is if it has been exhausted. And I don't have to tell you how debilitating even simple illnesses are; at some time in your life you must have had a common cold, or a reaction to an infected tooth, or a cut. Can you imagine how much energy was constantly being drained from your system by things as commonplace as that? Energy that could have gone to doing work or maintaining the growth and repair functions of your body?" He was shifting back and forth between the two of us now. We kept looking at him blankly because there wasn't any need to encourage him and we weren't planning to interrupt him. And he kept trying to get through to us—trying to get us to smile, or pat his hand and say. "It's all *right*."

"Can you imagine what the population of this town is like? It's free to devote full energy to life. There's none of that gray, dragging stuff they used to come in to me with in the old days, that I couldn't diagnose, and made them miserable, and I'd write tonics for. Do you realize how much tension has been wiped out of their lives? They're not nagged by a hundred little illnesses. They're not terrified by sudden stomach-twinges and mysterious rashes or coughing spells. They don't find themselves spitting or passing blood. They don't worry themselves into stomach ulcers, and they don't come down with nervous diseases. When you add that to the fact that they no longer have many of the old social tensions . . . Don't you see? It's like a miracle for them! It's like perpetual springtime—they're alive—they're vital. They don't tire as fast, they don't mope—"

"And they laugh all the time," I said. "Artel and I could see that; running and dancing and singing and clapping their hands when they saw us. Like a bunch of happy South Sea islanders in a book. Nature's Children."

Sherman ducked his head again. "They were pretty well off until you showed up," he muttered.

"No arthritis, Doctor?" Artel said. "No athlete's foot, no kidney stones?"

"I didn't say that," the doctor said. "If you had something like that before the Klarri came, there's nothing that can be done for you except to make you generally healthier. That helps." His head came up a little farther, "There is something interesting about that, though. I don't see any new cases starting. You can't tell with a sample this size, but it just may be we won't have any of that after this generation.

"There's a lot I don't know about it. What I've got does the job it has to. But I'm not going to pretend to you that my extraction methods are exact. I haven't got the time or equipment to isolate the precise effective fraction, whatever it is. I've got a bundle of stuff there, and some part of it does the job. The rest doesn't do any harm." He was starting to gather the little pieces of himself back together again. Talking shop was doing him good. Well, that had to be one of his reasons for talking shop.

"What does it do for cancer, Doc?" I asked.

"I think it prevents it. I know it doesn't cure it."

"That's fine, Doctor." I looked at him from a long way away. I had an idea I was about to smash him again.

I looked over at Artel. He had caught it in the doctor's choices of words. It was sad to see his face. "Doctor—where do you get this stuff?"

He had nearly made himself forget it. He had been talking, and talking, and all the time his mind had been putting the screens back up. He stared at me as if I'd belched in church, and then he took a little half step away from Artel; a little, sidling, sheepish step I'm sure he didn't know he was performing. "I extract it from human-infected Klarr blood," he said, his mouth blowing each word in its own bubble. Artel sighed and bowed his head.

I'd had my next question ready, and I was pretty sure of the answer to that one, too, but I had to stop and study him for a minute. Then I said. "And everybody in town knows where it comes from?"

Sherman nodded, two or three times, slowly. "All the adults. I *wish* you hadn't brought in Mr. Loovan."

"I think we'd better move, Artel."

He wasn't keeping all his mind on the spot we were in, but he nodded. "Yo." We pushed open the swinging door.

"Wait!" Sherman cried behind us. "If you try to run for it, they're *bound* to kill you."

• • •

Artel was moving quickly up the foyer. "We know that," I said over my shoulder. That kind of talk annoys me. I didn't need him to teach me my business. Sherman's wife and his kids were hanging over the bannister three-quarters of the way up the stairs, staring down at us. Artel hit the front door as hard as he could, slamming it back against the wall, and then kneed the screen door open so that it spanged against the outside wall. The people standing around out there jumped. Well, that was the effect that he wanted.

"Good-by, Mister Boogeyman!" the little girl piped as Artel hit the veranda with his boots clattering. I went just as fast behind him, slamming both doors shut. Artel didn't slow; you never want to do that. I jumped the steps and picked up speed, so that we reached the crowd side by side. We went right by our bikes, picked the biggest man in the group, and stood with our toes practically on his. "Where do we find Luther Koning?" I barked in his face. The rest of the people were falling back. Artel and I were both glowering and obviously beside ourselves with rage. The man took a step back, and we took a step forward. Artel reached down and grabbed his belt. "Come on, you! You're fooling with the Government!" The man waved vaguely down the street toward the intersection.

"Right!" I said. "Let's go, buddy." Artel pushed the man back firmly, letting go of his belt, and the two of us swung down the sidewalk, marching side by side, our feet coming down regular as heartbeats, our faces grim, our arms swinging. Kids and housewives scattered out of our way. "You can't—!" somebody protested.

"Well, then, you run tell him," I said, and we kept going.

"Dorsey! Loovan!" Sherman shouted, coming down his veranda steps, his feet thudding across the lawn as he cut over to us. We kept marching. He came panting up to us. He was trying to keep up, but he lost speed as he turned to try to talk to us. I kept my eyes on the people down at the intersection; there were a fair number of them down there, and I saw one of them notice us coming and freeze.

"Dorsey!" Sherman panted. "You don't understand. It's not just—" He tripped over the cover of a water meter, stumbled, and lost pace. He came trotting up even with us again.

"Loovan—" Then he realized he'd picked the wrong one to tell the rest of it to. "Dorsey! We were dying. We were too weak to move. We hadn't eaten in days. We hadn't eaten enough in weeks, and all that time we'd been burning with fever. My wife was lying dead upstairs. For three days. And I couldn't get up there. I had the boy in my office; on the examining table. I was lying on the floor. I couldn't reach him. I had him strapped down. He was crying. I couldn't reach him. We were all like that."

"So were we," I said. I had run out of patience with him entirely.

But Sherman wanted to make his point. I had been waiting for him to tell me where their captive Klarrs were, and it seemed to me at the time that would be the only other interesting thing he could have left to tell us. Instead, he kept babbling on: "You weren't lost and cut off from the rest of the world! Do you know how bad the human animal wants to live? Do you know what it will do to keep alive? Do you know what it will keep trying to do, right up to the last minute? As long as it has its teeth and claws?"

I was listening for any footsteps coming up fast and determined behind us. I was paying most of my attention to that. There weren't any. We'd left them standing there. Now we were almost up to the intersection. The fourth corner was a big saloon-hotel thing, and I guess it was a town hall now, because I could see Koning and a bunch of other men come out quickly through the doors and stop dead, watching us. There was a grinning, jumping figure with them, pointing at us coming on and slapping his broomstick thigh, making the flapping cloth of his pants billow as if he had no bones at all.

"It was Tully!" Sherman puffed out. "There was a lot of Klarr-killing going on for a while. Then we got too weak, and we gave it up. But Tully wounded one someplace where they'd both crawled to die, I guess. Starving to death, both of them. Tully must have been just as far out of his head—just as far back to being a dying animal as you can get. You know what I mean?" he pleaded. "You know how Tully was? It was just him and this dying Klarr. It was Tully. It was Tully that was the animal. But it was Tully then that had sense enough to come and save me—and save little Walt—after he was back to being a man again." He barely got it out. "It was Tully who found out. I just refined his discovery. Made it nice and medical and sanitary. But you see how it is—they *can't* let the two of you go!"

Artel had stopped dead. He had turned to salt in the blink of an eye. "Move. Move." I said to him, "You've got to move," still looking straight ahead, stopping dead with him. Whatever we did, we had to do it together. "If you don't move, none of this gets back." We moved.

Now there were about fifteen or twenty people at the intersection. They were all men. They were wound up tight, moving their feet and hands back and forth. They stood on the corner in front of the hotel as we marched off the end of the sidewalk and across the street toward them.

Tully was bouncing and grinning at the crowd's left. He had a lot of energy; a lot of drive. You had to figure him for spunk. For him to be the historical personage he was, he had to have had the persistence to have haggled hot raw meat with loose teeth in a mouth full of open sores.

You won't often find that kind of grit, even in your really desperate person. Even so, the nearest man to him was drawn a little away from him. Like the others in the crowd, he was watching Artel and me, but he kept darting side-glances at Tully, too.

We walked up to Koning, who was trying to keep his face blank and was keeping it tense instead. I looked only at him; straight into his eyes. It was important to hit him before he could say or do anything. I said casually: "Well, it worked out the way you were hoping. Sherman cracked wide open and told us all about it. So you didn't do it. It's all out of your hands and off your mind."

Koning started to frown. "What do you mean by that?"

Artel said "Look, Mr. Koning," with his voice patient, "if you really didn't want it taken off you, you would have made sure to ask the supply trucks for some drugs now and then. Whether Doc wanted to deprive the poor sick outside world or not."

"Now you can just be mayor," I said. "That'll be a lot easier, won't it?"

"Well, we've got things to do, Mr. Koning." Artel said.

"Let's go, Ed. That building's four blocks down and over to our right."

Sherman had been trying to catch his breath over to my right for the last few moments. He said: "I never—"

I gave him something that might pass for a smile. "We know where the lifeboat is, too, Dr. Sherman. And those over there." I waved my hand in the direction of the neat houses, off beyond the bulk of the hotel. "Well, you can see we have to open that casino building, Mr. Koning. Care to come along?"

Koning's jaw flexed a couple of times. He looked around, and once you do that, of course, you've lost it.

He took a deep breath. And then nodded hastily, looking back at the crowd. "All right. Okay."

Artel and I stepped out. We walked down the middle of the street, with Koning walking along beside us, and having to compromise between a casual walk and a trot, until he finally settled for keeping in step with us. Doc Sherman tagged along. One or two other people started to follow, and then the rest of them, and with the group that had slowly followed us down from Sherman's house, it made a respectable bunch. Tully had set out down the sidewalk. He was keeping pace with us the best he could. He kept trying to attract the attention of people who passed near him. I could hear him saying: "Where do you think you're going, you chicken punk?" He said it to young and old, irrespective of sex. "Where do you think you're going, you chicken punk?" I could hear it as a fading mutter in the background. People were looking at him and then looking away. They were dodging around him, and twitching their feet nearer the center of the street. Except for him, nobody was talking.

X

In daylight, the building was painted green. Not new—from before. Artel and I trotted up the steps. Koning pushed himself ahead and unlocked the doors into the lobby. The crowd waited out in the street.

The lobby was dark and musty. It was floored in a checkerboard pattern of red and brown vinyl tiles with a black rubber runner laid down over them. There were office doors opening on the lobby, but Koning went ahead toward a flight of stairs leading to the left. "Lantern around here somewhere," he said.

"Never mind," Artel said, taking his flashlight out of his windbreaker. We went up the stairs with it whirring. At the top of the stairs there was another set of double doors. Koning unlocked those. The smell kept getting stronger.

There was some light coming in from one window near us. They had bricked up the rest from the inside. The entire second floor was one big room from here on back, and the open window was on this side of the row of bars and cyclone fencing they had put in from one wall to the other. Artel shone his light in through the bars.

We could see six iron cots with mattresses on them. There were two Klarri lying on two of them. The mattresses were turned back and rolled over on three others. There was another Klarr sitting on the edge of the remaining bed. He was wearing what was left of his shipboard clothes, I guess.

"All right, unlock that," I told Koning, pointing to the pipe-and-cyclone-mesh gate that went from floor to ceiling. Some master craftsman had worked hard and expertly, custom-building that. Koning nodded, went over to it and trembled the key into the lock. He pushed in on the gate, and it swung back. He turned around and looked at Artel and me expectantly.

"I don't think anything much is going to happen to you, Koning," I said. "We don't mess with communities if we can possibly help it. We all had to live through a bad time, and we all found out things about ourselves."

Koning nodded.

"We didn't find out what you found out. I'll give you that," I said.

"But that was just luck," Artel said; he took a deep breath before each phrase. "Just your luck. Instead of somebody else's, somewhere else."

Koning shook his head. "Listen—that Tully—"

"I'm sure Artel understands," I said. "After all, you couldn't do anything to Tully."

Koning said bitterly: "The son of a bitch kept reminding us

and mocking us. He'd ask us if our arms were sore from Doc's needle."

"I wish you'd go away," Artel told him.

Koning nodded again and went around us to go back down the stairs. He went down quickly, and then we could hear his footsteps in the lobby, and the sound of him going out through the double doors outside. He was not a bad man. Not the sort who would eat the flesh of a Klarr, no matter how hungry. Just the sort who would take a Klarr's blood to make medicine out of it. And take. And take.

As soon as it was all quiet, Artel began to tremble. He shook like a leaf. He put one hand on my shoulder and squeezed. "Oh, Ed."

"Easy, easy, easy."

"Chicken punks," Artel muttered.

The Klarr who'd been sitting on his bed had gotten up. He came shuffling forward, peering ahead.

"Artel, I don't see any reason why it might not work the other way. Maybe I'm wrong, but I don't see why Klarr-infected human blood fractions wouldn't do it for your people."

"They didn't try that, though, did they?" Artel said with his eyes shut.

"Well, they couldn't," I said. "They needed these Klarri to stay infected."

Artel nodded. "I understand that."

The other two Klarri had noticed something was different and had turned over on their beds. I speak a pretty good version of Klarr. "Hey," I said to them. "We're policemen. You can come out."

"What are we going to do with them, Ed?" Artel said.

"Move 'em into one of the houses. I'll stay with them until you send a truck down to pick them up. If you take a bike out to the Camden route, you'll probably be up at the Old Man's maybe late tonight, tomorrow morning for sure."

Artel nodded. "All right." He put his hand back on my shoulder as the white-haired Klarr came closer, got to the gate, and stood in it with one hand on each upright, leaning forward and looking out at us.

"I am Eredin Mek, Sub-Assistant Navigating Officer. My

companions here are very weak and may be frightened. Could one of you go in and speak to them, please?" He came closer.

"Go ahead, Artel," I said, and he ducked through the gate and walked quickly toward the back of the cell.

"Is it possible to go outside?" Eredin asked me.

"Certainly," I said.

"I'd like that."

We walked together to the stairs, and then, with him putting one hand on the bannister and the other over my shoulders, we got down the stairs and out into the lobby. I could see the crowd milling around outside, and for a minute I thought we were in trouble again, but their backs were to the glass doors. Then we got out through those, and stood at the head of the steps. Tully was across the street. He was standing on the sidewalk, and he was saying something to the people. They were ducking their heads away from him.

Tully saw Eredin and me. He pointed over at us. "Hey, critter!" That made them raise their heads. They all turned, and when they saw Eredin leaning against me, they sighed like an extra wave. Sherman and Koning were in the middle of them, pale. They could all see what it meant, the Klarr up there on the steps with me, stinking and sick, but out. Only Tully didn't see what it meant to him. He thought he still had something going for him.

He laughed. "Hey, critter! I b'lieve you're even scrawnier than me! What's the matter—ain't we been feedin' you right?" He looked around for his effect.

"Who is that man?" Eredin muttered, peering, groping like any sensible person will when he's weak and is in a world he doesn't understand; like somebody senile. "What's he saying?"

Klarr is a language that made my answer come out: "He is the savior of their tribe."

"Yah!" Tully was crying out. "Yah, ya bunch of needle-pushing arm-wipers—"

"Ah, God!" Sherman groaned and turned and rammed back through the crowd toward Tully. Then they were all as if they were being yanked on strings. They clustered suddenly around the squirrel-cheeked man in the green sunshade. I could see

Koning's face. The veins were standing out; his mouth was wide open, and what was coming out of him and all of them was what you might hear if all the lovers in the world were inside one big megaphone. The people at the back of the crowd tried to push in. The whole mass of them fell against a tall hedge.

Eredin looked up at me, squinting, his eyes watering; there had to be a lot of things he couldn't know the reasons for. "They—they kept taking our blood," he complained.

"I know," I said. I patted him on the shoulder.

The title is Frederik Pohl's; I forget how I had it when I sold this story to him for Galaxy, and that's a good sign I more than approve of his choice. I wrote it overnight, during a period when I was trying to see if I could understand what Cordwainer Smith was doing. The central Nemesis is drawn from my experience as a whilom investigator of unusual travelers' cheque refund claims for American Express. A clerical investigator, but the seed is father to the stalk.

I delivered the manuscript to Fred's house, not far from where we lived, and when I returned home Edna was washing her hair and hurrying to make me some breakfast. After breakfast, she asked me to drive her to the hospital, and a few hours later our second son, Steven, was born. Steve is now the junior chess champion of Illinois.

Wall of Crystal, Eye of Night

SOFT AS THE voice of a mourning dove, the telephone sounded at Rufus Sollenar's desk. Sollenar himself was standing fifty paces away, his leonine head cocked, his hands flat in his hip pockets, watching the nighted world through the crystal wall that faced out over Manhattan Island. The window was so high that some of what he saw was dimmed by low cloud hovering over the rivers. Above him were stars; below him the city was traced out in light and brimming with light. A falling star—an interplanetary rocket—streaked down toward Long Island Facility like a scratch across the soot on the doors of Hell.

Sollenar's eyes took it in, but he was watching the total scene, not any particular part of it. His eyes were shining.

When he heard the telephone, he raised his left hand to his lips. "Yes?" The hand glittered with utilijem rings; the effect

©1961, Galaxy Publishing Corporation

was that of an attempt at the sort of copper-binding that was once used to reinforce the ribbing of wooden warships.

His personal receptionist's voice moved from the air near his desk to the air near his ear. Seated at the monitor board in her office, wherever in this building her office was, the receptionist told him:

"Mr. Ermine says he has an appointment."

"No." Sollenar dropped his hand and returned to his panorama. When he had been twenty years younger—managing the modest optical factory that had provided the support of three generations of Sollenars—he had very much wanted to be able to stand in a place like this, and feel as he imagined men felt in such circumstances. But he felt unimaginable now.

To be here was one thing. To have almost lost the right, and regained it at the last moment, was another. Now he knew that not only could he be here today but that tomorrow, and tomorrow, he could still be here. He had won. His gamble had given him EmpaVid—and EmpaVid would give him all.

The city was not merely a prize set down before his eyes. It was a dynamic system he had proved he could manipulate. He and the city were one. It buoyed and sustained him; it supported him, here in the air, with stars above and light-thickened mist below.

The telephone mourned: "Mr. Ermine states he has a firm appointment."

"I've never heard of him." And the left hand's utilijems fell from Sollenar's lips again. He enjoyed such toys. He raised his right hand, sheathed in insubstantial midnight-blue silk in which the silver threads of metallic wiring ran subtly toward the fingertips. He raised the hand, and touched two fingers together: music began to play behind and before him. He made contact between another combination of finger circuits, and a soft, feminine laugh came from the terrace at the other side of the room, where connecting doors had opened. He moved toward it. One layer of translucent drapery remained across the doorway, billowing lightly in the breeze from the terrace. Through it, he saw the taboret with its candle lit; the iced wine in the stand beside it; the two fragile chairs; Bess Allardyce, slender and regal, waiting in one of them—all these, through the misty curtain, like either the beginning or the end of a dream.

"Mr. Ermine reminds you the appointment was made for him at the Annual Business Dinner of the International Association of Broadcasters in 1998."

Sollenar completed his latest step, then stopped. He frowned down at his left hand. "Is Mr. Ermine with the IAB's Special Public Relations Office?"

"Yes," the voice said after a pause.

The fingers of Sollenar's right hand shrank into a cone. The connecting door closed. The girl disappeared. The music stopped. "All right. You can tell Mr. Ermine to come up." Sollenar went to sit behind his desk.

The office door chimed. Sollenar crooked a finger of his left hand, and the door opened. With another gesture, he kindled the overhead lights near the door and sat in shadow as Mr. Ermine came in.

Ermine was dressed in rust-colored garments. His figure was spare, and his hands were empty. His face was round and soft, with long dark sideburns. His scalp was bald. He stood just inside Sollenar's office and said: "I would like some light to see you by, Mr. Sollenar."

Sollenar crooked his little finger.

The overhead lights came to soft light all over the office. The crystal wall became a mirror, with only the strongest city lights glimmering through it. "I only wanted to see you first," said Sollenar; "I thought perhaps we'd met before."

"No," Ermine said, walking across the office. "It's not likely you've ever seen me." He took a card case out of his pocket and showed Sollenar proper identification. "I'm not a very forward person."

"Please sit down," Sollenar said. "What may I do for you?"

"At the moment, Mr. Sollenar, I'm doing something for you."

Sollenar sat back in his chair. "Are you? Are you, now?" He frowned at Ermine. "When I became a party to the By-Laws passed at the '98 Dinner, I thought a Special Public Relations Office would make a valuable asset to the organization. Consequently, I voted for it, and for the powers it was given. But I never expected to have any personal dealings with it. I barely remembered you people had carte blanche with any IAB member."

"Well, of course, it's been a while since '98," Ermine said. "I imagine some legends have grown up around us. Industry gossip—that sort of thing."

"Yes."

"But we don't restrict ourselves to an enforcement function, Mr. Sollenar. You haven't broken any By-Laws, to our knowledge."

"Or mine. But nobody feels one hundred per cent secure. Not under these circumstances." Nor did Sollenar yet relax his face into its magnificent smile. "I'm sure you've found that out."

"I have a somewhat less ambitious older brother who's with the Federal Bureau of Investigation. When I embarked on my own career, he told me I could expect everyone in the world to react like a criminal, yes," Ermine said, paying no attention to Sollenar's involuntary blink. "It's one of the complicating factors in a profession like my brother's, or mine. But I'm here to advise you, Mr. Sollenar. Only that."

"In what matter, Mr. Ermine?"

"Well, your corporation recently came into control of the patents for a new video system. I understand that this in effect makes your corporation the licensor for an extremely valuable sales and entertainment medium. Fantastically valuable."

"EmpaVid," Sollenar agreed. "Various subliminal stimuli are broadcast with and keyed to the overt subject matter. The home receiving unit contains feedback sensors which determine the viewer's reaction to these stimuli, and intensify some while playing down others in order to create complete emotional rapport between the viewer and the subject matter. EmpaVid, in other words, is a system for orchestrating the viewer's emotions. The home unit is self-contained, semiportable and not significantly bulkier than the standard TV receiver. EmpaVid is compatible with standard TV receivers—except, of course, that the subject matter seems thin and vaguely unsatisfactory on a standard receiver. So the consumer shortly purchases an EV unit." It pleased Sollenar to spell out the nature of his prize.

"At a very reasonable price. Quite so, Mr. Sollenar. But you had several difficulties in finding potential licensees for this system, among the networks."

Sollenar's lips pinched out.

Mr. Ermine raised one finger. "First, there was the matter of acquiring the patents from the original inventor, who was also approached by Cortwright Burr."

"Yes, he was," Sollenar said in a completely new voice.

"Competition between Mr. Burr and yourself is long-standing and intense."

"Quite intense," Sollenar said, looking directly ahead of him at the one blank wall of the office. Burr's offices were several blocks downtown, in that direction.

"Well, I have no wish to enlarge on that point, Mr. Burr being an IAB member in standing as good as yours, Mr. Sollenar. There was, in any case, a further difficulty in licensing EV, due to the very heavy cost involved in equipping broadcasting stations and network relay equipment for this sort of transmission."

"Yes, there was."

"Ultimately, however, you succeeded. You pointed out, quite rightly, that if just one station made the change, and if just a few EV receivers were put into public places within the area served by that station, normal TV outlets could not possibly compete for advertising revenue."

"Yes."

"And so your last difficulties were resolved a few days ago, when your EmpaVid Unlimited—pardon me; when EmpaVid, a subsidiary of the Sollenar Corporation—became a major stockholder in the Transworld TV Network."

"I don't understand, Mr. Ermine," Sollenar said. "Why are you recounting this? Are you trying to demonstrate the power of your knowledge? All these transactions are already matters of record in the IAB confidential files, in accordance with the By-Laws."

Ermine held up another finger. "You're forgetting I'm only here to advise you. I have two things to say. They are:

"These transactions are on file with the IAB because they involve a great number of IAB members, and an increasingly large amount of capital. Also, Transworld's exclusivity, under the IAB By-Laws, will hold good only until thirty-three per cent market saturation has been reached. If EV is as good as it looks, that will be quite soon. After that, under the By-Laws, Transworld will be restrained from making effective defenses against patent infringement by competitors. Then all of the IAB's membership and much of their capital will be involved with EV. Much of that capital is already in anticipatory motion. So a highly complex structure now ultimately depends on the integrity of the Sollenar Corporation. If Sollenar stock falls in value, not just you but many IAB members will be greatly embarrassed. Which is another way of saying EV must succeed."

"I know all that! What of it? There's no risk. I've had every related patent on Earth checked. There will be no catastrophic obsolescence of the EV system."

Ermine said: "There are engineers on Mars. Martian engineers. They're a dying race, but no one knows what they can still do."

Sollenar raised his massive head.

Ermine said: "Late this evening, my office learned that Cortwright Burr has been in close consultation with the Martians for several weeks. They have made some sort of machine for him. He was on the flight that landed at the Facility a few moments ago."

Sollenar's fists clenched. The lights crashed off and on, and the room wailed. From the terrace came a startled cry, and a sound of smashed glass.

Mr. Ermine nodded, excused himself and left.

A few moments later, Mr. Ermine stepped out at the pedestrian level of the Sollenar Building. He strolled through the landscaped garden, and across the frothing brook toward the central walkway down the Avenue. He paused at a hedge to pluck a blossom and inhale its odor. He walked away, holding it in his naked fingers.

II

Drifting slowly on the thread of his spinneret, Rufus Sollenar came gliding down the wind above Cortwright Burr's building.

The building, like a spider, touched the ground at only the points of its legs. It held its wide, low bulk spread like a parasol over several downtown blocks. Sollenar, manipulating the helium-filled plastic drifter far above him, steered himself with jets of compressed gas from plastic bottles in the drifter's structure.

Only Sollenar himself, in all this system, was not effectively transparent to the municipal antiplane radar. And he himself was wrapped in long, fluttering streamers of dull black metallic sheeting. To the eye, he was amorphous and non-reflective. To electronic sensors, he was a drift of static much like a sheet of foil picked by the wind from some careless trash heap. To all of the senses of all interested parties he was hardly there at all—and, thus, in an excellent position for murder.

He fluttered against Burr's window. There was the man, crouched over his desk. What was that in his hands—a pomander?

Sollenar clipped his harness to the edges of the cornice. Swayed out against it, his sponge-soled boots pressed to the glass, he touched his left hand to the window and described a circle. He pushed; there was a thud on the carpeting in Burr's office, and now there was no barrier to Sollenar. Doubling his knees against his chest, he catapulted forward, the riot pistol in his right hand. He stumbled and fell to his knees, but the gun was up.

Burr jolted behind his desk. The little sphere of orange-gold metal, streaked with darker bronze, its surface vermicular with encrustations, was still in his hands. "Him!" Burr cried out as Sollenar fired.

Gasping, Sollenar watched the charge strike Burr. It threw his torso backward faster than his limbs and head could follow without dangling. The choked-down pistol was nearly silent. Burr crashed backward to end, transfixed, against the wall.

Pale and sick, Sollenar moved to take the golden ball. He wondered where Shakespeare could have seen an example such as this, to know an old man could have so much blood in him.

Burr held the prize out to him. Staring with eyes distended by hydrostatic pressure, his clothing raddled and his torso grinding its broken bones, Burr stalked away from the wall and moved as if to embrace Sollenar. It was queer, but he was not dead.

Shuddering, Sollenar fired again.

Again Burr was thrown back. The ball spun from his splayed fingers as he once more marked the wall with his body.

Pomander, orange, whatever—it looked valuable.

Sollenar ran after the rolling ball. And Burr moved to intercept him, nearly faceless, hunched under a great invisible weight that slowly yielded as his back groaned.

Sollenar took a single backward step.

Burr took a step toward him. The golden ball lay in a far corner. Sollenar raised the pistol despairingly and fired again. Burr tripped backward on tiptoe, his arms like windmills, and fell atop the prize.

Tears ran down Sollenar's cheeks. He pushed one foot forward . . . and Burr, in his corner, lifted his head and began to gather his body for the effort of rising.

Sollenar retreated to the window, the pistol sledging backward against his wrist and elbow as he fired the remaining shots in the magazine.

Panting, he climbed up into the window frame and clipped the harness to his body, craning to look over his shoulder . . . as Burr—shredded; leaking blood and worse than blood—advanced across the office.

Sollenar cast off his holds on the window frame and clumsily worked the drifter controls. Far above him, volatile ballast spilled out and dispersed in the air long before it touched ground. Sollenar rose, sobbing—

And Burr stood in the window, his shattered hands on the edges of the cut circle, raising his distended eyes steadily to watch Sollenar in flight across the enigmatic sky.

Where he landed, on the roof of a building in his possession, Sollenar had a disposal unit for his gun and his other trappings. He deferred for a time the question of why Burr had failed at once to die. Empty-handed, he returned uptown.

He entered his office, called and told his attorneys the exact times of departure and return and knew the question of dealing with municipal authorities was thereby resolved. That was simple enough, with no witnesses to complicate the matter. He began to wish he hadn't been so irresolute as to leave Burr without the thing he was after. Surely, if the pistol hadn't killed the man—an old man, with thin limbs and spotted skin—he could have wrestled that thin-limbed, bloody old man aside—that spotted old man—and dragged himself and his prize back to the window, for all that the old man would have clung to him, and clutched at his legs, and fumbled for a handhold on his somber disguise of wrappings—that broken, immortal old man.

Sollenar raised his hand. The great window to the city grew opaque.

Bess Allardyce knocked softly on the door from the terrace. He would have thought she'd returned to her own apartments many hours ago. Tortuously pleased, he opened the door and smiled at her, feeling the dried tears crack on the skin of his cheeks.

He took her proffered hands. "You waited for me," he sighed. "A long time for anyone as beautiful as you to wait."

She smiled back at him. "Let's go out and look at the stars."

"Isn't it chilly?"

"I made spiced hot cider for us. We can sip it and think."

He let her draw him out onto the terrace. He leaned on the parapet, his arm around her pulsing waist, his cape drawn around both their shoulders.

"Bess, I won't ask if you'd stay with me no matter what the circumstances. But it might be a time will come when I couldn't bear to live in this city. What about that?"

"I don't know," she answered honestly.

And Cortwright Burr put his hand up over the edge of the parapet, between them.

Sollenar stared down at the straining knuckles, holding the entire weight of the man dangling against the sheer face of the building. There was a sliding, rustling noise, and the other hand came up, searched blindly for a hold and found it, hooked over the stone. The fingers tensed and rose, their tips flattening at the pressure as Burr tried to pull his head and shoulders up to the level of the parapet.

Bess breathed: "Oh, look at them! He must have torn them terribly climbing up!" Then she pulled away from Sollenar and stood staring at him, her hand to her mouth. "But he *couldn't* have climbed! We're so high!"

Sollenar beat at the hands with the heels of his palms, using the direct, trained blows he had learned at his athletic club.

Bone splintered against the stone. When the knuckles were broken the hands instantaneously disappeared, leaving only streaks behind them. Sollenar looked over the parapet. A bundle shrank from sight, silhouetted against the lights of the pedestrian level and the Avenue. It contracted to a pinpoint. Then, when it reached the brook and water flew in all directions, it disappeared in a final sunburst, endowed with glory by the many lights which found momentary reflection down there.

"Bess, leave me! Leave me, please!" Rufus Sollenar cried out.

III

Rufus Sollenar paced his office, his hands held safely still in front of him, their fingers spread and rigid.

The telephone sounded, and his secretary said to him: "Mr. Sollenar, you are ten minutes from being late at the TTV Executives' Ball. This is a First Class obligation."

Sollenar laughed. "I thought it was, when I originally classified it."

"Are you now planning to renege, Mr. Sollenar?" the secretary inquired politely.

Certainly, Sollenar thought. He could as easily renege on the Ball as a king could on his coronation.

"Burr, you scum, what have you done to me?" he asked the air, and the telephone said: "Beg pardon?"

"Tell my valet," Sollenar said. "I'm going." He dismissed the phone. His hands cupped in front of his chest. A firm grip on emptiness might be stronger than any prize in a broken hand.

Carrying in his chest something he refused to admit was terror, Sollenar made ready for the Ball.

But only a few moments after the first dance set had ended. Malcolm Levier of the local TTV station executive staff looked over Sollenar's shoulder and remarked:

"Oh, there's Cort Burr, dressed like a gallows bird."

Sollenar, glittering in the costume of the Medici, did not turn his head. "Is he? What would he want here?"

Levier's eyebrows arched. "He holds a little stock. He has entree. But he's late." Levier's lips quirked. "It must have taken him some time to get that makeup on."

"Not in good taste, is it?"

"Look for yourself."

"Oh, I'll do better than that," Sollenar said. "I'll go and talk to him a while. Excuse me, Levier." And only then did he turn around, already started on his first pace toward the man.

But Cortwright Burr was only a pasteboard imitation of himself as Sollenar had come to know him. He stood to one side of the doorway, dressed in black and crimson robes, with black leather gauntlets on his hands, carrying a staff of weathered, natural wood. His face was shadowed by a sackcloth hood, the eyes well hidden. His face was powdered gray, and some blend of livid colors hollowed his cheeks. He stood motionless as Sollenar came up to him.

As he had crossed the floor, each step regular, the eyes of bystanders had followed Sollenar, until, anticipating his course, they found Burr waiting. The noise level of the Ball shrank perceptibly, for the lesser revelers who chanced to be present were sustaining it all alone. The people who really mattered here were silent and watchful.

The obvious thought was that Burr, defeated in business, had come here in some insane reproach to his adversary, in this lugubrious, distasteful clothing. Why, he looked like a corpse. Or worse.

The question was, what would Sollenar say to him? The wish was that Burr would take himself away, back to his estates or to some other city. New York was no longer for Cortwright Burr. But what could Sollenar say to him now, to drive him back to where he hadn't the grace to go willingly?

"Cortwright," Sollenar said in a voice confined to the two of them. "So your Martian immortality works."

Burr said nothing.

"You got that in addition, didn't you? You knew how I'd react. You knew you'd need protection. Paid the Martians to make you physically invulnerable? It's a good system. Very impressive. Who would have thought the Martians knew so much? But who here is going to pay attention to you now? Get out of town, Cortwright. You're past your chance. You're dead as far as these people are concerned—all you have left is your skin."

Burr reached up and surreptitiously lifted a corner of his fleshed mask. And there he was, under it. The hood retreated an inch, and the light reached his eyes; and Sollenar had been wrong; Burr had less left than he thought.

"Oh, no, no, Cortwright," Sollenar said softly. "No, you're right—I can't stand up to that."

He turned and bowed to the assembled company. "Good night!" he cried, and walked out of the ballroom.

Someone followed him down the corridor to the elevators. Sollenar did not look behind him.

"I have another appointment with you now," Ermine said at his elbow.

They reached the pedestrian level. Sollenar said: "There's a cafe. We can talk there."

"Too public, Mr. Sollenar. Let's simply stroll and converse." Ermine lightly took his arm and guided him along the walkway. Sollenar noticed then that Ermine was costumed so cunningly that no one could have guessed the appearance of the man.

"Very well," Sollenar said.

"Of course."

They walked together, casually. Ermine said: "Burr's driving you to your death. Is it because you tried to kill him earlier? Did you get his Martian secret?"

Sollenar shook his head.

"You didn't get it." Ermine sighed. "That's unfortunate. I'll have to take steps."

"Under the By-Laws," Sollenar said, "I cry *laissez faire*."

Ermine looked up, his eyes twinkling. "*Laissez faire?* Mr. Sollenar, do you have any idea how many of our members are involved in your fortunes? *They* will cry *laissez faire*, Mr. Sollenar, but clearly you persist in dragging them down with you. No, sir, Mr. Sollenar, my office now forwards an immediate recommendation to the Technical Advisory Committee of the IAB that Mr. Burr probably has a system superior to yours, and that stock in Sollenar, Incorporated, had best be disposed of."

"There's a bench," Sollenar said. "Let's sit down."

"As you wish." Ermine moved beside Sollenar to the bench, but remained standing.

"What is it, Mr. Sollenar?"

"I want your help. You advised me on what Burr had. It's still in his office building, somewhere. You have resources. We can get it."

Laissez faire, Mr. Sollenar. I visited you in an advisory capacity, I can do no more."

"For a partnership in my affairs could you do more?"

"Money?" Ermine tittered. "For me? Do you know the conditions of my employment?"

If he had thought, Sollenar would have remembered. He reached out tentatively. Ermine anticipated him.

Ermine bared his left arm and sank his teeth into it. He displayed the arm. There was no quiver of pain in voice or stance. "It's not a legend, Mr. Sollenar. It's quite true. We of our office must spend a year, after the nerve surgery, learning to walk without the feel of our feet, to handle objects without crushing them or letting them slip, or damaging ourselves. Our mundane pleasures are auditory, olfactory, and visual. Easily gratified at little expense. Our dreams are totally interior, Mr. Sollenar. The operation is irreversible. What would you buy for me with your money?"

"What would I buy for myself?" Sollenar's head sank down between his shoulders.

Ermine bent over him. "Your despair is your own, Mr. Sollenar. I have official business with you."

He lifted Sollenar's chin with a forefinger. "I judge physical interference to be unwarranted at this time. But matters must remain so that the IAB members involved with you can recover the value of their investments in EV. Is that perfectly clear, Mr. Sollenar? You are hereby enjoined under the By-Laws, as enforced by the Special Public Relations Office." He glanced at his watch. "Notice was served at 1:27 AM, City time."

"1:27," Sollenar said. "City time." He sprang to his feet and raced down a companionway to the taxi level.

Mr. Ermine watched him quizzically.

He opened his costume, took out his omnipresent medical kit, and sprayed coagulant over the wound in his forearm. Replacing the kit, he adjusted his clothing and strolled down the same companionway Sollenar had run. He raised an arm, and a taxi flittered down beside him. He showed the driver a card, and the cab lifted off with him, its lights glaring in a Priority pattern, far faster than Sollenar's ordinary legal limit allowed.

IV

Long Island Facility vaulted at the stars in great kangaroo-leaps of arch and cantilever span, jeweled in glass and metal as if the entire port were a mechanism for navigating interplanetary space. Rufus Sollenar placed its esplanades, measuring his steps, holding his arms still, for the short time until he could board the Mars rocket.

Erect and majestic, he took a place in the lounge and carefully sipped liqueur, once the liner had boosted away from Earth and coupled in its Faraday main drives.

Mr. Ermine settled into the place beside him.

Sollenar looked over at him calmly. "I thought so."

Ermine nodded. "Of course you did. But I didn't almost miss you. I was here ahead of you. I have no objection to your going to Mars, Mr. Sollenar. *Laissez faire*. Provided I can go along."

"Well," Rufus Sollenar said. "Liqueur?" He gestured with his glass.

Ermine shook his head. "No, thank you," he said delicately.

Sollenar said: "Even your tongue?"

"Of course my tongue, Mr. Sollenar. I taste nothing. I touch nothing." Ermine smiled. "But I feel no pressure."

"All right, then," Rufus Sollenar said crisply. "We have several hours to landing time. You sit and dream your interior dreams, and I'll dream mine." He faced around in his chair and folded his arms across his chest.

"Mr. Sollenar," Ermine said gently.

"Yes?"

"I am once again with you by appointment as provided under the By-Laws."

"State your business, Mr. Ermine."

"You are not permitted to lie in an unknown grave, Mr. Sollenar. Insurance policies on your life have been taken out at a high premium rate. The IAB members concerned cannot wait the statutory seven years to have you declared dead. Do what you will, Mr. Sollenar, but I must take care I witness your death. From now on, I am with you wherever you go."

Sollenar smiled. "I don't intend to die. Why should I die, Mr. Ermine?"

"I have no idea, Mr. Sollenar. But I know Corwright Burr's character. And isn't that he, seated there in the corner? The light is poor, but I think he's recognizable."

Across the lounge, Burr raised his head and looked into Sollenar's eyes. He raised a hand near his face, perhaps merely to signify greeting. Rufus Sollenar faced front.

"A worthy opponent, Mr. Sollenar," Ermine said. "A persevering, unforgiving, ingenious man. And yet—" Ermine seemed a little touched by bafflement. "And yet it seems to me, Mr. Sollenar, that he got you running rather easily. What *did* happen between you, after my advisory call?"

Sollenar turned a terrible smile on Ermine. "I shot him to pieces. If you'd peel his face, you'd see."

Ermine sighed. "Up to this moment, I had thought perhaps you might still salvage your affairs."

"Pity, Mr. Ermine? Pity for the insane?"

"Interest. I can take no part in your world. Be grateful, Mr. Sollenar. I am not the same gullible man I was when I signed my contract with IAB, so many years ago."

Sollenar laughed. Then he stole a glance at Burr's corner.

The ship came down at Abernathy Field, in Aresia, the Terrestrial city. Industrialized, prefabricated, jerry-built and clamorous, the storm-proofed buildings huddled, but huddled proudly, at the desert's edge.

Low on the horizon was the Martian settlement the buildings so skillfully blended with the landscape, so eroded, so much abandoned that the uninformed eye saw nothing. Sollenar had been to Mars—on a tour. He had seen the natives in their nameless dwelling place; arrogant, venomous and weak. He had been told, by the paid guide, they trafficked with Earthmen as much as they cared to, and kept to their place on the rim of Earth's encroachment, observing.

"Tell me, Ermine," Sollenar said quietly as they walked across the terminal lobby. "You're to kill me, aren't you, if I try to go on without you?"

"A matter of procedure, Mr. Sollenar," Ermine said evenly. "We cannot risk the investment capital of so many IAB members."

Sollenar sighed. "If I were any other member, how I would commend you, Mr. Ermine! Can we hire a car for ourselves, then, somewhere nearby?"

"Going out to see the engineers?" Ermine asked. "Who would have thought they'd have something valuable for sale?"

"I want to show them something," Sollenar said.

"What thing, Mr. Sollenar?"

They turned the corner of a corridor, with branching hallways here and there, not all of them busy. "Come here," Sollenar said, nodding toward one of them.

They stopped out of sight of the lobby and the main corridor. "Come on," Sollenar said. "A little farther."

"No," Ermine said. "This is farther than I really wish. It's dark here."

"Wise too late, Mr. Ermine," Sollenar said, his arms flashing out.

One palm impacted against Ermine's solar plexus, and the other against the muscle at the side of his neck, but not hard enough to kill. Ermine collapsed, starved for oxygen, while Sollenar silently cursed having been cured of murder. Then Sollenar turned and ran.

Behind him Ermine's body struggled to draw breath by reflex alone.

Moving as fast as he dared, Sollenar walked back and reached the taxi lock, pulling a respirator from a wall rack as he went. He flagged a car and gave his destination, looking behind him. He had seen nothing of Cortwright Burr since setting foot on Mars. But he knew that soon or late, Burr would find him.

A few moments later Ermine got to his feet. Sollenar's car was well away. Ermine shrugged and went to the local broadcasting station.

He commandeered a private desk, a firearm and immediate time on the IAB interoffice circuit to Earth. When his call acknowledgement had come back to him from his office there, he reported:

"Sollenar is enroute to the Martian city. He wants a duplicate of Burr's device, of course, since he smashed the original when he killed Burr. I'll follow and make final disposition. The disorientation I reported previously is progressing rapidly. Almost all his responses now are inappropriate. On the flight out, he seemed to be staring at something in an empty seat. Quite often when spoken to he obviously hears something else entirely. I expect to catch one of the next few flights back."

There was no point in waiting for comment to wend its way back from Earth. Ermine left. He went to a cab rank and paid the exorbitant fee for transportation outside Aresian city limits.

Close at hand, the Martian city was like a welter of broken pots. Shards of wall and roof joined at savage angles and pointed to nothing. Underfoot, drifts of vitreous material, shaped to fit no sane configuration, and broken to fit such a mosaic as no church would contain, rocked and slid under Sollenar's hurrying feet.

What from Aresia had been a solid front of dun color was here a facade of red, green and blue splashed about centuries ago and since then weathered only enough to show how bitter the colors had once been. The plum-colored sky stretched over all this like a frigid membrane, and the wind blew and blew.

Here and there, as he progressed, Sollenar saw Martian arms and heads protruding from the rubble. Sculptures.

He was moving toward the heart of the city, where some few unbroken structures persisted. At the top of a heap of shards he turned to look behind him. There was the dust-plume of his cab, returning to the city. He expected to walk back—perhaps to meet someone on the road, all alone on the Martian plain if only Ermine would forebear from interfering. Searching the flat, thin-aired landscape, he tried to pick out the plodding dot of Cortwright Burr. But not yet.

He turned and ran down the untrustworthy slope.

He reached the edge of the maintained area. Here the rubble was gone, the ancient walks swept, the statues kept upright on their pediments. But only broken walls suggested the fronts of the houses that had stood here. Knifing their sides up through the wind-rippled sand that only constant care kept off the street, the shadow-houses fenced his way and the sculptures were motionless as hope. Ahead of him, he saw the buildings of the engineers. There was no heap to climb and look to see if Ermine followed close behind.

Sucking his respirator, he reached the building of the Martian engineers.

A sounding strip ran down the doorjamb. He scratched his fingernails sharply along it, and the magnified vibration, ducted throughout the hollow walls, rattled his plea for entrance.

V

The door opened, and Martians stood looking. They were spindly-limbed and slight, their faces framed by folds of leathery tissue. Their mouths were lipped with horn as hard as dentures, and pursed, forever ready to masticate. They were pleasant neither to look at nor, Sollenar knew, to deal with. But Cortwright Burr had done it. And Sollenar needed to do it.

"Does anyone here speak English?" he asked.

"I," said the central Martian, his mouth opening to the sound, closing to end the reply.

"I would like to deal with you."

"Whenever," the Martian said, and the group at the doorway parted deliberately to let Sollenar in.

Before the door closed behind him, Sollenar looked back. But the rubble of the abandoned sectors blocked his line of sight into the desert.

"What can you offer? And what do you want?" the Martian asked. Sollenar stood half-ringed by them, in a room whose corners he could not see in the uncertain light.

"I offer you Terrestrial currency."

The English-speaking Martian—the Martian who had admitted to speaking English—turned his head slightly and spoke to his fellows. There were clacking sounds as his lips met. The others reacted variously, one of them suddenly gesturing with what seemed a disgusted flip of his arm before he turned without further word and stalked away, his shoulders looking like the shawled back of a very old and very hungry woman.

"What did Burr give you?" Sollenar asked.

"Burr." The Martian cocked his head. His eyes were not multi-faceted, but gave that impression.

"He was here and he dealt with you. Not long ago. On what basis?"

"Burr. Yes. Burr gave us currency. We will take currency from you. For the same thing we gave him?"

"For immortality, yes."

"Im— This is a new word."

"Is it? For the secret of not dying?"

"Not dying? You think we have not-dying for sale here?" The Martian spoke to the others again. Their lips clattered. Others left, like the first one had, moving with great precision and very slow step, and no remaining tolerance for Sollenar.

Sollenar cried out: "What did you sell him, then?"

The principal engineer said: "We made an entertainment device for him."

"A little thing. This size." Sollenar cupped his hands.

"You have seen it, then."

"Yes. And nothing more? That was all he bought here?"

"It was all we had to sell—or give. We don't yet know whether Earthmen will give us things in exchange for currency. We'll see, when we next need something from Aresia."

Sollenar demanded: "How did it work? This thing you sold him."

"Oh, it lets people tell stories to themselves."

Sollenar looked closely at the Martian. "What kind of stories?"

"Any kind," the Martian said blandly. "Burr told us what he wanted. He had drawings with him of an Earthman device that used pictures on a screen, and broadcast sounds, to carry the details of the story told to the auditor."

"He stole those patents! He couldn't have used them on Earth."

• • •

"And why should he? Our device needs to convey no precise details. Any mind can make its own. It only needs to be put into a situation, and from there it can do all the work. If an auditor wishes a story of contact with other sexes, for example, the projector simply makes it seem to him, the next time he is with the object of his desire, that he is getting positive feedback—that he is arousing a similar response in that object. Once that has been established for him, the auditor may then leave the machine, move about normally, conduct his life as usual—but always in accordance with the basic situation. It is, you see, in the end a means of introducing system into his view of reality. Of course, his society must understand that he is not in accord with reality, for some of what he does cannot seem rational from an outside view of him. So some care must be taken, but not much. If many such devices were to enter his society, soon the circumstances would become commonplace, and the society would surely readjust to allow for it," said the English-speaking Martian.

"The machine creates any desired situation in the auditor's mind?"

"Certainly. There are simple predisposing tapes that can be inserted as desired. Love, adventure, cerebration—it makes no difference."

Several of the bystanders clacked sounds out to each other. Sollenar looked at them narrowly. It was obvious there had to be more than one English-speaker among these people.

"And the device you gave Burr," he asked the engineer, neither calmly nor hopefully. "What sort of stories could its auditors tell themselves?"

The Martian cocked his head again. It gave him the look of an owl at a bedroom window. "Oh, there was one situation we were particularly instructed to include. Burr said he was thinking ahead to showing it to an acquaintance of his.

"It was a situation of adventure; of adventure with the fearful. And it was to end in loss and bitterness." The Martian looked even more closely at Sollenar. "Of course, the device does not specify details. No one but the auditor can know what fearful thing inhabits his story, or precisely how the end of it would come. You would, I believe, be Rufus Sollenar? Burr spoke of you and made the noise of laughing."

Sollenar opened his mouth. But there was nothing to say.

"You want such a device?" the Martian asked. "We've prepared several since Burr left. He spoke of machines that would manufacture them in astronomical numbers. We, of course, have done our best with our poor hands."

Sollenar said: "I would like to look out your door."

"Pleasure."

Sollenar opened the door slightly. Mr. Ermine stood in the cleared street, motionless as the shadow buildings behind him. He raised one hand in a gesture of unfelt greeting as he saw Sollenar, then put it back on the stock of his rifle. Sollenar closed the door, and turned to the Martian. "How much currency do you want?"

"Oh, all you have with you. You people always have a good deal with you when you travel."

Sollenar plunged his hands into his pockets and pulled out his billfold, his change, his keys, his jeweled radio; whatever was there, he rummaged out onto the floor, listening to the sound of rolling coins.

"I wish I had more here," he laughed. "I wish I had the amount that man out there is going to recover when he shoots me."

The Martian engineer cocked his head, "But your dream is over, Mr. Sollenar," he clacked drily. "Isn't it?"

"Quite so. But you to your purposes and I to mine. Now give me one of those projectors. And set it to predispose a situation I am about to specify to you. Take however long it needs. The audience is a patient one." He laughed, and tears gathered in his eyes.

Mr. Ermine waited, isolated from the cold, listening to hear whether the rifle stock was slipping out of his fingers. He had no desire to go into the Martian building after Sollenar and involve third parties. All he wanted was to put Sollenar's body under a dated marker, with as little trouble as possible.

Now and then he walked a few paces backward and forward, to keep from losing muscular control at his extremities because of low skin temperature. Sollenar must come out soon enough. He had no food supply with him, and though Ermine did not like the risk of engaging a man like Sollenar in a starvation contest, there was no doubt that a man with no taste for fuel could outlast one with the acquired reflexes of eating.

The door opened and Sollenar came out.

He was carrying something. Perhaps a weapon. Ermine let him come closer while he raised and carefully sighted his rifle. Sollenar might have some Martian weapon or he might not. Ermine did not particularly care. If Ermine died, he would hardly notice it—far less than he would notice a botched ending to a job of work already roiled by Sollenar's break away at the space field. If Ermine died, some other SPRO agent would be assigned almost immediately. No matter what happened, SPRO would stop Sollenar before he ever reached Abernathy Field.

So there was plenty of time to aim an unhurried, clean shot.

Sollenar was closer, now. He seemed to be in a very agitated frame of mind. He held out whatever he had in his hand.

It was another one of the Martian entertainment machines. Sollenar seemed to be offering it as a token to Ermine. Ermine smiled.

"What can you offer me, Mr. Sollenar?" he said, and shot.

The golden ball rolled away over the sand. "There now," Ermine said. "*Now,* wouldn't you sooner be me than you? And where is the thing that made the difference between us?"

He shivered. He was chilly. Sand was blowing against his tender face, which had been somewhat abraded during his long wait.

He stopped, transfixed.

He lifted his head.

Then, with a great swing of his arms, he sent the rifle whirling away. "The wind!" he sighed into the thin air. "I feel the wind." He leapt into the air, and sand flew away from his feet as he landed. He whispered to himself: "I feel the ground!"

He stared in tremblant joy at Sollenar's empty body. "What have you given me?" Full of his own rebirth, he swung his head up at the sky again, and cried in the direction of the Sun: "Oh, you squeezing, nibbling people who made me incorruptible and thought that was the end of me!"

With love he buried Sollenar, and with reverence he put up the marker, but he had plans for what he might accomplish with the facts of this transaction, and the myriad others he was privy to.

A sharp bit of pottery had penetrated the sole of his shoe and gashed his foot, but he, not having seen it, hadn't felt it. Nor would he see it or feel it even when he changed his stockings; for he had not noticed the wound when it was made. It didn't matter. In a few days it would heal, though not as rapidly as if it had been properly attended to.

Vaguely, he heard the sound of Martians clacking behind their closed door as he hurried out of the city, full of revenge, and of reverence for his savior.

Sometimes, I find myself playing with some object—in this case, a pair of slip-joint pliers, in another case a randomly bent paper clip—and entering some sort of daze in which the mechanical action or the superficially meaningless shape transforms itself into an image. I believe this derives from a semester of studying Gestalt Therapy under Ralph Hefferline at Columbia University. The paperclip became the consumable emitting element in a raygun—especially after I had seared it with a cigarette lighter, still for no conscious reason. From the gun grew the feeling for the thumbless man who had to replace its element, and he in turn became the tragic hero of a story called "The Burning World," which is in another collection.

The pliers—the pliers and the man who dealt with them—you will find here, both transmogrified.

All For Love

MALACHI RUNNER DIDN'T like to look at General Compton. Compton the lean, keen, slash-gesturing semi-demagogue of a few years ago had been much easier to live with than Compton as he was now, and Runner had never had much stomach for him even then. So Runner kept his eyes firmly fixed on the device he was showing.

Keeping his eyes where they were was not as easy as it might have been. The speckled, bulbous distortion in front of him was what Headquarters, several hundred miles away under The Great Salt Lake, was pleased to refer to as an Invisible Weapons Carrier. It was hard to see because it was designed to be hard to see.

But Malachi Runner was going to have to take this thing up across several hundred miles of terrain, and he was standing too close to it not to see it. The Invisible Weapons Carrier was, in fact, a half-tone of reality. It was large enough inside to contain a

©1962, Galaxy Publishing Corporation

man and a fusion bomb, together with the power supply for its engine and its light amplifiers. It bristled with a stiff mat of flexible-plastic light-conducting rods, whose stub ends, clustered together in a tight mosaic pointing outward in every conceivable direction, contrived to bend light around its bulk. It was presently conducting, toward Runner, a picture of the carved rock directly behind it.

The rock, here in this chamber cut under the eastern face of the Medicine Bow Mountains, was reasonably featureless; and the light-amplifiers carefully controlled the intensity of the picture. So the illusion was marred by only two things: the improbable angle of the pictured floor it was also showing him, and the fact that for every rod conducting light from the wall, another rod was conducting light from Runner's direction, so that to his eyes the ends of half the rods were dead black.

"Invisibility," Compton said scornfully from behind and to one side of Runner. Or, rather, he whispered and an amplifier took up the strain in raising his voice to a normal level. "But it's not bad camouflage. You might make it, Colonel."

"I have orders to try." Runner would not give Compton the satisfaction of knowing that his impatience was with the means provided, not with the opportunity. The war could not possibly be permitted to continue the thirty years more given to it by Compton's schedule. Compton himself was proof of that.

Not that proof required Compton. He was only one. There were many.

Runner glanced aside at the cadet officer who had guided him from the tramway stop to this chamber here, in one of the side passages of the siege bore that was being driven under the Medicine Bows in the direction of the alien spaceship that had dominated the world for fifty years. The boy—none of these underofficers were older than seventeen—had a face that looked as if it had been made from wet paper and then baked dry. His eyesockets were black pits from which his red eyes stared, and his hands were like chickens' feet. His bloated stomach pushed against the wide white plastic of his sidearm belt.

He looked, in short, like most of the other people Runner had seen here since getting off the tram. As he was only seventeen, he had probably been born underground, somewhere along the advancing bore, and had never so much as seen sunlight, much less eaten anything grown under it. He had been bred and educated—or mis-educated; show him something not printed in Military Alphabet and you showed him the Mayan Codex—trained and assigned to duty in a tunnel in the rock; and never in his life had he been away from the sound of the biting drills.

"You're not eager to go, Colonel?" Compton's amplified whisper said. "You're Special Division, so of course this isn't quite your line of work. I know your ideals, you Special Division men. Find some way to keep the race from dehumanizing itself." And now he chose to make a laugh, remembering to whisper it. "One way to do that would be to end the war before another generation goes by."

Runner wondered, not for the first time, if Compton would find some way to stop him without actually disobeying the Headquarters directive ordering him to cooperate. Runner wondered, too, what Compton would say if he knew just how eager he was for the mission—and why. Runner could answer the questions for himself by getting to know Compton better, of course. There was the rub.

Runner did not think he could ever have felt particularly civilized toward anyone who had married his fiancee. That was understandable. It was even welcome. Runner perversely cherished his failings. Not too perversely, at that—Runner consciously cherished every human thing remaining to the race.

Runner could understand why a woman would choose to marry the famous Corps of Engineers general who had already chivvied and bullied the Army—the organizing force of the world—into devoting its major resources to this project he had fostered. There was no difficulty in seeing why Norma Brand might turn away from Malachi Runner in favor of a man who was not only the picture of efficiency and successful intellect but was thought likely to be the savior of Humanity.

But Compton several years later was—

Runner turned and looked; he couldn't spend the rest of the day avoiding it. Compton, several years later, was precisely what a man of his time could become if he was engaged in pushing a three hundred mile tunnel through the rock of a mountain chain, never knowing how much his enemy might know about it, and if he proposed to continue that excavation to its end, thirty years from now, whether the flesh was willing to meet his schedules or not.

Compton's leonine head protruded from what was very like a steam cabinet on wheels. In that cabinet were devices to assist his silicotic lungs, his sclerotic blood vessels, and a nervous system so badly deranged that even several years ago Runner had detected the great man in fits of spastic trembling. And God knew what else might be going wrong with Compton's body that Compton's will would not admit.

Compton grinned at him. Almost simultaneously, a bell chimed softly in the control panel on the back of the cabinet. The cadet aide sprang forward, read the warning in some dial or other and made an adjustment in the settings of the control knobs. Compton craned his neck in its collar of loose gray plastic sheeting and extended his grin to the boy. "Thank you, Cadet. I thought I was starting to feel a little dizzy."

"Yes, sir." The aide went back to his rest position.

"All right, Colonel," Compton said to Runner as though nothing had happened. "I've been curious to see this gimmick of yours in operation ever since it was delivered here. Thank you. You can turn it off now. And after that, I'll show *you* something you've never seen."

Runner frowned for a moment. Then he nodded to himself. He crawled under the weapons carrier. From that close it was no longer "invisible," only vaguely dizzying to the eye. He opened the hatch and turned off the main switch.

Compton could only have meant he was going to show him the ship.

Of course, he had seen films of it often enough. Who had not? The Army had managed to keep spy-drones flying above the Mississippi plain. The ship ignored them unless they took on aggressive trajectories.

Presumably there was some limit to the power the ship felt able to expend. Or perhaps the ship simply did not care what Earthmen might learn from watching it; perhaps it underestimated them.

This latest in the long chain of Compton's command bunkers, creeping mole-like toward the ship, was lighted a sickly orange-yellow. Runner seemed to recall a minor scandal in the Quartermaster Corps. Something about a contractor who had bribed or cozened a Corps officer into believing that yellow light duplicated natural sunlight. Contractor and misled officer were no doubt long dead in one of the labor battalions at the bore face, but some use for the useless lights had had to be found. And so here they were, casting their pall, just as if two lives and two careers had not already gone toward settling the account.

But, of course, nothing settles an account as derelict as Earth's was.

In that light, Compton's cabinet rolled forward to the bank of hooded television screens jury-rigged against a somewhat waterproofed wall. A row of technicians perched on stools watched what the drones were showing them.

"Lights," Compton said, and the aide made the room dark. "Here, Colonel—try this one." He pointed his chin toward a particular screen, and Runner stepped closer. For the first time in his life, he saw something only a few hundred people of his time had seen in an undelayed picture; he saw the ship. It was two hundred miles away from his present location, and two hundred fifty miles high.

II

Fifty years ago, the alien ship landed butt-down in the northwest quadrant of the central plain of the United States. Stern-first, she had put one of her four landing jacks straight down to bedrock through the town of Scott's Bluff, Nebraska, and the diagonally opposite leg seventy-five miles away near Julesburg, Colorado. Her shadow swept fifty thousand square miles.

A tower of pitted dull green and brown-gold metal, her forepeak narrowing in perspective into a needle raking unseen through the thinnest last margins of the atmosphere, she had neither parleyed nor even communicated with anything on or of Earth. No one had ever seen anything of what her crew might look like. To this day, she still neither spoke to Earth nor listened to whatever Terrestrials might want to say to her. She was neither an embassy nor an invader.

For fifty years she had been broadcasting the same code group into space, hour after hour, but she had neither made nor received any beam transmissions along any portion of the electromagnetic spectrum. The presumption was she had a distress beacon out on general principles, but had no hope of communicating with a particular source of rescue.

She had come down a little erratically; there was some suggestion of jury-rigging in the plates over an apparently buckled section of the hull shrouding her stern tubes; there seemed to be some abnormal erosion at one segment of the lip around the main jet. Over the years, Headquarters Intelligence had reached the decision that she was down on Earth for a self-refit.

Landing, she had immediately put out surface parties and air patrols—there were turret-mounted weapons all along her flanks; she was clearly a warship of some kind—in a display of resources that badly upset the Terrestrial military forces observing her. The surface parties were squat-profiled, tracked, armored amphibious machines with sixteen-foot bogeys and a track-to-turtledeck height of seventy-five feet. They had fanned out over the surrounding states and, without regard to road, river, fence or farmhouse, had foraged for minerals. It had finally been concluded that the vehicles, equipped with power shovels, claws, drills, ore buckets and whatever other mining tools were necessary, were remote-controlled from the ship on the basis of local topography but not with any reference to the works of Man. Or to the presence of Man. The undeviating tracks made as much of a hayrick as they did of a company of anti-tank infantry or a battalion of what the Army in those days was pleased to call "armor."

Whatever had hurt her, there was no point in Earthmen speculating on it. No missile could reach her. She had antimissile missiles and barrage patterns that, in operation, had made the Mississippi plain uninhabitable. An attempt was made to strike her foraging parties, with some immediate success. She then extended her air cover to the entire civilized world, and began methodically smashing down every military installation and every industrial complex capable of supporting one.

It was a tribute to the energy and perseverance of Twentieth Century Man. And it was the cause of Twenty-First Century man's finding himself broken into isolated enclaves, almost all of them either underground or so geographically remote as to be valueless, and each also nearly incapable of physical communication with any other.

It did not take a great deal of Terrestrial surface activity to attract one of the ship's nearly invulnerable aircraft. Runner's journey between Salt Lake and the tunnel pit head had been long, complicated by the need to establish no beaten path, and anxious. Only the broken terrain, full of hiding places, had made it possible at all.

But the balance between birth and death rates was once more favorable, and things were no longer going all the ship's way— whether the ship knew it or not. Still, it would be another thirty years before this siege bore Compton was driving could reach, undermine and finally topple the ship.

Thirty years from now, Runner and the other members of Special Division knew, the biped, spindling, red-eyed creatures emerging from the ground to loot that broken ship and repay themselves for this nightmare campaign would be only externally human—some of them. Some would be far less. Special Division's hope—its prospects were not good enough to call it a task—was to attempt to shorten that time while Humanity was still human.

And if the human race did not topple the ship, or if the ship completed its refit and left before they could reach it, then all this fifty years of incalculable material and psychic expenditure was irretrievably lost. Humanity would be bankrupt. They were all living now on the physical and emotional credit embodied in that tower of alien resources. From it, they could strip a technology to make the world new again—nothing less could accomplish that; in its conquest, there was a triumph to renew the most exhausted heart. Or almost any such heart. Runner could only speculate on how many of the victors would be, like Compton, unable to dance upon the broken corpse.

If anyone on Earth doubted, no one dared to dwell aloud on the enfeebling thought.

They had to have the ship.

"She's got some kind of force-field running over her structure," Compton remarked, looking at the image on the screen. "We know that much. Something that keeps the crystals in her metal from deforming and sliding. She'd collapse. If we had something like that field, we could build to her size, too."

"Is there that much metal in the world?"

Compton looked sideward at Runner. "A damned sight more. But if we had her, we wouldn't need it."

Yes, Runner thought, keeping himself from looking at the screen now as faithfully as he had prevented himself from looking at Compton earlier. Yes, if we had the ship we wouldn't need this, and we wouldn't need that, or the other thing. We could even engineer such wonderful cabinets like the one in which Compton dwells that none of us would have to fear a stop to our ambitions, and we could roll along in glory on the wonderfully smooth corridor floors we could carve, away from the places where storms and lightning strike.

For how could you live, Compton, out there where I have to go tomorrow?

Compton, looking up at him, shrewdly said: "Do you know I approve of the Special Division? I think you people serve a very necessary function. I need the pressure of rivals."

Runner thought: You are ugly.

"I have to go to sleep," he had said and left Compton to his screens and schedules. But he did not take the lift down to the Bachelor Officers' Quarters where he had been given an accommodation—a two-man cubicle for himself alone; the aide, never having experienced solitude, as Runner had, had been envious. Instead, he puzzled his way through another of the branching temporary passageways that were crudely chopped out for living space near the advancing bore.

He searched until he found the proper door. The letter Norma had sent him did not contain the most exact directions. It had spoken in local terms: "Follow the first parallel until you reach the fourth gallery," and so forth.

He knocked, and the gas-tight door opened.

"I heard you would be here today," Norma said in a choked voice, and there was much for him to read in the waxiness of her skin and the deep wrinkles that ran from the corners of her nose to the corners of her bloodless mouth.

He took the hands she offered, and stepped inside.

There was one large room; that is, a room large enough for a free-standing single cot, rather than a bunk, and a cleared area, faintly marked by black rubber wheelmarks, large enough for a cabinet to turn around in.

"How are you, Norma?" he said as if he could not guess, and she did not trouble to answer him. She shut the door and leaned against it as if they had both just fled in here.

"Are you going out in the morning?"

Runner nodded. It seemed to him he had time at least to say a few conventional things to the girl who had been his fiancee, and then Compton's wife. But she apparently thought otherwise.

"Are you going to make it?"

"I don't know. It's a gamble."

"Do you think you'll make it?"

"No."

It had never seemed reasonable that he would. In the Technical Section of the Special Division there were men—fully his equals—who were convinced he could succeed. They said they had calculated the ship's weaknesses, and he believed they had figures and evaluations, right enough. He in his own turn believed there were things a man had to be willing to do whether they seemed reasonable or not, simply because they seemed necessary. So neither fact nor opinion could modify his taking the weapons carrier out against the ship tomorrow. "But I *hope* I'll make it," he said.

"You hope you'll make it," Norma said tonelessly. She reached out quickly and took his hands again. "What a forlorn thing to tell me! You know I won't be able to stand it down here much longer. How do we know the ship doesn't have seismic detectors? How do we know it isn't just letting us concentrate ourselves here so it can smash us before we become dangerous?"

"Well, we don't know, but it seems unlikely. They have geological probes, of course. The gamble is that they're only probes and not detectors."

"If they don't smash us, there's only one reason—they know they'll be finished and gone before we can reach them!"

This was all wrong; he could not talk to her about anything important before he had calmed her. He said, searching for some way to reach her: "But we have to go on as if they won't. Nothing else we've tried has worked. At least Compton's project hasn't failed."

"Now you're on his side! You!"

She was nothing like the way she had been with him. She would never have been like this. The way she was now, she and Malachi Runner could not meet. He understood, now, that in the years since she had left Headquarters with Compton she had come to think back on Malachi Runner not as a man but as an embodiment of that safe life. It was not him she was shouting out to. It was to all those days gone forever.

And so I must be those days of life in a place where shafts lead to the wine-rich air of the surface, and there is no sound of metal twisting in the rock. I am not Malachi Runner now. I hoped I could be. I should have read that letter as it was, not as I hoped it was. Good-by, Runner, you aren't needed here.

"No, I'm not on his side. But I wouldn't dare stop him if I could. I wouldn't dare shut off any hope that things will end and the world can go back to living."

"End? Where can they end? He goes on; he can't move an arm or a finger, but he goes on. He doesn't need anything but that box that keeps him alive and this tunnel and that ship. Where can I touch him?"

They stood separated by their outstretched hands, and Runner watched her as intently as though he had been ordered to make a report on her.

"I thought I could help him, but now he's in that box!"

Yes, Runner thought, now he's in that box. He will not let death rob him of seeing the end of his plans. And you love him, but he's gone where you can't follow. Can you?

He considered what he saw in her now, and he knew she was lost. But he thought that if the war would only end, there would be ways to reach her. He could not reach her now; nothing could reach her. He knew insanity was incurable, but he thought that perhaps she was not yet insane; if he could at least keep her within this world's bounds, there might be time, and ways, to bring her back. If not to him, then at least to the remembered days of Headquarters.

"Norma!" he said, driven by what he foresaw and feared. He

pulled her close and caught her eyes in his own. "Norma, you have got to promise me that no matter what happens, you won't get into another one of those boxes so you can be with him."

The thought was entirely new to her. Her voice was much lower. She frowned as if to see him better and said: "Get into one of those boxes? Oh, no—no, I'm not sick, yet. I only have to have shots for my nerves. A corpsman comes and gives them to me. He'll be here soon. It's only if you can't not-care; I mean, if you have to stay involved, like he does, that you need the interrupter circuits instead of the tranquilizer shots. You don't get into one of those boxes just for fear," she said.

He had forgotten that; he had more than forgotten it—there were apparently things in the world that had made him be sure, for a moment, that it really was fear.

He did not like hallucinating. He did not have any way of depending on himself if he had lapses like that.

"Norma, how do I look to you?" he said rapidly.

She was still frowning at him in that way. "You look about the same as always," she said.

He left her quickly—he had never thought, in conniving for this assignment with the letter crackling in his pocket, that he would leave her so quickly. And he went to his accommodation, crossing the raw, still untracked and unsheathed echoing shaft of the tunnel this near the face, with the labor battalion squads filing back and forth and the rubble carts rumbling. And in the morning he set out. He crawled into the weapons carrier, and was lifted up to a hidden opening that had been made for it during the night. He started the engine and, lying flat on his stomach in the tiny cockpit, peering through the cat's-eye viewports, he slid out onto the surface of the mountain and so became the first of his generation to advance into this territory that did not any more belong to Man.

When he was three days out, he passed within a hundred yards of a cluster of mining-machines. They paid him no attention, and he laughed, cackling inside his egg. He knew that if he had safely come so close to an extension of the ship—an extension that could have stepped over and crushed him with almost no extra expenditure—then his chances were very good. He knew he cackled. But he knew the Army's drones were watching, unobtrusively, for signs of his extinction or breakdown. Not finding them, they were therefore giving Compton and Headquarters the negative good news that he had not yet failed. At Headquarters, other Special Division personnel would be beginning to hope. They had been the minority party in the conflicts there for as long as they had been in existence at all.

But it did not matter, he thought as he lay up that night and sipped warm water from the carrier's tank. It didn't matter what party was winning. Surely even Compton would not be infuriated by a premature end to the war. And there were plenty of people at Headquarters who had fought for Compton not because they were convinced his was the only way, but only because his was a way that seemed sure. If slow. Or as sure as any way could be.

It came to Runner, for the first time in his life, that any race, in whatever straits, willing to expend so much of its resources on what was really not a surety at all, must be desperate beyond all reason.

He cackled again. He knew he cackled. He smiled at himself for it.

III

The interior of the weapons carrier was padded to protect him from the inevitable jounces and collisions. So it was hot. And the controls were crude; the carrier moved from one foot to another, like a turtle, and there were levers for each of his hands and feet to control. He sweated and panted for breath.

No other machine could possibly have climbed down the face of that mountain and then begun its heaving, staggering progress toward the spaceship's nearest leg. It could not afford to leave tracks. And it would, when it had covered the long miles of open country that separated it from its first destination, have to begin another inching, creeping journey of fifty-five miles, diagonally up the broadening, extensible pillar of the leg.

It stumbled forward on pseudopods—enormous hollow pads of tough, transparent plastic, molded full of stress-channels that curled them to fit the terrain, when they were stiffened in turn by compressed colorless fluid. Shifting its weight from one of these to another, the carrier duck-walked from one shadow to another as Runner, writhing with muscle cramps, guided it at approximately the pace of a drunken man.

But it moved forward.

After the first day Runner was ready to believe that the ship's radar systems were not designed to track something that moved so close to the ground and so slowly. The optical detection system—which Intelligence respected far more than it did radar; there were dozens of countered radar-proof missiles to confirm them—also did not seem to have picked him up.

He began to feel he might see Norma again. Thinking of that babbling stranger in Compton's accommodation, he began to feel he might someday see *Norma* again.

The ship's leg was sunken through the ground down to its anchorage among the deep rock layers sloping away from the mountains. It was, at ground level, so far across that he could not see past it. It was a wall of streaked and overgrown metal curving away from him, and only by shifting to one of the side viewports could he make out its apparent limits from where he now was.

Looking overhead, he saw it rise away from him, an inverted pylon thrust into the ground at an angle, and far, far above him, in the air toward which that angle pointed, something large and vague rested on that pylon. Obscured by mist and cloud, distorted by the curvature of the tiny lens through which he was forced to look at it, it was nothing meaningful. He reasoned the pylon led up to the ship. He could not see the ship; he concentrated on the pylon.

Gingerly, he extended a pseudopod. It touched the metal of the ship, through which the stabilizing field ran. There was an unknown danger here, but it hadn't seemed likely to Intelligence that the field would affect non-metallic substances.

It didn't. The pseudopod touched the metal of the ship, and nothing untoward happened. He drew it back, and cycled an entirely new fluid through the pseudopods. Hairline excretory channels opened on their soles, blown clean by the pressure. The pads flattened and increased in area. He moved forward toward the pylon again, and this time he began to climb it, held by air pressure on the pads and the surface tension on their wet soles. He began, then, at the end of a week's journey, to climb upon the ship no other aggression of Man's had ever reached. By the time he was a thousand feet up, he dared look only through the fore ports.

Now he moved in a universe of sound. The leg thrummed and quivered, so gently that he doubted anyone in the ship could feel it. But he was not in the ship; he was where the thrumming was. It invaded his gritted teeth and put an intolerable itching deep into his ears. This fifty-five miles had to be made without stop for rest; he could not, in fact, take his hands from the controls. He was not sure but what he shouldn't be grateful—he would have gouged his ears with his nails, surely, if he had been free to work at them.

He was past laughter of any kind now—but exultation sustained him even when, near the very peak of his climb, he came to the rat guard.

He had studied this problem with a model. No one had tried to tell him what it might be like to solve it at this altitude, with the wind and mist upon him.

The rat guard was a collar of metal, cone-shaped and inverted downward, circling the leg. The leg here was several miles in diameter; the rat guard was a canopy several yards thick and several hundred feet wide from its joining at the leg to its lip. It was designed to prevent exactly what was happening—the attempted entry of a pest.

Runner extended the carrier's pseudopods as far and wide as they would go. He pumped more coagulant into the fluid that leaked almost imperceptibly out of their soles, and began to make his way, head-downward, along the descending slope of the rat guard's outer face. The carrier swayed and stretched at the plastic membranes. He neutralized the coagulant in each foot in turn, slid it forward, fastened it again, and proceeded. After three hours he was at the lip, and dangling by the carrier's forelegs until he had succeeded in billowing one of the rear pads onto the lip as well.

And when he had, by this patient trial and error, scrambled successfully onto the rat guard's welcome upward face, he found that he was not past laughing after all. He shouted it; the carrier's interior frothed with it, and even the itching in his ears was lost. Then he began to move upward again.

Not too far away, the leg entered the ship's hull. There was an opening at least as large as the carrier needed. It was only a well;

up here, the gleaming pistons that controlled the extension of the leg hung burnished in the gloom, but there was no entry to the ship itself. Nor did he need or want it.

He had reasoned long ago that whatever inhabited this ship must be as tired, as anxious, as beset as any human being. He needed no new miseries to borrow. He wanted only to find a good place to attach his bomb, set the fuse and go. Before the leg, its muscles cut, collapsed upon the aliens' hope of ever returning to whatever peace they dreamed of.

When he climbed out of the carrier, as he had to, to attach the bomb, he heard one noise that was not wind-thrum or the throb of internal machinery. It was a persistent, nerve-torn ululation, faint but clear, deep inside the ship and with a chilling quality of endurance.

He hurried back down the leg; he had only four days to get clear—that is, to have a hope of getting clear—and he hurried too much. At the rat guard's lip, he had to hang on by his heels and cast the fore pads under. He thought he had a grip, but he had only half a one. The carrier slipped, jerked and hung dangling by one pad. It began to slide back down the short distance to the lip of the guard, rippling and twisting as parts of its sole lost contact and other parts had to take up the sudden drag.

He poured coagulant into the pad, and stopped the awful series of sticks and slips. He slapped the other pads up into place and levered forward, forgetting how firmly that one pad had been set in his panic. He felt resistance, and then remembered, but by then the pull of the other three pads had torn the carrier forward and there was a long rip through which stress fluid and coagulant dripped in a turgid stream.

He came down the last ten miles of the leg like a runaway toboggan on a poorly surfaced slide, the almost flaccid pads turning brown and burnt, their plastic soft as jelly. He left behind him a long, slowly evaporating smear of fluid and, since no one had thought to put individual shut-offs in the cross-valving system between the pads, he came down with no hope of ever using the carrier to get back to the mountains.

It was worse than that. In the end, he crashed into the indented ground at the base of the leg and, for all the interior padding, the drive levers bludgeoned him and broke bones for him. He lay in the wreck with only a faint awareness of anything but his pain. He could not even know whether the carrier, with its silent power supply, still as much as half hid him or whether that had broken, too.

It hadn't broken, but he was still there when the bomb exploded; it was only a few hours afterward that he came out of his latest delirium and found that the ground had been stirred and the carrier was lying in a new position.

He pried open the hatch—not easily or painlessly—and looked out.

The ship hadn't fallen. The leg had twitched in the ground—it was displaced by several thousand yards, and raw earth clung to it far overhead. It had changed its angle several degrees toward vertical and was much less deeply sunken into the ground. But the ship had not fallen.

He fell back into the carrier and cried because the ship hadn't come down and crushed him.

IV

The carrier had to be abandoned. Even if the pads had been usable, it was three-quarters buried in the upheaval the leg had made when it stirred. The machine, Runner thought contemptuously, had failed, while a man could be holed and broken and heal himself nevertheless.

He had very good proof of that, creeping back toward the mountains. Broken badly enough, a man might not heal himself into what he had been. But he would heal into something.

For a time he had to be very wary of the mining machines, for there had been a frenzied increase in their activity. And there was the problem of food and water. But he was in well-watered country. The comings and goings of the machines had churned the banks of the Platte River into a series of sinks and swamps without making it impossible for a thirsty, crawling man to drink. And he had his rations from the carrier while the worst of the healing took place. After that, when he could already scuttle on his hands and one knee, he was able to range about. In crawling, he had discovered the great variety of burrowing animals that live beneath the eye of ordinary man; once he had learned which ones made bolt-holes and which could be scooped out of the traps of their own burrows he began to supply himself with a fair amount of protein.

The ship, and its extensions, did him no harm. Some of this was luck, when he was in the zones traversed by the machines as they went to and from the ship. But after he had taken up a systematic trek back along the North Platte, and presumably ought to have stopped being registered in the ship's detectors as an aimless animal, he was apparently protected by his coloration, which was that of the ground, and again by his slow speed and ability to hug the terrain. Even without pseudopods and a fusion bomb to carry, his speed was no better than that.

When several months had passed he was able to move in a half-upright walk that was an unrelenting parody of a skip and a jump, and he was making fair time. But by then he was well up into the beginnings of the Medicine Bows.

He thought that even though the ship still stood, if he could reach Norma soon enough she might still not be too lost.

Not only the ship but the Army drones had missed him, until he was almost back to the now refilled exit from which he and the carrier had launched themselves. The passages were hurriedly unblocked—every cubic yard of rubble that did not have to be dispersed and camouflaged at the pithead represented an enormous saving of expenditure—and he was hauled back into the company of his fellow creatures.

His rescue was nearly unendurable. He lay on a bed in the Aid Station and listened to Compton's delight.

"They went wild when I told them at Headquarters, Colonel. You'd already been given a posthumous Medal of Honor. I don't know what they'll do now you're available for parades. And you certainly deserve them. I had never had such a moment in my life as when I saw what you'd done to the ship."

And while Compton talked, Norma—Norma with no attention to spare for Runner; a Norma bent forward, peering at the dials of Compton's cabinet, one hand continually twitching toward the controls—that Norma reached with her free hand, took a photograph out of a file folder clipped to the side of the cabinet and held the picture, unseeing, for Runner to look at while she continued her stewardship of Compton's dials. The cadet had been replaced. The wife was homemaking in the only way she could.

The ship no longer pointed directly away from the ground, nor was she equally balanced on the quadrupod of her landing jacks. The bombed leg dangled useless, its end trailing in the ground, and the ship leaned away from it.

"When the bomb went off," Compton was explaining, "she did the only thing she could to save herself for the time being. She partially retracted the opposite leg to balance herself."

Norma reached out and adjusted one of the controls. The flush paled out of Compton's face, and his voice sank toward the toneless whisper Runner remembered.

"I was always afraid she would do that. But the way she is now, I know—I *know* that when I undermine another leg, she'll fall! And she can't get away from me. She'll never take off with that leg dragging. I never had a moment in my life like the moment I had when I saw her tilt. Now I know there's an end in sight. All of us here know there's an end in sight, don't you, Norma? The ship'll puzzle out how you did it, Runner, and she'll defend against another such attempt, but she can't defend against the ground opening up under her. We'll run the tunnel right through the rock layers she rests on, get underneath, mine out a pit for the leg to stumble into and blow the rock—she'll go down like a tree in the wind, Runner. Thirty years—well, possibly forty, now that we've got to reach a farther leg—and we'll have her! We'll swallow her up, Runner!"

Runner was watching Norma. Her eyes darted over the dials and not once, though most of the gestures were abortive, did her hands stop their twitching toward the controls. When she did touch them, her hands were sure; she seemed quite practiced; Runner could calculate that she had probably displaced the cadet very soon after he had bombed the ship.

Runner comforted himself with the thought that the aliens in the ship had also gone mad. And he thought it was a very human thing to do—he thought, with some pride, that it was perhaps the last human thing—for him to refuse the doctors who offered to give him artificial replacements for the hopelessly twisted legs he had come back with.

"You will *not!*" he snapped, while up in the bunker, all unimaginable to him, Norma kissed Compton's face and said: "You *will* get her—you *will!*"

I drive, among other things, a rusty old Fiat 1500 cabriolet named Marcia. (Many Italian ignition switches bear that appellation). On a visit to Cambridge, Massachusetts, researching an article on nuclear power plants, I broke Marcia's clutch throw-out fork at the corner of Broadway and Prescott. When I chivvied her into Dino's foreign car repair shop on Lechmere Square, it appeared I needed $250 parts and labor to get out of town again. Dino eventually solved it for $75 in labor, and solved it well, but I was in a panic meanwhile. This story was written on the subway between MIT and Harvard Square, and written down as fast as I could type it immediately thereafter. The character of Michaelmas, who suddenly fit right in, is from the novel which I then had in progress. The rest, except for the reference to the really interesting environmental tents developed by my aunt and uncle, Aleksandra and Vytautas Kasuba, is all from Marcia.

So we know the name of my muse. She is Mobility.

A Scraping at the Bones

THE WASTES PROCESSING foreman was doughy and soft: looking at his greenish pallor and watching the convulsed workings at the corners of his mouth, Ned Brosmer wondered what would happen if the man lost hold of himself and began puking. Would it all come up—first the stomach, and then the very nearly similar material of the limbs, and then the pelvis and torso and ears, until finally the empty royal blue slick-finish coverall would be lying at his feet under a heap of something like oatmeal? "It's in there, Officer," the foreman was saying with a relinquishing gesture toward the open inspection plate, the wave of his arm ending with his hand in front of his mouth.

©1975, Conde Nast Publications, Inc.

"All right," Brosmer said. "I'll look."

Down here, many levels below the dwelling units that clambered skyward in the complex shape of Panorama Tower, it was all pumps and tubing and worklights. The particular duct from which the smell came was four feet in diameter, and was painted an ivory white. Coded red decal symbols identified it as the north tower branch feed to the central waste macerator.

The hatch was a three-by-two plate, swung back and up; an extension light dangled over it, swaying from the cord as the constant air currents within the duct came gusting out. "Are we going to get flooded?" Brosmer asked, and the foreman shook his head violently.

"Hell, no!" he said. "We got this branch shut off back there, where the tube comes straight down from upstairs and makes that bend, see? There's this surge tank there, like you got to have, and you can use that big valve to block everything between it and here."

"Got you," Brosmer said. "Would a body pass through that valve?"

"No way. Jam it, maybe. But most likely it would just stay in the tank until the next time we cleaned it out."

"So it probably went into the duct right through this hatch."

"That would figure, yeah. Somebody came down here and put it in."

"Or it's suicide."

"You're kidding! Who would want to drown himself in—"

"I was kidding," Brosmer said. He had taken a respirator from his kit bag and was putting it on. His voice sounded remote in his ears, as if he were on dope. He sighed and looked into the duct.

The air flow was backing up from the hydrolizing tanks beyond the macerator, whistling against the torn edges of the thin metal blade that terminated the duct. The blade was designed to rotate at high rpm; it had shattered against something in the body, which had been passing feet-first through it without incident up to that point. Brosmer clenched his teeth, grasped one of the shoulders, and turned it over. A white male, middle-aged, hair gray, eyes brown, several post-mortem abrasions and superficial lacerations, and the apparently fatal puncture wound in the upper right-hand quadrant of the thorax. Made with a thin, long, sharp weapon, Brosmer decided, for he had seen the exit wound below the left shoulder blade. It wouldn't have bled very much; whatever rags had mopped up the spill had probably preceded the corpse down the duct, and were on their way to the farmers by now. And—Brosmer looked more closely. Right. A stainless steel replacement ball and Teflon socket for the original left hip joint. That was what had stopped the blade.

Brosmer drew his head and shoulders back out of the inspection hatchway. "Recognize him, Mr. Johnson?" he said to the foreman. "Take a good look. Sorry." He kept himself out of the way and put a hand on Johnson's elbow to urge him forward.

Johnson craned briefly, then stepped back. "No—I don't know him."

"He's just about got to live in this unit," Brosmer said.

"I don't see none of them. They're up there and I'm down here. There's thousands of them and three guys in my crew and me. That's the way they want it, and that's the way I want it. This is a different kind of place down here."

"OK," Brosmer said. No matter what, the longest delay in making an identification would be a routine four-hour turnaround time for the Social Security print files in Omaha; sooner if anybody wanted to rush it. He stripped off his examining gloves and dropped them in a waste can. "Somebody'll be along to pick it up."

"Is this all?" the foreman asked.

Brosmer looked at him with the appearance of great wisdom. "You mean, where's the sergeant and the lieutenant and the Chief Medical Examiner of New York City? Well, the sergeant's tied up collating officers' reports, and the lieutenant's in a conference with some sergeants. There'll be a photographer with the meat wagon crew. You see," he explained patiently, "this isn't a stage set; this is real. We don't need a lot of mouths full of dialogue to establish the plot."

"You're all the cop we're going to get on this case?"

"I'm 3-D and in color, Mr. Johnson. You can even feel me, if you don't get personal. That's good enough for an unidentified male found in a sewer."

"Well, you sure as hell look young to me, to be handling something like this all by yourself."

"That's right, I do," Brosmer said, packing away his respirator. "You've got my card. Call me if anybody starts asking you questions about the plumbing. I'm getting out of here. I hate dismal places." He turned back once: "Don't tell anybody about this, or I'll bust your ass to someplace where they use buckets."

At the lobby level, Brosmer walked through one Kasuba environment after another, eschewing their invitations to energy or lassitude, until he had reached the lobby area. He rang Building Management.

"Please state your business," the hologram said, and then caught itself. "Oh, it's you, Officer." Her lips took on fullness, but her eyes widened with something other than love. "I'll put you through to Mr. Vermeil." She faded, to be replaced by a naively interesting sculpture that rotated gently under lights, and with the sound of Japanese wind chimes, which in turn yielded to a representation of a man all in body-fitting burgundy crushed velvet. It seemed to Brosmer it was a little soon in the evening for that, but perhaps the manager was an early riser.

"Yes, Officer?" Vermeil said busily, not having bothered to put down his frappe.

"There'll be a mortuary truck to get the body, so you'll want to alert your perimeter security people," Brosmer said. "A police photographer will take ID shots; you'll be expected to look at them, in case you can identify the victim. It's almost a sure thing he's one of your residents."

"Good heavens, Officer, *I* don't know every Tom, Dick and Harry who lives here! Why on Earth should I?"

"Nobody ever calls you up about anything? You know, there was a time when tenants hammered on pipes for more heat, or had their dripping faucets fixed by the super. And the manager came around every month to collect the rent. They've got to be in touch with you now and then."

"I *don't* remember them, Officer. The bank evicts them if their credit goes, and Central Services has the building maintenance contract. They can hammer all they want to on their . . . *pipes,* did you say? Why, yes, Officer, there *was* a time when pipes brought on the heat, wasn't there?" He smirked.

"Vermeil, when the photographer calls you up and shows you the pictures, look at them. And remember it's a sworn admissible communication, whatever you tell him. I'll be in touch when I need you." Brosmer rang off. He went to the lobby doors and flashed his buzzer at the sensing devices. The inner doors opened, and he stepped into the lock. "NYPD Shield number 062-26-8729," he said perfunctorily. "One man going out."

There was a pause, and the intervening sound of wind chimes. Then the outer doors opened. He stepped into the raw air, grimacing, and walked toward the transit station, keeping clear of low walls and shrubbery. Above him, the brownish precast concrete settings clambered heavenward to frame waterfalls of reflectorized glass. As he walked, he rang a police channel and talked to his sergeant, telling him the story.

"What do you think, Ned?" the sergeant asked when he had all the data.

"I think somebody knows in his heart he got away with it. Thinks our victim's a bag of nutrient for the rutabaga. I'm going to get that sucker."

"Why do you suppose he wanted to obliterate the body? How'd he know how plumbing works?"

"What are you, Sarge—an old fire horse? Those are *my* questions."

"All right. You gonna be home?"

"Ten minutes transit time first. Thereafter."

"Good. I'll call you on a landline as soon as we have a working collation."

"I'll be there when I'm needed."

"Say hello to Dorrie for me."

"Should I give any particular name?"

Once on the train, he punched his destination on the coder in his armrest. When the straps went around him, the back of his mind thought of Dorrie. The train took off as soon as his interlock was made, and the front of his mind busied itself reviewing the people in the other seats. There were two or three persons with lunchbucket faces: technicians. The rest were pimps and whores. All of us personal servants make up the subway-riding public, he thought.

In the middle of his mind, he pondered an individual who could stuff a stripped corpse into the Jakes, but was too overwhelmed by his or her accomplishment to cut down through an old orthopedic scar and just check to see what might lie behind it. An amateur. But then, professionals just left 'em lying. There weren't any more feckless people. Everyone was numbered. When they died, there was a hole in the credit banks, the dwelling occupancy budget, the place where ongoing supermarket billings might be. There were no unmarked graves: IBM's tombstone punches represented more substance than the incidental flesh could ever show.

Please note, he told the place where he stored his experience: With the lower limbs absent, the free-floating position is face down.

He lived in Riverscene Heights. In the lobby lock, he said, "City civil servant," which put him in the system's admissible tenant class, and then gave his Social Security number. "One man coming in," he said for the voiceprint. In the motionless elevator, he gave his apartment number. In this building, the systems played music during intervals. When he had been properly scanned, the elevator unlocked and took him to his floor. He got out and walked down Hall 114, which also recognized him, and came to Door 11489, which let him in. Dorrie moved toward him out of the forefront of a crowd of dancers.

She was slight and dark, wearing black openwork hip-huggers and bronze jewelery; her long ashy hair fell over one eye; the apartment lights reflected from the amber lens over the other.

"Hello," he said.

She touched her upper lip with her tongue. "Welcome home," she said softly. They touched each other.

He couldn't get enough of her. Wincing, he pulled his shirt open so more of them would be touching. "Can't stay long," he said. "Working." She had put perfume on the top of her head. Her hands passed gently over his deltoid musculature.

"Home tonight?" she asked softly.

"Don't know. Probably not."

"I'll go down the hall, then. Iris Ruthven asked me to join her Bezant class with her."

He grimaced into her hair.

"You know," she said quickly, "that's not something you can do by phone." She leaned back in his arms, took off her glasses, and looked directly into his eyes. "I mean, when you all get around the table, you actually have to *touch* hands, or it doesn't work."

"Does it work if you do?"

"Oh, don't be so *rational!*" She tapped his bicep mock-pettishly with her glasses.

And don't be such a liar, he thought. Another thing worked better in the flesh, too. Why she thought she had to be so convincing and yet so transparent, he couldn't imagine. Husbands weren't supposed to be selfish, were they? But he was; he was, and he was pretty sure she lied to reproach him subtly, come to think of it.

"Rational is as rational does," he said. "There's one fresh soul I'd sure like to contact. I'll bet he's got a story he'd love to tell."

She danced away from him a little, replacing her glasses. "Are you on a murder?" she asked, her lips parting.

"Over at Panorama." He moved toward a chair.

"Where the *artists* live? Did you go inside? What are the units like? I'll bet they're *fabulous!*"

"They don't get any more cubic feet per body than we do," he said, dropping into the chair. "Besides, I wasn't up on the dwelling levels." He put his feet up on the edge of the daybed and sighed. He reached out and touched Dorrie's thigh as she moved about him. "Listen, I hate to cut off the party, but I want to watch the news."

She nodded. " 'S OK." He switched off the hi-fi and the dancers winked out. Moving toward the bar, Dorrie rummaged, keeping one hip cocked so as not to break the contact between his hand and her leg. "Stick?" she asked.

Dialing the phone for Laurent Michaelmas, he shook his head. "Working," he reminded her.

"You're funny," she murmured fondly as the Michaelmas hologram formed a few paces to her left. "You wouldn't even be back downstairs before your head was all straight again."

"Working *now,*" he said, evading the central issue.

"Good evening," Michaelmas said. He was, as usual, in a plain black suit. Looking at him, Brosmer thought that the self-contained, square-bodied man, with his economical gestures and his lively, intelligent face, might understand him. He hoped that someday an assignment would let them meet. But it seemed 'hardly likely; Brosmer wasn't even sure whether Michaelmas lived in Manhattan, and he worked all over the world.

"I just want *local crime*," Brosmer said to him, uttering the last two words distinctly.

Michaelmas nodded. There was a slight flicker. "Local crime," he said. He began a series of expositions, some of which involved Brosmer in the chase of a stolen boat, hunting over the riparian complexes like a midge among the stock shelves of a glass shoe store, sweeping down over the Hudson with a flurry of vanes and surging rpm changes in the turbines, whirling skyward again among the glittering windows as the thieves throttled down and circled disconsolately in the bay. In another sequence, ambulances ran mugging victims toward resuscitation centers, whistling among the pylons and freight ramps of the streets. Michaelmas' voice was crisp and measured, his data succinct. Dorrie, the broken end of a stick trailing between her enameled nails, smiled roguishly toward Brosmer and intertwined her limbs with Michaelmas, running her hands over the shoulders of the suit, miming with such casual skill that Brosmer had to laugh as Michaelmas continued to speak and move obliviously. Only a few of his gestures surpassed her anticipation; at one point, his left arm protruded between her shoulder blades, but in the next she had recovered and was mock-biting gently with her white teeth along his forearm.

There was nothing about Panorama.

"All right," Brosmer said to himself, and to Michaelmas by way of good-bye as he dialed him off. The hologram disappeared from Dorrie's caresses. She turned and faced Brosmer slump-shouldered, dangling her glasses in one hand against her thigh and looking at him through her lashes. Her lower lip was tentatively between her teeth. She moved her feet. She reached behind her to fully opaque the window wall.

Grinning awkwardly, Brosmer shook his head. "You know we're on an open police landline. George Holmeir could be calling any time now."

Well, what would he see that he didn't know first-hand? Brosmer thought as Dorrie smiled at him sadly. But her expression did change slightly at the mention of the sergeant's name.

What would he see? Brosmer finished the thought. He'd see me. He might feel it was inappropriate.

And in fact Holmeir formed without preliminaries, between Dorrie and Brosmer. "OK, Ned," he said. "Here's what there is."

Brosmer shifted in his chair so the pickup would give Holmeir eye-contact with him. "Go ahead."

"Your DOA is Charles Castelvecchio. Resident at 25609 Panorama North, accompanied by Nola Furness Castelvecchio and one infant son. Castelvecchio was a writer on the *Warbirds of Time* series. Here's the stats on them; want to take it?" Holmeir held up the sheet. Brosmer nodded and activated his camera.

"Got it."

Holmeir put the sheet down on his desk. "OK. Now that's a positive ID. Positive. Fingerprints, dental charts, surgical records, every way we could do it."

Brosmer raised his eyebrows. "Thorough."

"Had to be. He's still doing business; we reviewed his phone calls. He was part of a story conference half an hour ago. Seemed a little jumpy, but did his fair share."

"While he was down in that duct all the time."

"Dead twelve hours, Forensics says, and soaking in that thing for an hour before he was found."

"Killed in the building."

"Had to be. He didn't just materialize." Holmeir looked at Brosmer expectantly.

"How do you mean?"

"He never went in or out through any door. But the elevator wasn't used once all day. That's what the building tapes say."

"It's a glitch. You're getting a false memory readout."

Holmeir nodded. "Sure. Something screwed up in the building system. It happens. Of course, maybe nobody *did* use the elevator. That happens, too. So maybe somebody's found a way to make a hologram you can feel. Only which one is it—the dead one or the one that suggested sending a squadron of Spads to strafe Charlemagne?"

"Come off it, Sarge."

"Well, I'll be damned if I can explain it. But I don't have to. Sergeants sit and officers walk."

"How about the widow? Did you talk to her?"

"Come off it, Ned. How would I know she didn't do it? It's all yours. He's not even officially dead."

Brosmer nodded. "It's a sweetheart of a case."

Holmeir grinned. "Yeah. I never heard of an MO like this. You're gonna be breaking new ground. They'll give it your name at the Academy—every time it ever comes up again, they'll call it a Brosmer. It'll be good for you when you're tired enough to apply for sergeant."

"And I'll apply for green feathers and fly to the Moon," Brosmer said, trying to picture himself as Holmeir, and wincing.

"OK," he said. "I'll call in when I've got something."

"Right. I'm going off-shift in about an hour. But I'll leave a cue in my phone for you."

"OK."

Dorrie had moved around to where the pickup could find her. "Hello, George," she said.

"Hello, Dorrie."

"See you, Sarge." Brosmer said.

As soon as he was gone, Dorrie turned to Brosmer with her glasses off and her eyes full of stick. Hearing himself gasp, he knew there was nothing he could do to prevent it, or wanted to. Afterward, soft in his arms, blurred with lassitude, full of confidentiality, she murmured: "You silly, don't you know I don't see George any more; I've even mostly forgotten where he lives in this building. And besides, it's *you* I want to live with. You're so gentle with me," and he wished she didn't try so hard to teach a coherent understanding of the world to him.

It was funny how it all fell together. He had decided to call on the widow and see if there was any sense to be made of it. Appropriately dressed, his pockets full of supporting data, he walked up to her door as if it hadn't been his buzzer that had gotten him in, but when he rang at the door, nothing happened for a while. Brosmer stood plumped-out in the hall, thinking now about calling in for a warrant unlock, but instead the next door opened, and a man was standing there. "May I help you?" he said from under unceasingly restless eyes.

Brosmer shifted his feet in awkwardness and scratched the back of his neck. "Well, I don't know . . ." he said.

The man was tall and fleshy, dressed in a floor-length robe of figured iridescent orange. The flesh under one eye was jumping regularly, and his upper lip was wet, "It's all right. It's all right. I often come out," he said reassuringly. "The Castelvecchios aren't home; were they expecting you?"

"Well, yeah, Charlie left a cue in the system for me, and . . ."

"Strange. Yet he's not here. I'm Timothy Fortnum."

"Lou Marchant," Brosmer said. "I'm his cousin."

"Of this city?"

"Chicago," Brosmer said, having been there on a fugitive pickup once. Originally, he had been a young writer from the Bronx, for the widow's benefit, and he was shifting things around inside, watching Fortnum, looking nonplussed, wondering how a man could look so guilty and still keep talking.

Fortnum was calming down. "I knew he had no relatives in New York," he said, "Well, come in—let me offer you some hospitality while we straighten this thing out." He took Brosmer by the upper arm to urge him inside. Brosmer had to relax his muscles instantly to come off the pressure plates in the police undersuit beneath his garments, but his arm was only humanly resistant when Fortnum's hand closed on it.

Fortnum was much bolder now. His hip swung to bump Brosmer past him. Most of his attention was concentrated on closing and locking the door with swift, complex motions of his fingers.

"Sit down . . . sit down!" Fortnum said heartily, moving up behind him. "This is my wife, Martita. Darling, this is Mr. Marchant, Charles Castelvecchio's Chicago cousin, come to us unexpectedly."

Brosmer found himself having to look up. Martita Fortnum was leaning over the railing of an area to his left whose floor began at normal ceiling height. She was a slim, blonde woman in a red veil khaftan, her limbs long and straight, but aging as she descended a circular staircase. The elevated area, he saw, occupied the unit's worth of space above the Castelvecchio unit. Over his head, the ceiling, two ceilings high, supported a crystalline chandelier with soft lights playing upon it. Hanging gardens of opaque silky fabric draped the wall where three window frames ought to have been visible.

"I've never seen a place like this!" Brosmer said.

"Yes. I'm an architect. It's amazing what you can do. *Sit down*, Mr. Marchant. Tell us about yourself." His hand pressed Brosmer's shoulder. "Martita—bring our guest something, will you?"

The wall in the far corner was for shelves of books, a swing-down drawing board, and a prose encoder. Beside the encoder was a roughly similar machine—if he had not seen one in a documentary on popular music he would not have known it was for editing tune material. All that space was occupied. These people had no visible food preparation area.

Fortnum's hand was still pressing. Brosmer let himself fall into the chair beside the wall between the Fortnum and Castelvecchio units.

Martita Fortnum had reached this floor. She turned with a fluidity strongly reminiscent of youth and passed through an opening behind the staircase. Its edges were fresh: unfinished. There were wallboard fragments on a dropcloth laid in the opening, and it led into the next unit. Martita Fortnum threw Brosmer a fleeting smile as she moved out of sight.

"What are you *doing*?" Brosmer asked, turning his face up to Fortnum.

"Why, we're entertaining you," Fortnum said heartily. "There's so much I want to know about you. Any visitor of Charlie's is bound to be such a surprise to me. He was saying to me just yesterday that he never received any callers." Fortnum put one buttock on the arm of another chair, which stood where the daybed ought to have been, and eyed Brosmer's face intently. A pair of huge antique geometrician's dividers, massive in bronze, each slender two-foot arm ending in a glistening steel point, hung on the wall near his right shoulder.

"It's an old cue," Brosmer said. "I called him weeks ago and said I'd be in town on business, and he put it into the building system for me right then."

"What business are you in, Mr. Marchant?"

"I'm a writer," Brosmer answered, slapping his pocket so

Fortnum could hear the impact on the casette he'd put there when he still thought Castelvecchio had any survivors.

"Like Charles. Talent runs in families. Ah, here's Martita with some refreshment. Do you have any gifted children, Mr. Marchant? But you're so young—are you even married?"

"I'm a bachelor," Brosmer said. "In fact, I'm an orphan. Charlie's my only relative." He watched Fortnum's eyes widen in satisfaction. It was always so easy to believe what you hoped for. Brosmer reached out and took the goblet Martita Fortnum handed him silently, her broad mouth pursed quizzically, her eyes peering pale blue through dark cosmetics.

"Have a drink," she said in a husky whisper when he held the rim to his lips. "Both of us have just had some, or we'd join you."

Ah, Jesus, he thought as he inhaled. It was a thing they called Swindle on the street; none of the successful pimps would use it, but the whores all did. It made things so easy. And she hadn't lied; you could see it in both their eyes—they were drifting and dreaming of tense cleverness, lazily riding the hurtling nightmare.

"A harmless relaxant," Fortnum was saying.

Oh, yes, yes, yes, Brosmer thought. In a little while, you can play music and I can dance, I can toss up my hair and be one with the wind, and when you speak to me, I shall answer in tongues that I learned as a child and forgot that I knew.

He pressed his arm against his side, firing Dexedrine into his body, and took a long draught. Amateur animals, he thought, gazing amiably, his nostrils tingling with fumes.

"Isn't that better?" Martita Fortnum whispered.

"Mm-hmm," He smiled at Fortnum. "Do you know where Charlie is? He must have taken his whole family with him."

"Oh, as a matter of fact, they went slightly ahead of him." Fortnum said, and Martita Fortnum giggled.

He could feel it working on him; not just the Swindle gradually winning over the clumsily saurian rages of the Dexedrine, but the rightness, the inevitability of these monsters and what had been swimming in their systems long before entertainment chemistry had come along with snappily saleable products to validate it. What the hell am I doing here? he thought. I fly a Spad and these people are propelled by turbines.

He lolled his head back in his chair and looked up. There were brass placards in bronze frames hanging over where the door to 25709 could still be faintly made out in mid-air. Over the door to 25711, and over a bed, he imagined, was a nearly wall-width painting which, he deduced from what he could see of it, was of the ocean as one might glimpse it from a bower in a sea cave. The brass placards over the (permanently locked) door to 25709 were bas-reliefs of people in coveralls tearing patches off their clothing, baring buttocks and breasts.

"You killed them for their space," he whispered. "You chewed away their walls, and you stuffed them in the duct for their dwelling allocations."

Fortnum sprang to his feet. Martita recoiled. Fortnum stared at him goggle-eyed: "You're a cop!"

Brosmer lolled in his chair. He gestured idly with his goblet. "Cousin Fuzz." He keyed his phone to the DA's channels. "NYPD shield number 062-26-8729 arresting Timothy and Martita Fortnum, 25609 North Panorama, charge Murder I three counts with additional pending. Attempted Murder of Police Officer, one count. Stand by and monitor. Sit down, Fortnum," he said.

Martita Fortnum sat down at the foot of the circular stairs, one hand over her eyes, the other wandering idly, clambering unconsciously up the bannister to its fullest extension, then trailing swiftly back down to the newel post and clambering again.

Brosmer smiled from very far away. He held out his goblet to Fortnum. "Drink me," he said. "That's an order. You are being questioned."

Breathing sharply through white nostrils, Fortnum complied.

"How do you do it?" Brosmer said after the proper interval.

Fortnum sprawled. "Do what? Get through the walls? That's no trick—you just scrape away the material without nicking the sensors; you know, they're just all elementary. Thermocouples and manometers and things; standard hardware. After you get the wall structure cleared out, you swing all the wiring up so the sensors are reading each other; all the damn building systems care about is whether things are burning or flooding, or if the windows are broken. Then you hang drapes over it."

"Do architects know about plumbing?"

Fortnum raised his head and snorted. "What the hell do you

think architecture is, these days? Everybody's got the same space allocation, and the building code's uniform, isn't it? What the hell makes a difference between units except the efficiency of the services? The hell, man, *you* could do it—dial up the library. It's all in there. Plumbing, phone systems . . . everything." A spasm crossed his face. "But *you* never thought of that. You're going home to your place, wherever it is, and dial up *Warbirds,* or do you watch cop shows?"

"I get along," Brosmer said. "Is that how you got to the elevator memory? Do you know about that from the library?"

"*You'd* have to. I *learned* it." It was amazing how much scorn and pride were getting through the Swindle. Brosmer took it in through the buzzing in his ears.

"The story conference," he said. "I can see how you might have learned to intercut tapes of Castelvecchio, but how did you fake being a writer?"

Fortnum giggled shockingly. He wiped his open lips. "Fake being a writer," he grinned. "Fake. Writers." He stood up suddenly and pulled the covering off the chair. Underneath was a metal cabinet. "There she is," he said fondly, running his hands over the home-joined crackled panels. He peered over his shoulder at Brosmer. "This is what it takes," he said, "you know. It's just an assembly of standard logic circuits. Nothing Buck Rogers about it. It's a synthesizing phone switchboard. You give it a lot of tapes of Charlie Castelvecchio sitting in a chair and babbling his life away, and when you speak into it, it puts his face on the phone and talks in his voice. Every time it can't match a lip-movement, it shows him turning his face away from the point of view or putting his hand in front of his mouth. It makes him look like he's got the jerks, but who's gonna notice that?"

"And it does the writing for you?"

"Writing? You simple boob, all you need is a hero the audience can identify with, and you give him an immediate serious problem. Then you introduce complications that get him in deeper and deeper, but in the end he does something characteristic on his own hook, and gets out of it. The rest is just atmosphere. You think that stuff in your living room is *art?* Listen—" He waved his arm and dialed. Music swelled up in the room. It thrummed and shook in the air. "That's art," Fortnum said, bracing himself against the wall with one hand. "That's a little ditty called *Jesu, Joy of Man's Desiring,* by Johann Sebastian Bach, the mightiest voice in the Public Domain." He dialed it off hastily. "You know what you can do with that? You can give it an up-tempo, write a set of words that make sounds like screwing but don't use the word, and you're rich. That's how that *momser* upstairs makes his living," Fortnum gasped, waving at the chandelier. "And over *there,*" he panted, pointing into the emptiness above his bed, "is the woman who sculpts by dipping paper strands in epoxy and throwing them into the air just before they harden. I can be any of them. I can be all three of them and me, too, all at the same time. And what do you think of that, cop?" He turned, and for a moment his hand rested on the antique scriber. He looked over his shoulder guiltily at Brosmer. Brosmer shook his forefinger at him.

It was the woman who moved—who sprang from her place and flew to the wall, and so it developed that it was for her—for the To Be Widow Fortnum—that Brosmer had worn his suit. She gaped at him unbelievingly as his servos operated the auxiliary mesh skin over his body and gave him the speed and strength of ten, so that though she flew as a gannet, he struck as a hawk. And then it was over; she and her husband sat comforting each other with justifications, a police lock on their open phone and police locks on their door(s) as Brosmer made his way home.

Dorrie greeted him. Her eyes did not meet his. "You—you're home very soon," she said. "I haven't left yet. Do you want me to stay?"

He went over to his chair, walking around her as best he could, thinking. He thought of what would happen. Perhaps already, the libraries were being restricted in access. Only those with certain credentials, such as police buzzers, would be able to obtain certain classes of data.

"Ned?"

"What? Oh—no, no, you go ahead and do what you've promised. I've been thinking," he said. "Panorama owes me the standard rate on about seven Murder I's, and even after I give George his 25-percent commission, and pay the bill from

Forensic, that's pretty good. I think maybe we should get mirrors put in. On the walls . . . maybe on the ceiling."

Dorrie put her fingertip to her mouth. "It'll make it so much sexier in here," she murmured.

"Bigger," he said. "For a while."

I must lead a fascinating interior life. Although about half my work comes from conscious thought, the other half simply erupts, complete with all the little details you would swear I spent days researching or polishing. The research in this story consisted of walking over to my album of the Verdi Requiem Mass *and getting the right Latin spellings for ". . . nil inultum remanebit" and what precedes it. I may have been playing with a cigarette case; I can't remember. When I was done, I had written a one-act, one-set play, and here it is.*

Jim Blish, music buff, purchased it for the nonexistent second issue of Vanguard Science Fiction. *It appeared, complete with his blurb, in* The Magazine of Fantasy and Science Fiction, *but without the free illustration I had foisted off on my old friend with it. Jim is dead, God damn it, and I have never sold an illustration to an SF magazine, and I never will.*

The Price

THERE WERE THREE MEN; one fat, one thin, one very old. They sat together behind a long desk, with scratch pads and pencils before them, passing notes back and forth to each other while they questioned him. The very old one spoke most often, in a voice full of the anticipation of death.

"Your name?"

The ugly hunchback in the gray tunic glowered back at them from his uncomfortable wooden chair. "No name," he growled. His knotted fingers were spread to cup his knees. His thick jaw was prognathous even at rest. Now, with the muscles bunched under his ears and his thick neck jutting forward, his lower teeth were exposed.

"You must have a name."

"I must nothing. Give me a cigarette."

©1960, Mercury Press, Inc.

The fat man whispered gently: "We'll give you a cigarette if you tell us your name."

"Rumpelstiltskin," the hunchback hissed. He extended his hand. "The cigarette."

The thin man slid a silver case across the table. The hunchback snatched it up, bit the filter from the end of the cigarette he took, spat it out on the floor with a jerk of his head, and thrust the case into the front of his tunic. He glared at the thin man. "A match."

The thin man licked his lips, fumbled in a pocket, and brought out a silver lighter to match the case. The old man covered the thin man's hand with his own.

"I am in charge here," he said to the hunchback. "I am the President."

"You have been that too long. The match."

The President hopelessly released the thin man's hand. The lighter slid across the table. The hunchback touched its flame to the frayed cigarette end. Then he slid it back, grinning without visible mirth. The thin man looked down at it without picking it up.

"I'm not as old as you," the President said. "No one is as old as you."

"You say."

"The records show. You were found in 1882, in Minskva Guvbernya, and taken to the Czar. You told him no more than you will tell us, and you were put away in a cell without light or heat until you would talk. You were taken out of the cell in 1918, questioned, and treated similarly, for the same reason. In 1941, you were turned over to a research team for study. In 1956, you were placed in the Vorkuta labor camp. In 1963 you were again made the subject of study, this time in Berlin. The assembled records show you learned more from your examiners than they learned from you. They learned nothing."

The hunchback grinned again. "A equals pi r squared. *Judex ergo cum sedebit, quidquid latet apparebit, nil inultum remanebit.*"

"Don't be so pleased with yourself," the fat man whispered, gently.

The President went on. "In 1967, you were taken to Geneva.

In 1970, you were given shelter by the Benedictine monks in Berne, remaining with them through most of the Seven Decades' War. Now you're here. You've been here for the past eight months, and you have been treated well."

The hunchback ground his cigarette into the desk's polished mahogany.

"We need you," the thin man said. "You must help us."

"I must nothing." He pulled the case out of his tunic, took a fresh cigarette, spat out the end, and held the case in his hand. "A match."

The thin man slid the lighter across the desk. The hunchback lit his cigarette and returned the lighter. He ground out the cigarette and took another. "A match." The thin man pushed the lighter across the desk, and the hunchback cackled in glee.

There were heavy drapes on the windows behind the President, who gestured abruptly. The thin man yanked them aside.

"Look," the President said. Sputtering fires and swirling ropes of smoke cast their lights and shadows through the window and into the room. "It's all like that, everywhere. We can't put it out, but if we could learn what let you walk through it out of Europe. . . ."

The hunchback grinned slyly and swallowed the glowing coal from the end of his cigarette. He looked from one man to the other with great delight.

The fat man whispered: "I'll pull you apart with chains and hooks."

The hunchback said: "Once I was straight and tall."

"For God's sake!" the President cried out, "there are no more than a hundred of us left!"

"What do you want?" the thin man asked. "Money? Women?"

The hunchback took the cigarette case and crumpled it over between his hands. He threw it on the table before the thin man. Then he sat back and smiled, and smiled. "I will tell you how you may be saved."

"What do you want?" the thin man whispered breathily.

"Nothing! Nothing!" the hunchback cackled. "I will tell you from the mercy of my own good heart."

"Tell us," the fat man cried. "Tell us, then!"

"*Wait—*" It was the President stumbling over his own urgency. "Wait—this thing, this process—this treatment—will it turn us into something like you?"

The hunchback smiled, and grinned, and laughed. "Inside and out. Yes."

The President hid his face in his hands. Then he gestured importantly to the thin man. "Draw the curtains! Quickly!" His voice was hoarse with emotion.

But the fat man dragged the President from his chair and held him so that he was forced to face the open window. "Look out at it," he said harshly. "Look."

The President hung from the fat man's hands for a moment, and then he mumbled:

"All right. Tell us, hunchback."

And the hunchback leaped from his chair up onto the top of the table. He stamped his feet in joy and bayed his triumph from his open throat. He leaped and capered, his boots splintering the oil-rubbed veneer of the table and scattering the scratch pads. The pencils flew into the corners of the room, and the three men had to wait for him to finish.

This one is easy. My grandfather, the village tailor of Marijampole, Lithuania, was a wonderful man, replete with attributes a child could love. He was magnificent when he filled his mouth with water, sprayed a loud, joyous mist over the clothes on the board, and applied a flatiron from the wood-stove. He had a cow, a well with a sweep, a vegetable garden, a house with a tin roof, and I helped carry the pickets for the new white fence in front of his house. To honor him, I piddled in his galoshes. The Russians took many of his children.

This story is not about him; it is about another man, whom I would not have thought of.

The Ridge Around The World

STENN HUNCHED HIS shoulders and lifted the plow. With his back against the split-rail fence that marked the end of his field, he swung it around, dropped it, and wiped the back of his heavy wrist across his forehead. Squinting into the sun, he twitched the reins and began following his bony horse back across the cramped field.

As he walked, his bare feet set themselves doggedly in the turned earth. He had walked over every fist of dirt in this hectare, so many times that the earth was like cream. Every stone, every root, had been found and thrown aside long ago. He kept his head down and his eyes on the furrow. He could trust the horse to walk straight. Horses were dependable, though they died too often.

He heard an automobile stop on the crushed-stone road beside his field, and growled to himself. Automobiles meant somebody from outside the village.

"You, there!" a harsh voice called out. "Come here."

He growled to himself again and went on as though he hadn't heard. Sometimes that was good enough. The stranger, whoever

©1957, Algis Budrys

he was and whatever he wanted, might simply curse him and then go away.

The automobile door slammed. "You—I said come here!"

Stenn yanked the reins, stopped the horse, wound the reins deliberately, in no hurry, wrapped them around the plow handles, and finally turned around. Scowling out from under his lowered eyebrows, he looked at the man standing impatiently on the other side of the fence.

He was wearing a uniform and boots, with a pistol in a holster at his waist. Stenn shuffled forward, taking off his hat in the way he'd learned from his father, long ago in other times when strangers in uniforms spoke to him. He reached the fence and stopped.

"Didn't you hear me?" the man demanded. His face was set in the hard, angry mask that Stenn expected of such men. Expecting it, he ignored it and grunted to show he was here now.

"What's your name?" the man barked.

Stenn gave it, and the man nodded. "All right. You're coming with me to see the Commissioner."

Stenn hunched his shoulders. Here was half a day wasted.

"Now!" the man rasped.

Stenn kept his face set, looking at the man woodenly. The man was powerful, with his uniform and his Commissioner behind him, so there was no question of not going. The half day was wasted, and that was that.

"I'll stall my horse," he grunted.

The man grinned. "The devil with your horse. You won't have to worry about him where you're going. Get in the car!"

Still expressionless, Stenn bent through the fence and shuffled to the automobile. There was only one seat. The uniformed man took a set of handcuffs out of his pocket, pulled Stenn's right wrist across his body, and manacled it to the left-hand assist handle on the dashboard. Then the uniformed man started the automobile, turned it around, and drove them back the way he had come.

Stenn twisted his head to look back at the horse standing in the middle of the field. Then he faced front, his arm hanging by its wristlet, and said nothing all the way into the town on the far side of the village. He had never been in an automobile before. He didn't like riding in one.

In the Commissioner's office, he sat stiffly in the hard chair facing the light, his knotty fingers curled over his knees.

"What is your name?" the Commissioner asked.

Stenn gave it again, and the Commissioner grunted. "That's the name on your papers here. Now, what's your real name? Who sent you here?"

Stenn gave his name again. He didn't understand the second part of the question, so he didn't say anything beyond that.

"Who forged these records?" the Commissioner asked. "What is your assignment—sabotage?"

Stenn looked at him woodenly. He made no sense out of what the Commissioner was saying. This was often true of questions strangers asked. It did not upset him.

"Come, now," the Commissioner said softly, "these records are a ridiculous forgery. Did your masters think that even the former regime here could make such mistakes in its birth archives?"

Stenn had no answer for him.

The Commissioner's voice remained smooth. "Let's be sensible. Your masters obviously couldn't have cared much about your safety if they permitted themselves to be so clumsy. All I want you to tell me is when you were sent into this country, and who sent you. If you cooperate, nothing more will be made of the matter. It is even possible that the new regime might have a good offer for you. Now, despite your present appearance, you must be an intelligent man. I'm sure we can reach an agreement."

Stenn's expression remained the same. He stared uncomprehendingly and said nothing. Not one word of what the Commissioner had said was in any way understandable. He knew from experience that eventually all strangers grew tired of talking to him, and that sooner or later he would be able to go back to his farm.

"Listen, my friend, you'd better say something fairly soon," the Commissioner said.

Stenn shrugged.

The Commissioner called in another man, who was carrying a truncheon. The new man took a position beside Stenn and waited.

"Now," the Commissioner said, "What is your name?"

Stenn told him again. The Commissioner nodded to the new man, and Stenn was hit across the top of his left shoulder.

"How long have you lived in the village?"

Stenn told him, and the man with the truncheon hit him in the same place.

"Who are your associates?"

"I keep to myself. I live alone." He was hit on the left shoulder again. The Commissioner was growing furious because Stenn showed no reaction.

"Where do you come from?"

"I was born in the village."

He was hit.

"Who were your parents?"

He gave his mother's and father's names, and was hit.

"Where are they?"

"Dead." He volunteered his first piece of information, since the Commissioner was now asking something he understood. "I have no brothers or sisters."

Instead of hitting him, the man with the truncheon felt his shoulder.

"Pardon, Commissioner, but there is something here I don't understand. This man's collarbone should be broken. It is not."

"To hell with his collarbone! If you don't know your business, learn it! Now, you—again. When were you born?"

Stenn told him, and was hit harder.

Finally, the Commissioner said: "Very well. We're going to put you on a train."

He pulled a blank record card out of his desk and in a taut, savage hand scrawled a few sentences on it in his own language. "By the time you come back, my friend—" He looked at Stenn, who returned his stare woodenly, just as expressionless now as he had been before he'd worn the stranger down. "By the time you come back, you will be as old again as these ridiculous papers make you out to be."

Stenn spent some years in the labor camp, keeping to himself, and shuffling wordlessly down into the shaft each day. He had noted that men here died even faster than his plowhorses did, but this did not concern him except that sometimes he was asked more questions to which he did not have answers. After a time, the men in charge of the camp had been replaced by crippled men in worn uniforms, and these men also shared his habit of silence, toward him and among themselves.

From time to time he looked up at the airplanes crossing overhead, especially when the camp siren gave the alarm, as it did more and more often. Finally, a day came when the few men remaining in charge of the camp locked themselves in a blockhouse and stayed there. Soon afterward, the other men who worked in the camp got the gates open. One or two of them ventured outside the gate. When the men in the blockhouse showed no reaction, everyone in the camp went wild. Some spilled out onto the snowy plains, and others broke into the blockhouse. Stenn shuffled down the railroad track alone, going back the way he'd come.

In due time, he arrived back at his farm. The house was burned down, and the fence broken. Also, there was a new regime, but very few of these new strangers as yet were able to talk his language, and, in any case, they found a great deal of work to do. Stenn went down to the woods with an ax he'd found, cut down some trees, built new fences, and then a new house. The new regime gave him a plow and a horse. He was satisfied.

Stenn hunched his shoulders and lifted the plow. He put his back against his fence, swung the plow, and twitched the reins. His horse settled into the collar and began to move. It was a very old horse, and it plodded slowly. Stenn growled at it as his bare feet followed the furrow.

He came to the end of the field, pushing the plow stubbornly forward as the horse turned away from the fence. He had seen other men plow, wasting ground at each end of the field because they followed the horse as it turned. He did not, and he knew how much ground he'd gained, an extra half-meter a year for the whole width of the field. If one only considered the time since he'd gotten this old plow; which was now almost worn out, it was still a great gain.

He lifted the plow and turned it around, lifting his head to wipe his face, but not bothering to look past the borders of his field at the buildings that surrounded it. The buildings were no concern of his, since they were low enough on the south side so the sun could fall on his crops.

As he started forward again, he saw someone standing at the other end of the field, watching him. He growled and walked doggedly forward, his head down.

But the stranger had not gone away by the time he reached the opposite fence. Stenn ignored him and lifted the plow.

"May I talk to you a moment?" At least, that was what Stenn thought it must be the man had said. He spoke peculiarly, pronouncing his words in a different way from Stenn, and he spoke too fast. Stenn grunted and twitched the horse's reins.

The man persisted. "I'll come back later, if you're too busy now."

Stenn stopped the horse and hunched his shoulders. Better to get this over now, in that case. He wrapped the reins and turned around with a grunt.

The man was dressed in soft clothing, and though it was still early Spring and Stenn was wearing a coat, the man only wore that one garment, and a belt with little boxes attached to it.

"I was wondering if you needed anything," the man said. "New clothes, perhaps? You've had those a long time, haven't you?"

Stenn looked at the man. These people had bothered him earlier, when they wanted to buy this land and build buildings on it. He remembered they'd been quick to offer, before they went away and left him alone. For that reason, he distrusted them.

"What do you have to trade?" the man asked.

Stenn grunted. Now, that was better. He looked at the man narrowly. "I have cabbages. I have potatoes. I will have sugar beets."

The man nodded. "What do you need?"

"I need a new horse. And a plow."

"Anything else?"

Stenn shook his head.

The man looked thoughtful. "Well, we can give you a new plow. We can give you one that doesn't need a horse."

"I don't want a tractor." Stenn scowled at the man. The regime that had given him this plow had first tried to explain a tractor to him.

The man, who looked shrewd enough so Stenn could respect him, shook his head. "I don't mean a tractor. I mean a plow that moves by itself. It is very much like your plow. You only have to push and pull on the handles to work it, and that's all. I'm afraid that's the best I can do. There aren't very many horses at all, any more."

"I'll look at it," Stenn grunted. He wasn't surprised. Horses died too often. Furthermore, they ate and had to be cared for.

"All right," the man said. "I'll bring it over later."

"What do you want for it?"

"Potatoes and cabbages, I suppose," the man said. "Twenty bushels of each."

"Ten."

"Eighteen."

Stenn spat in a furrow and turned away.

"All right, fifteen," the man said.

"Eleven," Stenn said grudgingly.

The man seemed to consider for a moment. "All right," he said.

Stenn grunted to himself. The man was no bargainer, that was certain. "Remember," he said, "it's no bargain if I don't like the plow."

The man nodded. "I'll be over with it tonight." He started to turn away, and then he stopped. "Tell me—what do you eat? Do you eat your potatoes and cabbages and beets?"

"That and my pigs. What else would a man eat?"

"Well, *why* do you eat?"

Stenn looked at the man. Why did he eat? Why did any man eat? He turned away and unwrapped the horse's reins. Giving the reins a twitch, he started the new furrow. He ate because everybody ate. Hadn't his father eaten before him? It was true a man didn't have to, as he'd found out for himself. If food was short he could go without eating. But usually, a man ate. What else were his teeth for?

"I'll see you tonight," the man reminded him, turning to depart.

Stenn ignored him. The man was a fool, as he'd suspected at first. If he brought the plow, well and good. If he didn't, earth could always be spaded.

The man brought the plow. Stenn examined it carefully, and tried it out. There wasn't much to using it—a twist of the handle to the right, a twist to the left, a push for forward and a pull for backing up. The motor was inside the share, and didn't need gasoline. Also, it was obviously handmade, and that made the man an even greater fool for bargaining so poorly on such an expensive thing. Then, in addition, the man threw in some clothes—good, honest clothes—and these were also hand-woven. For his throw-in, the man asked for the horse, and Stenn nodded contemptuously. Now the fool was taking that useless mouth off his hands, and doubtless thinking he'd made a great gain.

The man left, and Stenn's mouth twisted into a grin. Now he had something better than a horse, and furthermore with this plow he could turn a furrow right up to the fences.

The long succession of days that followed were no different from those that had gone before. Sometimes he was left alone, and sometimes he was not. Sometimes there were good regimes. Sometimes not. Several times, he was taken away from his farm, and there were certain times he spent in hospitals. There was also a time he lived in a cage. But he always wore the strangers down in the end.

Stenn stopped his plow at the bottom of the fence surrounding his field. He glared up at the dim sun, its light cut into two halves by the metal structure that sank its one pier into the lawn beyond his fence and then shot up at an angle, thickening out into a joint at a point some kilometers over his head and then fusing into one slender finger that disappeared over the horizon without touching ground.

As he looked up, he saw four of the silent firescythes go across the sky, trailing silver dust that vanished as they left it behind. They touched the four curving masts that rose out of the east and instantly shot back again, the way they had come. In a few minutes, the clear chime from the masts came to him across the distance.

In the shrubbery a few meters beyond his field, a bird answered the chime. Stenn turned his plough and touched the handles. As he walked forward, he thought that probably now he would have quiet times all summer. It had been quiet for several years, and he was beginning to think that such quietness was now a permanent thing. For many years before that, quiet times and loud times had alternated unpredictably, and though it made no difference to the crops, it had annoyed him not to know whether to put the plugs in his ears or not.

Still, it wasn't so bad, even in loud times. The new regime left him entirely alone, though he could tell they disliked him. None of them had come near here in a long time, though he knew they had put a great deal of patience into planting the shrubs just so and tending the lawn. The gardener firescythes did that work now—machines, like his plow. He saw *them* often enough, darting back and forth over the lawn and parks that surrounded his field as far as he could see.

He looked up and growled as one of the cloudleaves passed its shadow across the field. They moved with the wind, rising and falling, flowing softly with all sorts of colors, and they never stayed still over his field long enough to hurt the crops. But still they angered him.

Then he saw one of the new regime come into being at the edge of his field. He stopped his plow and stood looking at it, his jaw pushed very sharply forward.

It swayed slightly in the breeze, and began talking to him. As always, it had great difficulty speaking so a man could understand it.

"Listen—listen . . ." Its voice, as the new regime's voices had always lately been, was bitter and angry. "Listen—day—*your* day has finally come . . ."

Stenn grunted and looked at it.

"We knew—knew there was no—help for it. Had to come. We fought it—but had to come. I am here to tell you . . . We knew one—one of us someday must . . . But why did it have to be me? Listen—I am the last human being alive on Earth. There are no more . . . not *you*—certainly not you."

It bent in a ripple of agony. "I am killing the machines." It swam its head around at the horizons. "I am over. All this work—all this beauty—all our life, everything in this world I am leaving—*yours!*" It spat the word out, curling in contempt.

Stenn watched it go out of being. He grunted, started the plow, and moved forward.

At dusk, he looked back along the way he had come. One single dark furrow stretched through the shrubs and the old fence through which he had driven the plow. He would have liked to turn around and put another furrow beside it, but he hadn't yet come to the end of his field.

This was written around an illustration that leaned against the wall at Royal Publications, where I free-lanced and illustrated for Car Speed and Style, Custom Rodder, Cars *Magazine,* Gunsport, Untamed, Lion Adventures, *and* Knave. *(I am the author of "Love-Starved Arabs Raped Me Often," as well as "I Shot Down Castro's China-Commie Air Force.") I had the use of a typewriter, the publisher's patience, and the unfailing forebearance of Larry Shaw, the editor. Casting about for something else to sell Irwin Stein, the publisher, I noted the illustration, which he owned but had nothing to publish with, and provided same.*

But the illustration, of soldiers in combat, it seems did not belong to Irwin. And he was not about to buy it simply so he could then buy my story. I was, incidentally, on diet pills I hadn't yet realized were Dexedrine. I didn't tell that to the people who eventually bought the story and published it unillustrated. The artist was Ed Emshwiller, who probably never knew.

The Girl in the Bottle

THE NEW MAN rolled over with a groan and woke up with his face jammed against the corner of a broken brick. He jerked himself upright in his end of the two-man foxhole, and looked at Folley. "Why—?"

"Hello," Folley said. "My name's Zach Folley."

The man continued to look numbly up from under the brim of his helmet, which had been blackened and blistered by the countless times it had been used as a cooking pot. His eyes were puffy and threaded with blood. From the way in which he was twitching his lips tentatively, like a fish not sure of being in water, Folley could see the man was still nine-tenths asleep.

©1959, Great American Publications, Inc.

A missile went by overhead and the new man shuddered, drawing muddy knees up under his bearded chin, and wriggling his back in against the side of the hole.

"It's all right," Folley pacified him, because he was now afraid that the man was completely battlehappy and might become violent. "They're not after you or me. They don't know we're here. It's just our machines fighting their machines, now. It's all being done by the automatic weapons systems. There's nobody alive in the cities anymore. Not since the nerve gas."

The new man muttered something that sounded like: ". . . alive in the cities . . ." and Folley, who thought the man was arguing with him, said:

"No. Not anybody. I know it's hard to believe. But they told me last month, when I was a clerk up at Battalion, before Battalion got smashed up, there's nobody alive anywhere in the world except around here in North America." Folley's jaw quivered involuntarily, as it always did when he tried to picture the world empty of life, bare of movement except for the dust-fountains where the automatic missiles kept coming in like meteorites hitting the barren Moon.

"I said," the other man replied with patient distinctness, "I *know* there's nobody left alive in the cities. But I don't care." He fumbled around behind his back and suddenly held up a bottle—a flat, half-pint glass bottle, unbroken, with only mildewed traces of a label but with most of its contents still there. "Not as long as I've still got *her*."

"What do you mean 'her'?" Folley was badly upset, now. The other man had showed up out of nowhere, last night, mumbling and calling softly to find out if anybody was still alive on the defense perimeter. When Folley answered, he had stumbled down into the hole with him and had fallen in a heap without saying another word. Folley knew nothing about him, except that he obviously wasn't one of the enemy from across the valley, and now he began to wonder whether this might not be some kind of traitor, or propaganda spreader, or at any rate some kind of enemy trying to get him drunk. If Folley got drunk, then the enemy would be able to sneak past him to the rear, without warning. Folley did not know what lay in the rear, anymore— he was deathly afraid there was so little left in the world that if the enemy once got by him, they would have won the war.

Folley could not be clear in his mind about this. He knew he wasn't being completely sane, himself. But he was doing the best he could, for a man who had been a clerk up until last month and had then been given a rifle for the first time since Basic Training, which was ten years ago. He had stayed in his hole, living off the rations of the other men who had been killed on either side of him, and he always fought off the few enemies who were left to make attacks. They would come up through the barbed wire and the minefields, always losing some men, and being driven back at last, but they had been closer and closer to Folley with each attack, even though there were only five of them left.

Folley was practically out of ammunition, and had to choose his shots carefully, and this gave them time to get in close. They had been getting close enough so that he had learned to recognize them as individuals—there was a tall, scar-faced one for instance, who was very cautious but persistent, and a short, stubby one with a nervous grin who shouted insults in pidgin English—and he was sure they knew by now he was all alone on the perimeter. Today they would be braver than ever, and he was down to one clip of eight shots. He had been hoping the new man—who had been such a great hope, for a while—would have more ammunition, but he didn't have as much as a sidearm. All he had was his bottle, and Folley shied away from it like poison.

"Throw that away!" he cried out.

The man hugged the bottle and hunched himself over it, to protect it from the sweep of Folley's arm. "Oh, no!" he said doggedly. "No—I'm not going to throw *her* away!"

The fact that he did not offer to fight, but only tried to protect the bottle, impressed Folley very deeply. It was such an unusual way for someone to react that Folley decided it must be because the new man really did feel the bottle was more important than anything else in the world.

"What about her?" he asked soothingly.

"The girl," the new man explained, his face as innocent as a child's under the beard, and the dirt, and the blood, and the sallow, doughy texture of his skin. "The girl in the bottle."

On the other side of the valley, Folley could see the enemy moving around, now. It was too far away for an accurate rifle shot, and neither he nor the enemy men had any other weapons. The enemy soldiers did not bother to hide themselves or their movements. Folley would have been badly upset if they had tried.

It occurred to him that if either side—they or he—were to violate established routine in some way, it would be a disconcerting and possibly fatal tactic to the opposition. But he could not seem to draw any conclusions from this thought, or to fully understand what to do with it. It drifted out of his mind as foggily as it had first entered, and he looked at the new man again. "The girl in the bottle," he said. "Is there a girl in there?"

"Always," the new man said. He weighed the bottle in his hand. Earlier, it had seemed to Folley, that the glass was brown. Now he saw it was actually a delicate shade of green. A flash of sunlight sparkled on it as the new man held it up. It was like the sudden sideward turning of a young girl's eyes as she walks by on a park path. Folley blinked.

"Who is she?"

The new man said: "The girl." He became shy. "You know," he said under his breath, not because he was trying to keep Folley from hearing but because he was afraid of how Folley would react if he did grasp his meaning.

But Folley only looked at him blankly. "I don't—"

"Here," the man said tenderly, offering him the bottle.

With his hand carefully cupping the bottle, for fear his fingers might shake and loose their grip, Folley uncapped it and touched his lip to the rim. He winced away from the contact. Then, tilting the bottle very cautiously, he took a few swallows. Lowering the bottle, he slowly recapped it and handed it back. The taste slid down the back of his throat, warm, musky, and bittersweet.

He looked around him, at the rubble and the torn-up equipment, and the fly-clustered things like water-logged feather pillows in too-tight dirty olive drab pillowslips, and the cracked old stumps of trees. He could feel that there was no longer any clear separation between the raw soles of his feet and the glutinous fabric of his socks. He plucked absently at his shirt, and shifted his seat uncomfortably. A V of slow antipersonnel missiles went hunting by overhead, and he cowered, though he knew that the minimum concentration of men required to attract such a missile was twenty within a hundred yard radius. Abruptly, the missiles seemed to lurch in the air. Bits of machinery whirled out of their noses, and then they fell forward and glided steeply into the ground down in the valley bottom. They had run out of fuel, and had jettisoned their warhead fuzes before crash-landing in open territory.

Folley shook his head violently, having followed the missiles' downward arc all the way to the ground. "She was the first girl I ever loved," he said to the new man, his voice confidential. "We were walking hand-in-hand, along the glassy gray lake where the pelicans swam in the park, under the eyes of the buildings. There were forsythia bushes like soft phosphorus explosions beside us, and there were squirrels fat enough to eat that scampered along beside us. She was wearing a pale green gown and black slippers, and her russet hair came down to her shoulders. I remember I was afraid strands of it would catch on the thorny trees which hung their branches low over the walk, like barbed wire.

"My God," he said, staring in awe at the bottle, "it was beautiful!" He sprang to his feet and shouted across the valley: "Beautiful! Beautiful, you sons of bitches! You and your bombs and your gas and your chemicals—you and your war, your death, your rapine! Beautiful, you bastards!"

Folley crumpled back down into the hole, shuddering. He hugged his knees and rubbed his cheeks against the old camouflage cloth stretched over his bones. He had forgotten why he was here, and now that he had been reminded, he was trying desperately to forget, again. But he remained aware that the bottle was infinitely precious—that the new man was perfectly right in having saved it.

"What's your girl like?" he asked the new man.

"As lovely as yours," the man answered. He looked over the side of the hole, down into the valley. "They're coming," he said. "The enemy. It's another attack."

"The last attack," Folley said. "We've got to save her!" he cried out in panic. "I don't care what else they get—we can't let them get her!"

The new man smiled. "There's nothing else."

"*Nothing* else?"

"Just you and I, and the few of them down there. There's nothing else left in the whole world."

Folley believed him. There was no uncertainty in the new man's voice at all. But Folley was so shocked at believing him; at finding himself so ready to give up what he thought to be a proper attitude of confidence, that he burst out indignantly: "What do you mean? Not as long as General Gaunt's still alive. He can save us if anyone can, and we would have heard if he was dead!" He clung bitterly to his belief in the genius of General Gaunt, who was his personal hero of the war.

"I am General Gaunt," the new man said, tears in his eyes. He lifted the bottle in salute.

"General Gaunt?" Folley said.

The new man nodded. He extended the bottle. "Would you like another?" He turned his glance momentarily in the direction of the enemy, who were scurrying across the valley floor like baby spiders. "There's time before they get into range."

"No," Folley whispered, "no, we've got to *save* her!"

"Save her?" Gaunt pawed brutally with the back of hand under his eyes. "Save?" He stood up, feet apart, back arched arms outflung to embrace the world. "Save!" he cried, and the long echo coursed down the valley. He collapsed forward, the enemy bullet bulging a lump from the inside at the back of his thonked helmet. Folley snatched the bottle as he fell, and patted it.

The enemy were leaping up the rocks, and twisting in behind old guns and trucks, hurdling up over the gassy old bodies and the broken ammunition boxes. The short, stubby one was in the lead, screaming out: "Now die! Now die! Now die!" The scar-faced one was bringing up the rear, and this one Folley shot, the carbine banging his shoulder so hard that he clapped his left hand over the shirt pocket where he had put the bottle.

The other four enemies did not stop, and Folley saw that they had nerved themselves for this attack, and would not stop, but would soak up his ammunition until it was gone, and would overrun him. Two of them were firing at him, keeping him down, while the short one and another man advanced.

Then there was nothing to do, for the short one and his companion would soon be at the lip of the hole, and once they did that, all was lost. Folley carefully put the bottle down and sprang to his feet, firing his carbine. He was immediately hit by shots from the two covering riflemen, but he had known that would happen. He shot at them, and killed them, because it made no difference what happened with the nearer two if the others were alive. Then he turned his gun toward the short one's companion, and shot him, but that was the end of it, for he had used up all his ammunition.

"Now die!" shouted the little enemy. "Now we have your all!" He did not seem to know he was alone, and he held his rifle arched up, ready to thrust down with his bayonet.

Folley pushed him back with a nudge of his carbine butt, like a man stumbling in a crowd, but there was blood running down over his hands, and the carbine slipped away. The little enemy recovered his balance and came forward again. "You die!" he shouted, froth at the corners of his mouth because he was so frightened, "Now you die!"

And it was true. Folley could feel the pain like the teeth of a pitchfork in him, and the cut strings of his muscles would not hold him up.

"Now we rule!" the enemy cried, bayonet flashing down, and for a long moment Folley hung on the point of his rifle, all the wind knocked out of him as it had been once before in his life, when he ran down the long park slope after the girl and tripped over a root, and never afterward could be sure of her admiration.

Then he was flung back, and he lay kicking at the bottom of the hole. "Now ours!" the enemy cried. "All world!" He was straddling the hole, and his victorious glance flashed around him. Slowly, as he looked, dismay crept into it. "All world?"

Folley reached toward the bottle. He began to inch forward very quietly and painfully. Before the enemy saw what he was doing, he broke the bottle against a stone.

The enemy heard the sound, and stared down. He leaped into the hole and scrabbled at the wet splotch on the ground. Then he whirled up, his fingers bleeding, and slapped Folley's face:

"Why you break? Why you break?" He slapped Folley again, and began kicking him. "I wanted! Why you no give me?" He spun back toward the shards of glass in the sun, trying to find a few drops caught in the hollow of some curved fragment, but whatever had been there was evaporated, and the glass had turned dull brown. Folley saw it through a glistening fog the color of a gray lake.

Over the years, I have written any number of stories around illustrations. They serve as convenient objects for the fantasizing part of my mind. Many writers do this, and often develop close relationships with illustrators in part because they find they can cross-flow not ideas, so much, as a spark of creativity which can jump in either direction. Frank Kelly Freas and I did quite a bit of that at one time. He created the art to which I reacted spontaneously with stories called Who?, "The Executioner," and "Despite All Valor," among others. I wrote a number of stories—"The End of Summer," "In Clouds of Glory," "Cage of a Thousand Wings" (originally "Priestess of the Witch-Wings")—for which Kelly produced illustrations that delighted me.

This story was written at and for Playboy, around an 8 × 10 Ektachrome of a plywood woman with buzz-saw breasts bolted on. The photo of this assemblage was the best of a series taken while the plywood, soaked in lighter fluid, burned. Having bought the art, from a talented person whose name escapes me, Playboy hung it on my office wall, down in Siberia where I was attempting to do something useful with the book-publishing department. It so happened I was then driving a Sunbeam Rapier—which had both a warning light and an ammeter—and had wound up in Warren, Ohio, under circumstances exactly like those in this story, omitting, I fear, the ladies listed herein. Even the rerun of Only Angels Have Wings actually happened. But as to the important events in the story, those are either a phantasie in the classical psychiatric sense or a new kind of ghost story, take your pick.

The Last Brunette

SHORTLY AFTER HOBBS had crossed the Indiana-Ohio border, headed east, his ammeter needle veered over to the left and lay implacably against the peg. His warning light came on a full,

©1965, HMH Publishing Co., Inc.

startling red. He cut his radio, his heater fans and finally his dash lights, but his headlights yellowed, and when he shone his flashlight on the dark ammeter, the needle had not moved.

He rolled onto the shoulder, stopped and looked under the hood, but the steady water-temperature gauge had already told him it wasn't anything as simple as a loose or broken fan belt. The generator was out, and that was all there was to it. For luck, he tested the firmness of as many electrical connections as he could reach, but nothing came of that. It was now just a question of driving as far as he could on his battery, which, thank God, was up to full charge from all the mileage since Chicago.

Forty miles down the road, practically groping by now and praying against state troopers, he got into a service plaza and had them give his battery a kick with their quick-charger while he went in and ate a disgusted meal. He already knew nobody was going to do anything about a foreign generator this side of Toledo and certainly not at this time of night. He made it into Toledo at three, found a motel operated by a motherly woman who hated him on sight, and slept until morning.

In Toledo, he was sold his own generator, rebuilt, and a new voltage regulator. Two hundred miles later, his ammeter began flashing back and forth like a man waving a shirt on a life raft and then went dead again. His voltage regulator began to buzz, and that was how he came to be in Warren, Ohio, when he ought to have been in New York. In New York, he often pondered in later years, an otherwise respectably married lady either did or did not spend two whole, entire, positively humiliating hours sitting in a hotel lobby waiting for him. It was his private opinion that she had done no such thing. If she had, he had missed the only occasion in their relationship on which she did not chicken out. He could stand missing her; he regretted missing the occasion.

Meanwhile, in Warren, Ohio, he had fallen in love.

Love in Warren was very much like love everywhere; he had found a motel for himself, since the Toledo stop had arranged his timing to get him into trouble after all the garages were closed, and had asked the desk clerk for the name of a decent place to eat. Directed to a place which was "good but not dressy," he found it was mediocre but dressy; the hostess moved him quickly to a very quiet table in an alcove beside the kitchen doors. He sat there in his printed shirt and green twill slacks, wishing idly that he were dead and in hell, looking forward to a fried steak, and wondering what had ever possessed him to think Ohioans considered anything less than a sports coat and white shirt not dressy. Shortly after he had reached the customary peak of irritation, the next table turned out to be occupied by a stunning, sad-faced, full-mouthed, medium-sized brunette with skin like velvet so golden it was almost visibly tinged with green.

Oh, Christ, he thought, I should have known, and noticed that she was drinking a light Scotch in an old-fashioned glass, with just a hint of bubble in it. Four or five loves ago, this had become established as the drink his loves drank, just as they had developed long legs when he was twenty-two, had acquired sad eyes when he was twenty-seven, had become medium tall at about that same time, but had not really produced high, firm breasts until the time early last year when his engine had burned out on his way to New Orleans. They had always been brunettes, of course. This one had by far the best skin, and it seemed reasonable to suppose that he could look forward to this feature from now on, for each was always like the last but better. Meeting them was becoming more and more of a hammer blow; being with them and then watching himself leave them was costing him more each time. If they improved much more, it would become totally unbearable.

"Sam Hobbs," he said to her, and she raised one eyebrow markedly.

"I beg your pardon?"

"My name is Sam Hobbs, I'm in town overnight with bad electricity in my car, I've got one hundred eighty-seven dollars cash and a checkbook, and a week's time."

"How very interesting." She tapped an ash from her cigarette with quick precision.

"Now, you, on the other hand, are married, engaged or someone's good friend. You have a well-paying job you don't like, a staggering load of debts public and psychic, a taste for quiet good living, few of the common inhibitions but a number of uncommon ones, and a sexy mouth."

"You're insane."

"So are you," he said with the certainty of a man watching a piano fall down a stairwell. "There is no argument between us. If I were king, nothing now could ever part us."

She looked at him as if over the tops of a pair of glasses and said, "I must say, your finesse staggers me."

"Darling, I've been in Ohio—a two-hundred-and-fifty-mile state—for eighteen hours, and I'm only in Warren, but I am also all used up until such time as you renew me. If you don't like it, screw it, but that is the shape of things that are."

"I don't like bad language."

"Neither do I. Let me tell you some. You can always cover your ears. How about 'It's too early,' and 'It's too late,' or 'Not *here*!'? How's that for obscenity? Want some more?"

She looked at him like a live human being and shook her head. "You may be right," she said.

He conquered the impulse to reply, "And I may be wrong; you know you're gonna miss me when I'm gone." Instead, he said politely, "Join me for dinner?"

She looked startled and glanced around as if every friend and relative she had were packed into the place, instead of the desultory scattering of good, honest faces that were bent over their soup plates hither and thither about the room. "Where are you staying?" she asked.

He told her the name of the motel and she nodded gravely, indicating she had it memorized, or that she approved his taste, or something equally positive. They went back to minding their own business, she being joined in due course by a chap who apologized for leaving her by herself and looked like a rising young man from a larger city, possibly Youngstown.

Hobbs ate his steak, gathered himself up and took his battery-driven car back to the motel, where he decided in favor of a shave and against a shower. He called his partner collect, told him he was in car trouble and would probably be a little late about everything and not to fret.

Sometime later in the evening, his phone rang and he picked it up while killing the volume on a spottily cut run of *Only Angels Have Wings*. Trapped in fog, knowing the Andean pass was a nesting place of stupid condors, Thomas Mitchell was groping for an opening through which to urge his laboring old trimotor mailplane.

"Sam," he said.

The girl said, "How are you, Eleanor?"

"Fine," Sam said. "Thomas Mitchell just got a condor through his windshield."

"Oh, no!" the girl said. "Are you hurt?"

"Lonely."

"Is there anything I can do? Do you want me to come over?"

"I can't run the car more than a mile or two at night."

"Yes. Of course. I'll be there in about half an hour. Is there anything you want me to pick up on the way?"

"I don't have anything drinkable on the premises."

"All right, fine. I'm sure I can find a drugstore open."

"See you."

"Yes. Please don't worry—it's no trouble for me at all. It's a shame about your car. It sounds to me as if it might take days to fix."

"Could be."

"I'm sure I'll be there soon."

On the screen, blinded Thomas Mitchell was spinning to his doom in a cloud of condors.

"Hurry," Hobbs said, thinking that by now his fine, leggy blonde wife was certainly in a saloon with his fretful partner.

"You are my cousin Eleanor," the girl explained gravely, setting a paper bag down on the dressing table and lifting out a bottle of White Label. "You were in a little bitty car accident and I may have to take care of you for a couple of days."

"All right, I got that," Hobbs said with equal solemnity, closing the door, wondering what it felt like to come all the way from Youngstown to hear a story about Cousin Eleanor. "What do you do in this town and what's your name?"

"Well, my name is Norah and I teach dancing. Social dancing." She moved her body in her olive silk sheath with a motion that was neither dramatic nor explicit but summed up what it was she did when she danced.

"Style," Hobbs said. "Fine style." He smiled at her suddenly, feeling the sudden outbreak of pure pleasure at having her to smile at, to move his mouth in a way that nothing else ever moved it. She was resting her weight lightly against the edge of the dressing table, her hands flat on the wood-grained Formica beside her hips, and he was thinking that another woman would have her ankles crossed negligently and her shoulders back, but she did not, and that her eyes were growing larger and larger as he drew nearer.

"I run a little outfit that designs and manufactures custom furniture," he said. "Executive desks at a grand a copy. Stuff like that."

"All right," she was saying. "And you're beautiful."

"Something like that," he said as he reached her.

There had not been much conversation between them. At dawn, he said, "Is somebody going to recognize your car out front?" She shook her head.

"My car is at my cousin Eleanor's," she said with a soft chuckle, warm, sleepy and full of herself. "I switched them," and this seemed to be a full and satisfactory solution to all the possible problems involved.

"What about this Eleanor?" he asked. "How many relatives do you have in this town? How tied up are you?"

She smiled at him like a little jam-faced girl blaming it all on her brother. "Me?" she asked incredulously. "I'm never tied up. When a beautiful man with a bad car came along, how tied up was I?" She closed her teeth lightly on the round of his shoulder. "Why? Do you want to take me somewhere?" she murmured with the tip of her tongue.

"I want— I want," he said, "I want to inhabit faery lands forlorn with you." And he did. He did. He wanted to take her with him through the pass in the Andes and on beyond, to where the Incan roads swept straight and new from way station to way station, innocent of wheel tracks, and at night the torchbearing runners ran lightly, tirelessly, naked and the color of earth, bearing the messages of the emperor.

She was murmuring with pleasure. "Do you say things like that a lot?" she whispered.

"Only to my love."

She turned sleepily, stretching her body, her hair and smooth arms brushing his face and neck. "Am I your love?" she asked lightly.

"My perfect love."

"You are my best."

"And you."

"Mmm!" She turned farther and kissed him, warm and like velvet come alive, light as pale clouds over the face of the full summer moon, her eyes glossy and dark as a river at midnight. Hobbs laughed softly. He was half-asleep, and he had been thinking of her as a princess of the Incas, as the magic woman who had come over the mountains and walked without looking left or right to the palace of the emperor and had found him.

The girl put her mouth lightly against his ear. "Happy?"

"Uh-huh. It's always fun being king." He ran his hand from her shoulder to her hip as if creating her in a dream.

Later he woke up, feeling as if he would live forever and be glad of it. She was drowsing against him, light as a cat. When he moved to slide away carefully off the edge of the bed, she made a soft, mewing, discontented noise and pulled the cover around her shoulders with a lithe, instantaneous twist of her body that left her curled facing him, her breathing once more serene. He looked at her, shaking his head fondly, and went to shower and wake up, making a rumbling, purring sound instead of singing. When he felt adequate, he came back out, drying his shoulders, and stood looking at her again. She had uncurled and was lying sprawled face down, one leg bent up, her arms outstretched toward the corners of the headboard, her face peeping out of the swirled nest of her hair. She was moving her shoulders and hips uncertainly and whimpering in her sleep. Her fingers flexed against the sheets.

He almost got back into the bed, but instead he went to the telephone book.

He found a Volkswagen dealer who said he knew nothing about Hobbs's kind of car but was willing to learn. Fair enough. Hobbs began walking softly around the room, pulling on his clothes. He couldn't keep himself from sneaking occasional glances at the girl in the bed, though he knew in his belly he was only acting like a man with a fresh, salty hole where a tooth had been. A man with other bad teeth biding their time in his jaw.

When he touched the doorknob, the girl sat up, smiled and arched her eyebrows.

"Car," Hobbs said.

"Oh." She sat warm and glowing, looking softer than the girl he had met in the restaurant last night, as if all her pores had opened. But he had seen something very much like that many times before, he reminded himself. "Do you have to go now?"

He shrugged, but he kept his hand on the doorknob.

"Well," she said uncertainly, "if they tell you it'll be a long thing, please call me here. I'll pick you up and we can come back to wait."

He smiled and nodded.

He went out and found the garage, where, after a certain amount of talking and poking back and forth, it was discovered that the too slack new wires leading from his generator had burned through against the exhaust manifold on their way to the regulator. The mechanics fixed it in ten minutes.

He stood there watching them do it. It was something he should have been able to find out for himself and repair on the road, but he had been too sick of it to go look. He shrugged sadly, thinking of the girl and how he always met them, and it was obvious to him once again that there was nothing he could do about it. So he went back to the motel with his car in good shape and his mind uneasy.

She was there, sitting with her back against the headboard, wearing her coral-colored bikini panties, her bare heels digging into the spread on the made-up bed. She was reading a paperback of the great plays of the 1950s, which she apparently carried in her purse. The reading light burnished her combed-out hair and her shoulders while filling her eyes with darkness. Hobbs thought of Frankie and how she had ached to be a member of the wedding. But if this girl wanted to talk about plays, he would say he didn't know much about them, because he had had that talk in other times and places. He stood just inside the closed door, feeling uncertain.

The girl said, "Hello." She smiled fondly at him. "That didn't take long. How's the car?"

"All fixed."

"Oh."

"Listen, about this dance teaching. Do you have to be at the studio a certain time or what?"

"Not if I don't want to."

"Do you want to?" he asked, remembering how he had smiled the night before.

She looked at him with her head cocked, alert and suddenly wary. "That's up to you. What's the matter?"

And there it was. She had put the book down and was looking closely at him; it was hard to read her eyes, with the light behind her, but suddenly she was not the same in anything, and he could feel himself groping inside.

"If it's up to me, nothing's the matter," he said and went over to the bed, kissing her, but it was just brave words, and he held the kiss as long as he could, because he did not want them looking at each other's faces any sooner than they had to. He reached out and touched her with every evidence of love and skill.

But at the wane of the sunny afternoon, she finally said, "I'd better go to work. There's somebody important coming in. I forgot."

He lay back on his back, smoking a cigarette and looking up into a corner of the ceiling. "Youngstown?"

"Who?"

"The boy from last night?"

She made a snorting noise through her delicate nostrils and shook her head scornfully. "No, I just have to go." She had good control, but control is not the same as self-, and he reached out to touch her thigh, because he wanted it registered in heaven that he felt compassion for her. And he said, "Please don't."

She looked at him with her neck arched and her eyes turned sideward out of her thoroughbred profile. "Why not?"

"Because I don't want you to," he said to the corner of the ceiling. And he didn't want her to. It seemed to him morally wrong that a girl should be told the things he'd told her and be unwanted in the morning.

"That's bullshit. Your car's fixed and you want to get back on the road. You've wanted to leave since this morning."

And so they were into it, and looking at her he felt the cold fear of discovery, once again, of how vicious they could be, of how the magic woman was more various than the emperor could have guessed when he created her for himself. But what he said, because he was honestly trying to find out why it always went like this, was, "That's not reasonable. You know I'm on my own time. Can there be anything I want in New York that isn't much better here?"

He tried to look at her tenderly, but the fact was that something about her face or his voice made it worse. He thought about the road, about the long, roaring miles between here and New York, the engine and gearbox screaming, the trucks gusting back and forth across the lane markers in crosswinds, the potholes clubbing his tires and suspension, the freeze of his mind and muscles behind the wheel, his burnt eyes locked on whatever was coming toward the windscreen, the narrow, dripping tunnels with their awful lights, the rough asphalt burring him with vibration on the blind downhill mountainside turns before Harrisburg, the cops, the hot rodders out at night in their Chevies with their clinging girls. Always he managed to hit Pennsylvania sleepless and at night, where they were forever trying to patch up their crumbling cart track and marking it with burned-out lanterns. Always he finished up on that Jersey Pike with its too low speed limit and the tar run into the cracks like the stitching on Frankenstein's monster. And then into Manhattan at some hour between two and eight, when the clerks in his kind of hotel hated giving you a single room, and once you had one you couldn't get to sleep, with your body still on the road. And when you finally did wake up, it was some hour you couldn't use for anything and didn't know whom to call, or what you were going to do, and wound up going around the city with your face numb and your eyes defensive.

"What in hell would make you say a thing like that?" he said, realizing that if he got out on the road now, that was exactly how it would be.

"You would, you son of a bitch," she said, pulling the sheet around herself and looking at the bottle and his overnight bag on the dressing table beside her purse. "Ever since you got back. What the hell made you go to that garage this morning, anyway? Didn't you say you had a whole week?"

Well, no, he'd had as long as the car would let him. But—

"Look," he said clumsily, reaching out for her rigid arm. "Look, I want to stay. But I can't. I want to take you with me. I want—"

She said slowly, her arm cold in his hand, "You've had what you want. You've had me—fooled."

He felt the terrible dismay of knowing they were getting smarter, too. Of having it confirmed that his fear was real. He had, once again, an ever-clearer vision of how beautiful and terrible the last one would be. "Listen—it's—"

"I want to get dressed now," she said, looking down at his hand.

He let go reluctantly. He still, with some of himself, wanted to awake her to softness and sleep. But that portion of him was only the part he kept to show to God. "All right, Norah," he said. She got up, pulling the sheet from the bed and holding it around herself as she picked up her things. Even though she moved only for herself now, she moved with grace and pride, and he watched her longingly, though he knew it was past time to long for this one.

"This thing happens with me."

"Don't let it bother you. You're not the only man it happens with."

"I meet you over and over again."

Her mouth pulled sharply at one corner.

"Norah," he said, "I mean it. I wind up driving a lot. To a lot of places. I don't really have a reason. I always have some excuse. I don't *want* to go. I want to stay with you." He always wanted to stay home, too, with the cheated girl he'd married. But in the long afternoons over the drafting table, his hand would stop moving properly and his brain would turn to porridge, and he'd put it all down and in a matter of minutes he'd have a reason for getting out into the rusting, unwashed car, just pouring gas into the tank and maybe checking the oil and maybe not. It was a good thing he had a partner to stay home and take care of things.

And now his own lips seemed to move of their own accord. "Look, I can't explain it; I don't know why it happens, but I do meet you over and over again."

"What you mean is, you make it with bitchy-looking brunettes in safe places."

He looked around the room. "Not safe. No, not safe places. I—"

"Would you mind not talking to me?"

"Norah, I want you to understand—"

"*Please.*" He saw that there were tears starting in her eyes, and when he saw that, he saw that he was through, because there were some things he would not break even to express himself nearer to his heart's desire. He got into his own clothes again and followed her out to her car, which looked new and massive beside his own. She did nothing to stop him, but it was as if he had gone long ago, or as if she had arrived the night before and waited all night and day in the wrong room.

He stood with his hand on the doorframe beside her, leaning in. She started the car and sat waiting, looking out through the windshield, wanting to close her door. Finally she looked at him as he tried to think of exactly the right thing to say, and said, "Would you mind?"

"I want you to understand something. It's something I can't help. It's not your fault."

"I know it's not my fault. Now I have to go tell my cousin why I took her car last night."

He was watching her graceful left hand. He reached out to touch it and she winced away. He watched the closing door swing toward his fingers. It seemed to him he watched it for a great many heartbeats and with detached interest. At the last possible instant, he gasped and pulled his hand out of the way. He had the impression there had actually been very little time between the jerk of her shoulder and the thud of the door closing tight in the frame. He stood now looking at his hand, at the intricate bones moving under the flesh, while she pulled out of the motel lot. Then he went back inside and packed quickly.

He drove the first 200 miles with his face motionless. By then he was well into the mountains and tunnels. At intervals, he said "Look, Norah," softly, only his mouth moving, the words becoming inaudible only inches from his lips. But as the road took hold of him, the spells of thinking about this particular girl became shorter and more widely separated. He began paying attention to things around him: to the readings on the dash, the signs flashing toward him in the night. He smiled a little, thinking about good moments from the night before.

He was beginning to be like himself again, he thought. He felt accustomed to himself. He began, with a certain sadness, to think about the first girl, about the crying, intense love of his youth. "Look," he said to her loudly as he cut out around a semitrailer and shifted the wheel a little to take the blow from the wind, automatically registering the slap of his top as he entered the pod of rapidly moving air it carried down the road. "Look, what do you want me to do?"

But he knew what she wanted him to do. She wanted him to go back and change the past, to keep the promises of his youth. He could still remember what it had been like, parked in front of her house that last night and listening to her babble on about how even if he did have to quit school, it didn't matter—they could get married, and both work, and he could finish school at night, and the whole thing going on like that. But the truth of it was, he couldn't think of any way of breaking up with her without quitting school, because the look in her eyes had begun to frighten him.

He remembered looking at her and realizing she wasn't even good-looking, that her waist and legs were too short, and her neck was too thin, and she was going to be coarse-skinned and dough-faced in a few years. That all the virtues and attractions he had seen in her had been judged by too many men before him, and there was a reason why all of them had left her. He remembered the many times she had wept in his arms and named the others, and enumerated the injustices they had done her, and of the thousand petty things she had said and done to get back at them afterward, and he had realized he was actually frightened of what she would do to him. And he had thought that he had a lot to learn about women, but not any more from her.

He had sat there, hunched over, the sick knot growing in his stomach, listening to her run through a dozen plans for them, each wilder and more abject than the last, and each more savagely delivered, and he had realized suddenly that if he let this go on, she would break him. And he had turned toward her quickly and said, "Look—it's over. Thanks for everything, but it's over. I've got all my clothes and stuff in the trunk, and I'm gonna be three hundred miles away from here by breakfast time. So good-bye. Even if I stayed, I wouldn't be any good to you anymore."

"You won't ever be any good," she had cried bitterly. "I'm the only one who knows how to make you feel like a king. I'm warning you, Sam—if you betray me this way, I'll—"

And that had done it. The digging of her fingertips into his arm, drawing blood through the sweater and shirt, or maybe the threat he didn't want to hear.

"Christ Almighty, get out of the car!" he had cried and shoved her door open, reaching across her and, probably on purpose, pushing with his shoulder against her thin rib cage. She had gone sprawling out of the car, onto the sidewalk in front of the sooty brick row house with the chipping limestone steps, and a drunk hanging around a stoop three or four houses down had laughed.

Hobbs had found himself staring deep into her eyes as she sat there with her shocked mouth open, and he had seen something there that had nearly made his heart stop. He was already lunging across the seat to slam the door shut as she scrambled to her knees and reached to grab the doorframe.

Now, as he automatically checked a pair of headlights growing in his rearview mirror, coming up a hell of a lot faster than his own 73 mph, Hobbs felt his arms grow rigid and his fingers lock on the greasy wood of his steering wheel until the flesh was aching against the bones. He was remembering the sound and then her cry, and the sight of her standing rigid, her back arched, her head thrown back, holding the hand aloft, the blood like ribbons wound around her trembling forearm.

She had gone tottering down the street then, knees stiff, the hand clasped to her stomach, her face white as lightning, and the drunk had come stumbling toward her uttering, "Hey! Hey, Jesus, miss, can I do anythin' for you?"

"Nobody," Hobbs muttered now as the headlights turned into full quads on high beam and made him duck away from his mirrors, "nobody can do anything for us." He was remembering how he had realized that the only thing for him to do was to get the hell out of there. And he was remembering how his brain had turned over the first time he had been down in a strange town with a broken gearbox and had thought it was she behind the magazine counter in the third-rate hotel.

But it had only been a girl like her. Very much like her, but better. Better for an hour or two. And he was remembering other hours and other towns as the big Caddy came booming up behind him and cut out at the last second and hung head and head with him for a moment, the driver staring curiously at Hobbs's infrequently seen kind of car, while Hobbs watched his wheels and waited for the blowout or the dropped tie rod that would send the Caddy into him. He held the wheel steady, staring across, listening to the beating of his wheels across the expansion joints, feeling his car try to pitch back and forth, listening for the sound of breaking metal anywhere in his car, his shoulders hunched against the sudden wrench in his own steering, wondering if he would hold it.

But that was all reflex, just the way it always was. Nothing was going to happen to the Caddy, and nothing was going to happen to him, because the other car's driver was a man, alone. Hobbs smiled reassuringly across at him. Then he turned his vision back to the road ahead of him, feeling all right, feeling that a man couldn't ask for more than to know exactly how it was all going to end. He wondered, as he sometimes did, where she was at this moment—the last brunette of all, moving toward him somewhere in the space and time of this world. He was content to wait; he assumed she was, too, if she had any idea of what they would do to each other.

The Caddy had pulled away and was gone down the road to its own appointments with speed traps and justices of the peace. Hobbs drove on, watching ahead and behind, and to each pair of headlights gaining on him, he thought, I love you, just in case it's you at last. He wondered if, when the metal broke and the gasoline erupted into their marriage bed, she would cry out in answer.

I have never felt I couldn't write anything but SF. When the late Rogers Terrill put out word that Ziff-Davis Publishing Co., which then paid well for pulp fiction, was looking for sea stories in a hurry, I provided. I was living in an apartment house on the corner of Eighth Avenue and 23rd Street in New York. The rent was more per month than I was earning in six months. Ziff-Davis paid a respectable sum for the story, and gave me the feeling that I was breaking into the general fiction market. Then the magazine failed, and this story has, twice, appeared in Fantastic, *a former Z-D property, presumably because I had an established SF byline. I apologize to all SF magazine buyers who felt done-on by this tactic; it wasn't mine. Now here it is again—the story and the tactic, both—but the circumstances are more appropriate.*

Scream at Sea

THE PRINCIPAL FEATURE of Harry Meglow's life had been his ability to escape from seemingly complete disaster. True, his means of escape usually required flight to out-of-the-way corners, but Harry had been tailored by some Providence with the foresight to ensure that he would feel at home in them.

Consequently, he had found life in Venezuela not disagreeable, and not financially unrewarding. However, it became necessary, as a result of the latter circumstance, to find urgent employment as a cook's helper on a Panamanian tanker which had the desirable quality of departing for Lisbon almost immediately. He might have preferred a more elevated position, but he was completely ignorant of the sea. Moreover, hustling slops is still preferable to a South American jail and the good offices of the Venezuelan penal code.

The tanker was a thousand miles into the Atlantic when Meglow's special kind of good fortune reasserted itself. He was

©1954, Ziff-Davis Publishing Company, Inc.

standing casually on deck, scratching the ears of the cook's cat, when some spark touched off the cargo of casing head.

Gasoline vapor is one of the more vicious explosives. Meglow found himself in the sea, and it was not until he tried to scramble aboard a raft that had whirled into the water near him that he became sufficiently conscious of what had happened to notice that the cat was still in his arms. He tossed it aboard and pulled himself up after it.

He and the cat were equally uncomprehending observers as the tanker tore itself completely open with one final blast, fountaining debris and fire.

It was near twilight. Meglow found no survivors in the darkening water—or, rather, none cried out or swam toward him as the raft drifted away. This fact did not particularly bother him, for he was used to the undemanding company of himself. The thought that he was alone in the Atlantic was not particularly disquieting either, for by now the roots of his faith in the inevitable survival of Harry Meglow were sunk deep into the past, so thoroughly intertwined with every significant event in his life that it was a fundamentally optimistic Harry Meglow whose raft carried him farther and farther from the place where the tanker had wallowed down into the sea.

So, once he had accustomed himself to the raft's staccato motion on the choppy water, he was able to sleep without first giving any special thought to his present situation, the sequence of preceding events which had brought him to it, or the course of the future.

He woke up once during the night. The chop had subsided, but an overcast had left the ocean almost completely black, without stars or moonlight. He stared around him at the featureless unfamiliarity of the Atlantic at night, hearing no sound except the slap of water against the raft and the sibilance of his breath.

The water around him was pouring out the warmth it had stored up during the day. Nevertheless, his wet clothing was a cold and clinging shell around him. He tried to peel off his sweater, but the sodden wool bound around his neck and shoulders, smothering him, and he fought his face free with a flail of his arms and a frantic twist of his body. Breathing in spasms, he pulled the sweater back down over his stomach, but in a few minutes he managed a chuckle, and a little later he was asleep again.

He was awakened in the morning by the clawing and meowing of the cat. He rolled over, pushed the animal away from him, and stretched. The slats of the raft's superstructure were 1 × 2 lumber, spaced a half inch apart—an unyielding surface that stiffened muscle, bruised bone, and cut into skin. His sweater had shrunk, and clung tightly to his chest and arms. Both it and his dungarees were stiff and crusted with salt. His skin itched. He put his hand up to his eyebrows and hair. They were clogged and sticky. He grimaced in disgust.

It was too early to tell, but he thought he might be getting a cold. His nasal passages were congested, and his throat was raw. Perhaps it was merely irritation from salt water inhaled during his frantic lunge for the raft. If it was a genuine cold—well, at least he was alive to have it.

He stood up and moved about in bursts of energy, quickening his circulation. It took him a while to become accustomed to the yielding surface the raft presented, but he was soon able to adjust his movements to it. He began to look around the raft.

The raft itself was more properly a float. It consisted of a slat superstructure around and on a series of metal drums—one of them, a makeshift replacement, actually was an empty oil drum—and stood about a foot out of the water. It was well in keeping with the ship from which it had come.

He found the food locker and watertank after a short while, sunken into the superstructure. There was a considerable supply of biscuits and some canned stuff with a Spanish label that turned out to be ham. He had no way of estimating how long it would last him, but there certainly seemed to be enough of it for some time to come. The watertank was full, and he had no great worries there, either, though again he did not know how many days' supply this actually was. To the problem of survival and rescue, he brought only his perversely optimistic fatalism.

He dug some ham out of the can with his fingers and began to eat it. When the cat rubbed up against his leg and wailed, he bent down absently and put some food on the deck for her, where she ate it hungrily. As he ate, he continued to survey his surroundings.

The raft was on smooth water, with a clear blue, white-flecked sky overhead. The wooden slats of the raft were warped in places, and some pieces of the deck—the top of the raft could be called a deck, he decided—had been replaced, the newer wood contrasting with the old, which was weathered and dotted with black pockmarks where the heads of nails had lost their paint and corroded. The entire raft needed repainting badly.

He finished the ham and threw the can overside, after which he bent down to the watertank for a drink.

The tank, as far as he could see, was the only piece of modern—or almost modern—equipment on the raft. It had a lid with a cup clipped to the underside, and a rubber seal to prevent as much evaporation as possible. He drank thirstily, then refilled the cup and set it down on the deck for the cat.

Idly, he swept his glance around the horizon, not especially hoping to see a ship, and was only mildly disappointed when he did not. There was something vaguely disquieting about the empty sea, not for its lack of any sign of rescue, but because of the sense that he was the only living man in at least thirteen hundred square miles—that is, if his memory was right about the horizon line being about twenty miles away, and if the formula for the area of a circle *was* $A = pi\ R^2$. The raft, hencoop of a structure that it was, embodied the only evidence that anything of Man had ever stirred this featureless water.

Meglow had never in his life been twenty miles away from another human being. The visualization of himself alone in the middle of a vast circle of emptiness was completely outside his experience.

He looked at the water around him again. It was no different in one direction than in another. It was all smooth water, apparently changing from dirty green to blue as it stretched farther away, but he knew that actually, even beyond the horizon, it was still dirty green.

Becoming conscious for the first time of the volume of sheer emptiness that an ocean could present, he lost some of the sense of romantic adventure which he had felt up to now—and still felt, but to a lesser degree. Still optimistic, if somewhat subdued, he spent the remainder of the day simply sitting on the raft with his hands around his knees, occasionally stroking the cat, which seemed to be having little difficulty in adjusting to a ten-by-ten environment. After eating some more ham, and drinking another cupful of water, he fell asleep.

He was awakened by the pitching and bucking of the raft, which shook with a completely unfamiliar and mechanical vibration. The cat, somewhere in the darkness beside him, was scratching at the slats.

He looked to his left, and saw something huge and gray slipping past him in the blackness. Running lights tracked a colored line across the sky, and the open door of a radio shack was a moving square of light. Paralyzed, he crouched on the bucking raft, riding the white froth of the ship's wake. When he finally managed to shout, the sound was thin and empty under the beat of the propeller in the water, and he knew it had not carried to the deck.

"Hey! Hey there! *For God's sake*—"

He shouted after the retreating ship for a long time, rasping his throat, and it was only after the raft had steadied down once more that he stopped, realizing with even greater force just how large an ocean was, how rare a thing had just occurred, and passed him by. Even on the deck of a ship, the closeness of bulkheads and cargo booms made the sea a thing that was somehow not as desolate as it actually was. Only a man alone on a miniscule platform of warped and dirty slatting could appreciate the closeness, the immediacy of the ocean. To a man on a ship, the sea was a stretch of broad uniformity which carried him on its back. To a man on a raft, the sea was a wilderness.

His heart was pounding. He could not sleep. When it began to rain shortly thereafter, he lay down flat on his stomach, his hands over the back of his head, the slats digging into his face. He felt the cat burrowing against him, but he continued to lie stiff and unmoving. It was up to her to take care of herself.

It rained into daylight. He was stiff and wet, and now he definitely had a cold. Moreover, either because the raft was bobbing on a chop even heavier than that of the first day, or as a reaction to his disappointment during the night, he was feeling sick. His eyes were burning, and his mouth was full of a thick spittle that tasted like corroded copper. The back passages of his nose felt swollen, he was nauseous, and his throat was ragged from the periodic rushes of bile that fought their way up into his esophagus. He was coughing a little.

He looked at the cat, which was huddled miserably against him, and this somehow made him feel better. He managed to chuckle at her unintelligible cries.

The fact that he was still able to laugh made him feel better, and once the mood had been cracked, it broke and left him optimistic again, in spite of the steady downpour of rain and his coughing, which was complicating his nausea.

All right, so he'd missed the ship. For all he knew, it was headed for Venezuela, where the police would be only too happy to have him. As a matter of fact, the more he thought about it, the more he became convinced that something unpleasant would have awaited him aboard that vessel. No disaster in his life, no matter how serious it had been at first look, had ever really been as bad as it seemed. He had gotten into trouble in the States, and had found his way to South America. Once there, he had gotten quite a bit of money. Of course, he'd had to run for it, but the tanker had been readily available. And when the tanker exploded, he had survived. Come to think of it, it was probably because some harm waited for him in Lisbon that the ship had sunk.

He stared out over the white-capped ocean at the steel-gray horizon, and some of this new mood left him. He began to worry about the possibility of a full-fledged storm. Somehow, the sea seemed to be outside the abilities of his protecting destiny. On the raft, he was still Harry Meglow, still a living human being, with faith in himself and the future. But the Atlantic ran a foot below him, and in the Atlantic he would be a chip, an insignificant, purposeless something that would drift through the water for days before the pulped and fish-eaten remains settled down to the soundless bottom.

He tried to visualize the death of Harry Meglow. He tried to picture a world without him—and failed.

It rained until very late in the day, when the clouds broke and left the ocean in sunset. He was able to eat and drink a little. He fed the cat at the same time. She seemed to have come through the rain without any harm, and although her fur was still damp, it was drying rapidly. He became conscious of his own wetness. The temperature had dropped, and he began to shiver. His cough had gotten worse, and the glands in his throat had swollen, so that every time he swallowed, a painful pressure caught him around the neck. The breath whistling out of his nostrils was hot, and he knew he had a fever.

This time, he managed to get the sweater off. He sat with the wind chilling his bare skin, until finally he stood up, took off the dungarees as well, and began to exercise violently. He was warm and dry in a few minutes, but it would be hours before his clothes would dry. He was caught with the choice of putting them on again, or of remaining naked, in which case he would have to keep moving around.

Even as he considered the matter, he cooled off again, and began swinging his arms and running in place.

After five hours, the dungarees were dry enough to wear, and he put them on gratefully. The sweater was still wet, and he crouched on the slats with his arms folded over his chest. He tried hugging the cat for warmth, but she clawed at his arms and finally bit his hand. He dropped her with a curse and barely restrained himself from flinging her into the ocean.

The following day, the fever was worse, and his eyes were burning badly. Each time he swallowed, his eardrums popped, and his throat was almost closed. His bones ached, and there was a sharp pain in his chest. His vision was a little blurred.

When he got to his feet, the headache that pounded his skull made him stagger, and he closed his eyes at the pain. The cat was hungry again, and he opened a can of ham. By now, he had come to hate the salty taste and the mushy consistency, but he forced down a few mouthfuls and left the rest for the cat, which had a difficult time eating out of the flat, narrow can, but made the best of it. He opened the lid of the watertank and drank a cupful of water, setting another cupful down for the cat, but when he lurched away, his foot struck the cup, and kicked it overside.

He stared at the place where it had gone over, his face dull, but then he shrugged. He could always use an empty ham can to bring water up out of the tank. The cat would go thirsty in the meantime, but that was the cat's problem. He collapsed on the deck, and lay staring at the sea.

On his side, as he was, his eyes were only a little more than a foot above the water. The illusion that he was actually in the sea had grown more powerful, and a corresponding fear of the Atlantic had grown with it.

It was not merely the realization of the ocean's incredible area that overwhelmed him. It was the knowledge that the ocean was as old as all the Earth itself, and as enduring. Where the wrecked tanker had been, there was not even a dimple in the water. A ship had passed him in the night, tossing the water under his raft. Where was the ship? Where was the wake? They had existed for a few moments, then disappeared, and left the sea unmarked.

He realized that the sea could take him, and that the ripples would not reach a hundred yards. There would be no marker, no sign to the world that it had lost him.

"No!" The word burst out of him, a croaked shout. He sat up, trembling, sharp chills running through his body, his chest heaving as he coughed. Somehow, he would live through this. The sea would not have him.

He fell back, his jaw clenched, his body rigid, his hands in tight fists.

But that night it rained again, a cold, sharply driven rain from the north that first cooled his dry and feverish skin, but which was soon an icy slick that shot his temperature up and had him delirious by morning. He thrashed about on the raft, retching past the agony in his throat. The raft was tossing badly, and the cat had dug its claws into one leg of his dungarees in an effort to hang on.

Enough consciousness returned to permit a lance of fear at the thought that he might roll off the raft. Shuddering with chills, his teeth chattering, he got to his hands and knees and took off his belt. He passed it around a slat and buckled it around his waist again. Then the bone-wrenching fever took hold of him once more, and he lost consciousness.

He regained consciousness another time and lay staring up into the bright sky, with his eyes running from the fever. The pain in his chest was like a spike transfixing him. He tried to move, could not, and remembered the belt. His cracked lips twisted into a grimace as he plucked at it feebly but could not find the buckle. He heard a scratching sound, and turned his head. The cat was clawing at the trap over the food locker and the watertank. His own mouth was dry, and he tried to open the belt once more, but when he finally located the buckle, he could not open it. His hands were weak, robbed of strength.

Dully, he turned his head in the opposite direction, and looked at the sea.

Once again, and for the last time, his perverse luck had made sure that things were not as bad as they might have been. The sea would not get him.

He coughed, and smiled at the pain. His breath was hoarse—harsh, labored. No, the sea had not killed him. He was going to die of pneumonia. He had not starved, or died of thirst, or been swept overboard. The sea had lost. He snorted again, a painful "huh" that gusted from his nostrils.

The cat was clawing at his leg. He managed to raise his hand and swing it through the air, and the cat jumped back, mewing.

"Sor—sorry, cat," he grunted. "Nobody's going to—be around—to open—any food for—you."

His head fell back, and he chuckled. He had even managed to leave a living thing behind to regret his passing. Somehow, the thought appealed to him.

And then he realized to what precise end his special Providence had brought him, and he found the energy, buried deep in his system somewhere, to cry out, the harsh yell flinging itself over the whitecaps. He braced his shoulders against the deck and tried to break free, but the effort drained him, and he collapsed. He lay motionless, except for the tears that poured from his eyes.

The raft was picked up three weeks later by a Brazilian tramp. The cat had not starved to death. It was not even hungry.

This story won an "Edgar" special award from the Mystery Writers of America. First, it haunted me for many years, in disconnected pieces. The locale is nearly actual; off Route 35 in New Jersey, there are, I'm sure, stranger places than this. The Colonel's appearance is that of any number of angular protagonists drawn by Van Dongen for Astounding Science Fiction. He appeared earlier, without his physical disabilities, as a psychically crippled man in an SF story called "The Man Who Tasted Ashes." He is a Royal Marine because the British "Man Who Never Was," created by Ewen Montagu, carried the credentials of an RME officer when he washed ashore on Spain. The dogs, and his commands to them, have been in my mind for years, as a potential practical joke. But none of that came together until I saw what is still one of my favorite movies, The Great Escape. *I love it as I love pulp fiction; I have seen it a dozen times, and I will see it a dozen more. But it is a travesty on Paul Brickhill's book based on the real circumstances of that prison camp, just as Brickhill in turn, like all other prison camp descriptors, necessarily glosses over the real burdens and actual grim duties of any senior officer of captured military personnel.*

One day, therefore, long after we had left the Jersey coast, I sat bolt upright in my bed in Evanston, Illinois, and a month later I had a check from the Saturday Evening Post, *which is gone—check, and old* Post, *too— but the story remains. I am proud of it not because of the ending, which I like, but because I did not really understand how the Colonel was going to be until he appeared, sentence by sentence, effortlessly. And I do not watch reruns of* Hogan's Heroes. *Or I say I don't.*

The Master of the Hounds

THE WHITE SAND road led off the state highway through the sparse pines. There were no tire tracks in the road, but, as Malcolm turned the car onto it, he noticed the footprints of dogs, or perhaps of only one dog, running along the middle of the road toward the combined general store and gas station at the intersection.

"Well, it's far enough away from everything, all right," Virginia said. She was lean and had dusty black hair. Her face was long, with high cheekbones. They had married ten years ago, when she had been girlish and very slightly plump.

"Yes," Malcolm said. Just days ago, when he'd been turned down for a Guggenheim Fellowship that he'd expected to get, he had quit his job at the agency and made plans to spend the summer, somewhere as cheap as possible, working out with himself whether he was really an artist or just had a certain commercial talent. Now they were here.

He urged the car up the road, following a line of infrequent and weathered utility poles that carried a single strand of power line. The real-estate agent already had told them there were no telephones. Malcolm had taken that to be a positive feature, but somehow he did not like the looks of that one thin wire sagging from pole to pole. The wheels of the car sank in deeply on either side of the dog prints, which he followed like a row of bread crumbs through a forest.

Several hundred yards farther along, they came to a sign at the top of a hill:

©1966, Curtis Publishing Co., Inc.

Marine View Shores! New Jersey's Newest, Fastest-Growing Residential Community. Welcome Home! From $9,990. No Dn Pyt for Vets.

Below them was a wedge of land—perhaps ten acres altogether that pushed out into Lower New York Bay. The road became a gullied, yellow gravel street, pointing straight toward the water and ending in three concrete posts, one of which had fallen and left a gap wide enough for a car to blunder through. Beyond that was a low drop-off where the bay ran northward to New York City and, in the other direction, toward the open Atlantic.

On either side of the roughed-out street, the bulldozed land was overgrown with scrub oak and sumac. Along the street were rows of roughly rectangular pits—some with half-finished foundation walls in them—piles of excavated clay, and lesser quantities of sand, sparsely weed-grown and washed into ravaged mounds like Dakota Territory. Here and there were houses with half-completed frames, now silvered and warped.

There were only two exceptions to the general vista. At the end of the street, two identically designed, finished houses faced each other. One looked shabby. The lot around it was free of scrub, but weedy and unsodded. Across the street from it stood a house in excellent repair. Painted a charcoal gray and roofed with dark asphalt shingles, it sat in the center of a meticulously green and level lawn, which was in turn surrounded by a wire fence approximately four feet tall and splendid with fresh aluminum paint. False shutters, painted stark white, flanked high, narrow windows along the side Malcolm could see. In front of the house, a line of whitewashed stones the size of men's heads served as curbing. There wasn't a thing about the house and its surroundings that couldn't have been achieved with a straight string, a handsaw, and a three-inch brush. Malcolm saw a chance to cheer things up. "There now, Marthy!" he said to Virginia. "I've led you safe and sound through the howlin' forest to a snug home in the shadder of Fort Defiance."

"It's orderly," Virginia said. "I'll bet it's no joke, keeping up a place like that out here."

As Malcolm was parking the car parallel to where the curb would have been in front of their house, a pair of handsome young Doberman pinschers came out from behind the gray house across the street and stood together on the lawn with their noses just short of the fence, looking out. They did not bark. There was no movement at the front window, and no one came out into the yard. The dogs simply stood there, watching, as Malcolm walked over the clay to his door.

The house was furnished—that is to say, there were chairs in the living room, although there was no couch, and a chromium-and-plastic dinette set in the area off the kitchen. Though one of the bedrooms was completely empty, there was a bureau and a bed in the other. Malcolm walked through the house quickly and went back out to the car to get the luggage and groceries. Nodding toward the dogs, he said to Virginia, "Well! The latest thing in iron deer." He felt he had to say something light, because Virginia was staring across the street.

He knew perfectly well, as most people do and he assumed Virginia did, that Doberman pinschers are nervous, untrustworthy, and vicious. At the same time, he and his wife did have to spend the whole summer here. He could guess how much luck they'd have trying to get their money back from the agent now.

"They look streamlined like that because their ears and tails are trimmed when they're puppies," Virginia said. She picked up a bag of groceries and carried it into the house.

When Malcolm had finished unloading the car, he slammed the trunk lid shut. Although they hadn't moved until then, the Dobermans seemed to regard this as a sign. They turned smoothly, the arc of one inside the arc of the other, and keeping formation, trotted out of sight behind the gray house.

Malcolm helped Virginia put things away in the closets and in the lone bedroom bureau. There was enough to do to keep both of them busy for several hours, and it was dusk when Malcolm happened to look out through the living-room window. After he had glanced that way, he stopped.

Across the street, floodlights had come on at the four corners of the gray house. They poured illumination downward in cones that lighted the entire yard. A crippled man was walking just inside the fence, his legs stiff and his body bent forward from the waist, as he gripped the projecting handles of two crutch-canes that supported his weight at the elbows. As Malcolm watched, the man took a precise square turn at the corner of the fence and began walking along the front of his property. Looking straight ahead, he moved regularly and purposefully, his shadow thrown out through the fence behind the composite shadow of the two dogs walking immediately ahead of him. None of them was looking in Malcolm's direction. He watched as the man made another turn, followed the fence toward the back of his property, and disappeared behind the house.

Later Virginia served cold cuts in the little dining alcove. Putting the house in order seemed to have had a good effect on her morale.

"Listen, I think we're going to be all right here, don't you?" Malcolm said.

"Look," she said reasonably, "any place you can get straightened out is fine with me."

This wasn't quite the answer he wanted. He had been sure in New York that the summer would do it—that in four months a man would come to *some* decision. He had visualized a house for them by the ocean, in a town with a library and a movie and other diversions. It had been a shock to discover how expensive summer rentals were and how far in advance you had to book them. When the last agent they saw described this place to them and told them how low the rent was, Malcolm had jumped at it immediately. But so had Virginia, even though there wasn't anything to do for distraction. In fact, she had made a point of asking the agent again about the location of the house, and the agent, a fat, gray man with ashes on his shirt, had said earnestly, "Mrs. Lawrence, if you're looking for a place where nobody will bother your husband from working, I can't think of anything better." Virginia had nodded decisively.

It had bothered her, his quitting the agency; he could understand that. Still, he wanted her to be happy, because he expected to be surer of what he wanted to do by the end of the summer. She was looking at him steadily now. He cast about for something to offer her that would interest her and change the mood between them. Then he remembered the scene he had witnessed earlier that evening. He told her about the man and his dogs, and this did raise her eyebrows.

"Do you remember the real-estate agent telling us anything about him?" she asked. "I don't."

Malcolm, searching through his memory, did recall that the

agent had mentioned a custodian they could call on if there were any problems. At the time he had let it pass, because he couldn't imagine either agent or custodian really caring. Now he realized how dependent he and Virginia were out here if it came to things like broken plumbing or bad wiring, and the custodian's importance altered accordingly. "I guess he's the caretaker," he said.

"Oh."

"It makes sense—all this property has got to be worth something. If they didn't have someone here, people would just carry stuff away or come and camp or something."

"I suppose they would. I guess the owners let him live here rent-free, and with those dogs he must do a good job."

"He'll get to keep it for a while, too," Malcolm said. "Whoever started to build here was a good ten years ahead of himself. I can't see anybody buying into these places until things have gotten completely jammed up closer to New York."

"So, he's holding the fort," Virginia said, leaning casually over the table to put a dish down before him. She glanced over his shoulder toward the living-room window, widened her eyes, and automatically touched the neckline of her housecoat, and then snorted at herself.

"Look, he can't possibly see in here," Malcolm said. "The living room, yes, but to look in here he'd have to be standing in the far corner of his yard. And he's back inside his house." He turned his head to look, and it was indeed true, except that one of the dogs was standing at that corner looking toward their house, eyes glittering. Then its head seemed to melt into a new shape, and it was looking down the road. It pivoted, moved a few steps away from the fence, turned, soared, landed in the street, and set off. Then, a moment later, it came back down the street running side by side with its companion, whose jaws were lightly pressed together around the rolled-over neck of a small paper bag. The dogs trotted together companionably and briskly, their flanks rubbing against one another, and when they were a few steps from the fence they leaped over it in unison and continued across the lawn until they were out of Malcolm's range of vision.

"For heaven's sake! He lives all alone with those dogs!" Virginia said.

Malcolm turned quickly back to her. "How do you come to think that?"

"Well, it's pretty plain. You saw what they were doing out there just now. They're his servants. He can't get around himself, so they run errands for him. If he had a wife, she would do it."

"You learned all that already?"

"Did you notice how happy they were?" Virginia asked. "There was no need for that other dog to go meet its friend. But it wanted to. They can't be anything but happy." Then she looked at Malcolm, and he saw the old, studying reserve coming back into her eyes.

"For Pete's sake! They're only dogs—what do they know about anything?" Malcolm said.

"They know about happiness," Virginia said. "They know what they do in life."

Malcolm lay awake for a long time that night. He started by thinking about how good the summer was going to be, living here and working, and then he thought about the agency and about why he didn't seem to have the kind of shrewd, limited intuition that let a man do advertising work easily. At about four in the morning he wondered if perhaps he wasn't frightened, and had been frightened for a long time. None of this kind of thinking was new to him, and he knew that it would take him until late afternoon the following day to reach the point where he was feeling pretty good about himself.

When Virginia tried to wake him early the next morning he asked her to please leave him alone. At two in the afternoon, she brought him a cup of coffee and shook his shoulder. After a while, he walked out to the kitchen in his pajama pants and found that she had scrambled up some eggs for the two of them.

"What are your plans for the day?" Virginia said when he had finished eating.

He looked up. "Why?"

"Well, while you were sleeping, I put all your art things in the front bedroom. I think it'll make a good studio. With all your gear in there now, you can be pretty well set up by this evening."

At times she was so abrupt that she shocked him. It upset him that she might have been thinking that he wasn't planning to do anything at all today. "Look," he said, "you know I like to get the feel of a new thing."

"I know that. I didn't set anything up in there. I'm no artist. I just moved it all in."

When Malcolm had sat for a while without speaking, Virginia cleared away their plates and cups and went into the bedroom. She came out wearing a dress, and she had combed her hair and put on lipstick. "Well, you do what you want to," she said. "I'm going to go across the street and introduce myself."

A flash of irritability hit him, but then he said, "If you'll wait a minute, I'll get dressed and go with you. We might as well both meet him."

He got up and went back to the bedroom for a T-shirt and blue jeans and a pair of loafers. He could feel himself beginning to react to pressure. Pressure always made him bind up; it looked to him as if Virginia had already shot the day for him.

They were standing at the fence, on the narrow strip of lawn between it and the row of whitewashed stones, and nothing was happening. Malcolm saw that although there was a gate in the fence, there was no break in the little grass border opposite it. And there was no front walk. The lawn was lush and all one piece, as if the house had been lowered onto it by helicopter. He began to look closely at the ground just inside the fence, and when he saw the regular pockmarks of the man's crutches, he was comforted.

"Do you see any kind of bell or anything?" Virginia asked.

"No."

"You'd think the dogs would bark."

"I'd just as soon they didn't."

"Will you look?" she said, fingering the gate latch. "The paint's hardly scuffed. I'll bet he hasn't been out of his yard all summer." Her touch rattled the gate lightly, and at that the two dogs came out from behind the house. One of them stopped, turned, and went back. The other dog came and stood by the fence, close enough for them to hear its breathing, and watched them with its head cocked alertly.

The front door of the house opened. At the doorway there was a wink of metal crutches, and then the man came out and stood on his front steps. When he had satisfied himself as to who they were, he nodded, smiled, and came toward them. The other dog walked beside him. Malcolm noticed that the dog at the fence did not distract himself by looking back at his master.

The man moved swiftly, crossing the ground with nimble swings of his body. His trouble seemed to be not in the spine, but in the legs themselves, for he was trying to help himself along with them. It could not be called walking, but it could not be called total helplessness either.

Although the man seemed to be in his late fifties, he had not gone to seed any more than his property had. He was wiry and clean-boned, and the skin on his face was tough and tanned. Around his small blue eyes and at the corners of this thin lips were many fine, deep-etched wrinkles. His yellowish-white hair was brushed straight back from his temples in the classic British military manner. And he even had a slight mustache. He was wearing a tweed jacket with leather patches at the elbows, which seemed a little warm for this kind of day, and a light flannel pale-gray shirt with a pale-blue bow tie. He stopped at the fence, rested his elbows on the crutches, and held out a firm hand with short nails the color of old bones.

"How do you do," he said pleasantly, his manner polished and well-bred. "I have been looking forward to meeting my new neighbors. I am Colonel Ritchey." The dogs stood motionless, one to each side of him, their sharp black faces pointing outward.

"How do you do," Virginia said. "We are Malcolm and Virginia Lawrence."

"I'm very happy to meet you," Colonel Ritchey said. "I was prepared to believe Cortelyou would fail to provide anyone this season."

Virginia was smiling. "What beautiful dogs," she said. "I was watching them last night."

"Yes. Their names are Max and Moritz. I'm very proud of them."

As they prattled on, exchanging pleasantries, Malcolm wondered why the Colonel had referred to Cortelyou, the real-estate agent, as a provider. There was something familiar, too, about the colonel.

Virginia said, "You're the famous Colonel Ritchey."

Indeed he was. Malcolm now realized, remembering the big magazine series that had appeared with the release of the movie several years before.

Colonel Ritchey smiled with no trace of embarrassment. "I

am the famous Colonel Ritchey, but you'll notice I certainly don't look much like that charming fellow in the motion picture."

"What in hell are you doing *here*?" Malcolm asked.

Ritchey turned his attention to him. "One has to live somewhere, you know."

Virginia said immediately, "I was watching the dogs last night, and they seemed to do very well for you. I imagine it's pleasant having them to rely on."

"Yes, it is, indeed. They're quite good to me, Max and Moritz. But it is much better with people here now. I had begun to be quite disappointed in Cortelyou."

Malcolm began to wonder whether the agent would have had the brass to call Ritchey a custodian if the colonel had been within earshot.

"Come in, please," the colonel was saying. The gate latch resisted him momentarily, but he rapped it sharply with the heel of one palm and then lifted it. "Don't be concerned about Max and Moritz—they never do anything they're not told."

"Oh, I'm not the least bit worried about them," Virginia said.

"Ah, to some extent you should have been," the colonel said. "Dobermans are not to be casually trusted, you know. It takes many months before one can be at all confident in dealing with them."

"But you trained them yourself, didn't you?" Virginia said.

"Yes, I did," Colonel Ritchey said, with a pleased smile. "From imported pups." The voice in which he now spoke to the dogs was forceful, but as calm as his manner had been to Virginia. "Kennel," he said, and Max and Moritz stopped looking at Malcolm and Virginia and smoothly turned away.

The colonel's living room, which was as neat as a sample, contained beautifully cared for, somewhat old-fashioned furniture. The couch, with its needle-point upholstery and carved framing, was the sort of thing Malcolm would have expected in a lady's living room. Angling out from one wall was a Morris chair, placed so that a man might relax and gaze across the street or, with a turn of his head, rest his eyes on the distant lights of New York. Oil paintings in heavy gilded frames depicted landscapes, great eye-stretching vistas of rolling, open country. The furniture in the room seemed sparse to Malcolm until it occurred to him that the colonel needed extra clearance to get around in and had no particular need to keep additional chairs for visitors.

"Please do sit down," the colonel said. "I shall fetch some tea to refresh us."

When he had left the room, Virginia said, "Of all people! Neighborly, too."

Malcolm nodded. "Charming," he said.

The colonel entered holding a silver tray perfectly steady, its edges grasped between his thumbs and forefingers, his other fingers curled around each of the projecting black-rubber handgrips of his crutches. He brought tea on the tray and, of all things, homemade cookies. "I must apologize for the tea service," he said, "but it seems to be the only one I have."

When the colonel offered the tray, Malcolm saw that the utensils were made of the common sort of sheet metal used to manufacture food cans. Looking down now into his cup, he saw it had been enameled over its original tinplate, and he realized that the whole thing had been made literally from a tin can. The teapot—handle, spout, vented lid, and all—was the same. "Be damned—you made this for yourself at the prison camp, didn't you?"

"As a matter of fact, I did, yes. I was really quite proud of my handiwork at the time, and it still serves. Somehow, living as I do, I've never brought myself to replace it. It's amazing, the fuddy-duddy skills one needs in a camp and how important they become to one. I find myself repainting these poor objects periodically and still taking as much smug pleasure in it as I did when that attitude was quite necessary. One is allowed to do these things in my position, you know. But I do hope my *ersatz* Spode isn't uncomfortably hot in your fingers."

Virginia smiled. "Well, of course, it's trying to be." Malcolm was amazed. He hadn't thought Virginia still remembered how to act so coquettish. She hadn't grown apart from the girl who'd always attracted a lot of attention at other people's gallery openings; she had simply put that part of herself away somewhere else.

Colonel Ritchey's blue eyes were twinkling in response. He turned to Malcolm. "I must say, it will be delightful to share this summer with someone as charming as Mrs. Lawrence."

"Yes," Malcolm said, preoccupied now with the cup, which

was distressing his fingers with both heat and sharp edges. "At least, I've always been well satisfied with her," he added.

"I've been noticing the inscription here," Virginia said quickly, indicating the meticulous freehand engraving on the tea tray. She read out loud, " 'To Colonel David N. Ritchey, R.M.E., from his fellow officers at *Oflag* XXXI*b*, on the occasion of their liberation, May 14, 1945. Had he not been there to lead them, many would not have been present to share of this heartfelt token.' " Virginia's eyes shone, as she looked up at the colonel. "They must all have been very fond of you."

"Not all," the colonel said, with a slight smile. "I was senior officer over a very mixed bag. Mostly younger officers gathered from every conceivable branch. No followers at all—just budding leaders, all personally responsible for having surrendered once already, some apathetic, others desperate. Some useful, some not. It was my job to weld them into a disciplined, responsive body, to choose whom we must keep safe and who was best suited to keeping the Jerries on the jump. And we were in, of course, from the time of Dunkirk to the last days of the war, with the strategic situation in the camp constantly changing in various ways. All most of them understood was tactics—when they understood at all."

The colonel grimaced briefly, then smiled again. "The tray was presented by the survivors, of course. They'd had a tame Jerry pinch it out of the commandant's sideboard a few days earlier, in plenty of time to get the inscription on. But even the inscription hints that not all survived."

"It wasn't really like the movie, was it?" Virginia said.

"No, and yet—" Ritchey shrugged, as if remembering a time when he had accommodated someone on a matter of small importance. "That was a question of dramatic values, you must realize, and the need to tell an interesting and exciting story in terms recognizable to a civilian audience. Many of the incidents in the motion picture are literally true—they simply didn't happen in the context shown. The Christmas tunnel was quite real, obviously. I did promise the men I'd get at least one of them home for Christmas if they'd pitch in and dig it. But it wasn't a serious promise, and they knew it wasn't. Unlike the motion picture actor, I was not being fervent; I was being ironic.

"It was late in the war. An intelligent man's natural desire would be to avoid risk and wait for liberation. A great many of them felt exactly that way. In fact, many of them had turned civilian in their own minds and were talking about their careers outside, their families—all that sort of thing. So by couching in sarcasm trite words about Christmas tunnels, I was reminding them what and where they still were. The tactic worked quite well. Through devices of that sort, I was able to keep them from going to seed and coming out no use to anyone." The colonel's expression grew absent. "Some of them called me 'The Shrew,' " he murmured. "*That* was in the movie, too, but they were all shown smiling when they said it."

"But it was your duty to hold them all together any way you could," Virginia said encouragingly.

Ritchey's face twisted into a spasm of tension so fierce that there might have been strychnine in his tea. But it was gone at once. "Oh, yes, yes, I held them together. But the expenditure of energy was enormous. And demeaning. It ought not to have made any difference that we were cut off from higher authority. If we had all still been home, there was not a man among the prisoners who would have dared not jump to my simplest command. But in the camp they could shilly-shally and evade; they could settle down into little private ambitions. People will do that. People will not hold true to common purposes unless they are shown discipline." The colonel's uncompromising glance went from Virginia to Malcolm. "It's no good telling people what they ought to do. The only surety is in being in a position to tell people what they *must* do."

"Get some armed guards to back you up. That the idea, Colonel? Get permission from the Germans to set up your own machine-gun towers inside the camp?" Malcolm liked working things out to the point of absurdity.

The colonel appraised him imperturbably. "I was never quite that much my own man in Germany. But there is a little story I must tell you. It's not altogether off the point." He settled back, at ease once again.

"You may have been curious about Max and Moritz. The Germans, as you know, have always been fond of training dogs to perform all sorts of entertaining and useful things. During the war the Jerries were very much given to using Dobermans for auxiliary guard duty at the various prisoner-of-war camps. In action, Mr. Lawrence, or simply in view, a trained dog is far more terrifying than any soldier with a machine pistol. It takes an animal to stop a man without hesitation, no matter if the man is cursing or praying.

"Guard dogs at each camp were under the charge of a man called the *Hundführer*—the master of the hounds, if you will— whose function, after establishing himself with the dogs as their master and director, was to follow a few simple rules and to take the dogs to wherever they were needed. The dogs had been taught certain patrol routines. It was necessary only for the *Hundführer* to give simple commands such as 'Search' or 'Arrest,' and the dogs would know what to do. Once we had seen them do it, they were very much on our minds, I assure you.

"A Doberman, you see, has no conscience, being a dog. And a trained Doberman has no discretion. From the time he is a puppy, he is bent to whatever purpose has been preordained for him. And the lessons are painful—and autocratic. Once an order has been given, it must be enforced at all costs, for the dog must learn that all orders are to be obeyed unquestioningly. That being true, the dog must also learn immediately and irrevocably that only the orders from one particular individual are valid. Once a Doberman has been trained, there is no way to retrain it. When the American soldiers were seen coming, the Germans in the machine-gun towers threw down their weapons and tried to flee, but the dogs had to be shot. I watched from the hospital window, and I shall never forget how they continued to leap at the kennel fencing until the last one was dead. Their *Hundführer* had run away. . . ."

Malcolm found that his attention was wandering, but Virginia asked, as if on cue, "How did you get into the hospital—was that the Christmas tunnel accident?"

"Yes," the colonel said to Virginia, gentleman to lady. "The sole purpose of the tunnel was, as I said, to give the men a focus of attention. The war was near enough its end. It would have been foolhardy to risk actual escape attempts. But we did the thing up brown, of course. We had a concealed shaft, a tunnel lined with bed slats, a trolley for getting to and from the tunnel entrance, fat lamps made from shoe-blacking tins filled with margarine—all the normal appurtenances. The Germans at that stage were quite experienced in ferreting out this sort of operation, and the only reasonable assurance of continued progress was to work deeply and swiftly. Tunneling is always a calculated risk—the accounts of that sort of operation are biased in favor of the successes, of course.

"At any rate, by the end of November, some of the men were audibly thinking it was my turn to pitch in a bit, so one night I went down and began working. The shoring was as good as it ever was, and the conditions weren't any worse than normal. The air was breathable, and as long as one worked—ah—unclothed, and brushed down immediately on leaving the tunnel, the sand was not particularly damaging to one's skin. Clothing creates chafes in those circumstances. Sand burns coming to light at medical inspections were one of the surest signs that such an operation was under way.

"However that may be, I had been down there for about an hour and a half, and was about to start inching my way back up the tunnel, feetfirst on the trolley like some Freudian symbol, when there was a fall of the tunnel roof that buried my entire chest. It did not cover my face, which was fortunate, and I clearly remember my first thought was that now none of the men would be able to feel the senior officer hadn't shared their physical tribulations. I discovered, at once, that the business of clearing the sand that had fallen was going to be extremely awkward. First, I had to scoop some extra clearance from the roof over my face. Handfuls of sand began falling directly on me, and all I could do about that was to thrash my head back and forth. I was becoming distinctly exasperated at that when the fat lamp attached to the shoring loosened from its fastenings and spilled across my thighs. The hot fat was quite painful. What made it rather worse was that the string wick was not extinguished by the fall, and accordingly, the entire lower part of my body between navel and knees, having been saturated with volatile fat. . . ." The colonel grimaced in embarrassment.

"Well, I was immediately in a very bad way, for there was nothing I could do about the fire until I had dug my way past the sand on my chest. In due course, I did indeed free myself and was able to push my way backward up the tunnel after extinguishing the flames. The men at the shaft head had seen no reason to become alarmed—tunnels always smell rather high and sooty, as you can imagine. But they did send a man down when I got near the entrance shaft and made myself heard.

"Of course, there was nothing to do but tell the Jerries, since we had no facilities whatever for concealing my condition or treating it. They put me in the camp hospital, and there I stayed until the end of the war with plenty of time to lie about and think my thoughts. I was even able to continue exercising some control over my men. I shouldn't be a bit surprised if that hadn't been in the commandant's mind all along. I think he had come to depend on my presence to moderate the behavior of the men.

"That is really almost the end of the story. We were liberated by the American Army, and the men were sent home. I stayed in military hospitals until I was well enough to travel home, and there I dwelt in hotels and played the retired, invalided officer. After that journalist's book was published and the dramatic rights were sold, I was called to Hollywood to be the technical adviser for the movie. I was rather grateful to accept the employment, frankly—an officer's pension is not particularly munificent—and what with selectively lending my name and services to various organizations while my name was still before the public, I was able to accumulate a sufficient nest egg.

"Of course, I cannot go back to England, where the Inland Revenue would relieve me of most of it, but, having established a relationship with Mr. Cortelyou and acquired and trained Max and Moritz, I am content. A man must make his way as best he can and do whatever is required for survival." The colonel cocked his head brightly and regarded Virginia and Malcolm. "Wouldn't you say?"

"Y—es," Virginia said slowly. Malcolm couldn't decide what the look on her face meant. He had never seen it before. Her eyes were shining, but wary. Her smile showed excitement and sympathy, but tension too. She seemed caught between two feelings.

"Quite!" the colonel said, smacking his hands together. "It is most important to me that you fully understand the situation." He pushed himself up to his feet and, with the same move, brought the crutches out smoothly and positioned them to balance him before he could fall. He stood leaning slightly forward, beaming. "Well, now, having given my story. I imagine the objectives of this conversation are fully attained, and there is no need to detain you here further. I'll see you to the front gate."

"That won't be necessary," Malcolm said.

"I insist," the colonel said in what would have been a perfectly pleasant manner if he had added the animated twinkle to his eyes. Virginia was staring at him, blinking slowly.

"Please forgive us," she said. "We certainly hadn't meant to stay long enough to be rude. Thank you for the tea and cookies. They were very good."

"Not at all, my dear," the colonel said. "It's really quite pleasant to think of looking across the way, now and then, and catching glimpses of someone so attractive at her domestic preoccupations. I cleaned up thoroughly after the last tenants, of course, but there are always little personal touches one wants to apply. And you will start some plantings at the front of the house, won't you? Such little activities are quite precious to me—someone as charming as you, in her summer things, going about her little fussings and tendings, resting in the sun after weeding—that sort of thing. Yes, I expect a most pleasant summer. I assume there was never any question you wouldn't stay all summer. Cortelyou would hardly bother with anyone who could not afford to pay him that much. But little more, eh?" The urbane, shrewd look returned to the colonel's face. "Pinched resources and few ties, eh? Or what would you be doing here, if there were somewhere else to turn to?"

"Well, good afternoon, Colonel," Virginia said with noticeable composure. "Let's go, Malcolm."

"Interesting conversation, Colonel," Malcolm said.

"Interesting and necessary, Mr. Lawrence," the colonel said, following them out onto the lawn. Virginia watched him closely as she moved toward the gate, and Malcolm noticed a little downward twitch at the corners of her mouth.

"Feeling a bit of a strain, Mrs. Lawrence?" the colonel asked solicitously. "Please believe that I shall be as considerate of your sensibilities as intelligent care of my own comfort will permit. It is not at all in my code to offer offense to a lady, and in any case—" the colonel smiled deprecatingly "—since the mishap of the Christmas tunnel, one might say the spirit is willing but . . ." The colonel frowned down absently at his canes. "No, Mrs. Lawrence," he went on, shaking his head paternally, "is a flower the less for being breathed of? And is the cultivated flower, tended and nourished, not more fortunate than the wild rose that blushes unseen? Do not regret your present social situation too much, Mrs. Lawrence—some might find it enviable. Few things are more changeable than points of view. In the coming weeks your viewpoint might well change."

"Just what the hell are you saying to my wife?" Malcolm asked.

Virginia said quickly, "We can talk about it later."

The colonel smiled at Virginia. "Before you do that, I have something else to show Mr. Lawrence." He raised his voice slightly: "Max! Moritz! Here!"—and the dogs were there. "Ah, Mr. Lawrence, I would like to show you first how these animals respond, how discriminating they can be." He turned to one of the dogs. "Moritz," he said sharply, nodding toward Malcolm, "Kill."

Malcolm couldn't believe what he had heard. Then he felt a blow on his chest. The dog was on him, its hind legs making short, fast, digging sounds in the lawn as it pressed its body against him. It was inside the arc of his arms, and the most he could have done was to clasp it closer to him. He made a tentative move to pull his arms back and then push forward against its rib cage, but the minor shift in weight made him stumble, and he realized if he completed the gesture he would fall. All this happened in a very short time, and then the dog touched open lips with him. Having done that, it dropped down and went back to stand beside Colonel Ritchey and Max.

"You see, Mr. Lawrence?" the colonel asked conversationally. "A dog does not respond to literal meaning. It is conditioned. It is trained to perform a certain action when it hears a certain sound. The cues one teaches a dog with pain and patience are not necessarily cues an educated organism can understand. Pavlov rang a bell and a dog salivated. Is a bell food? If he had rung a different bell, or said, 'Food, doggie,' there would have been no response. So, when I speak in a normal tone, rather than at command pitch, 'kill' does not mean 'kiss,' even to Moritz. It means nothing to him—unless I raise my voice. And I could just as easily have conditioned him to perform that sequence in association with some other command—such as, oh, say, 'gingersnaps'—but then you might not have taken the point of my little instructive jest. There is no way anyone but myself can operate these creatures. Only when I command do they respond. And now you respond, eh, Mr. Lawrence? I dare say. . . . Well, good day. As I said, you have things to do."

They left through the gate, which the colonel drew shut behind them. "Max," he said, "watch," and the dog froze in position. "Moritz, come." The colonel turned, and he and the other dog crossed the lawn and went into his house.

Malcolm and Virginia walked at a normal pace back to the rented house, Malcolm matching his step to Virginia's. He wondered if she were being so deliberate because she wasn't sure what the dog would do if she ran. It had been a long time since Virginia hadn't been sure of something.

In the house, Virginia made certain the door was shut tight, and then she went to sit in the chair that faced away from the window. "Would you make me some coffee, please?" she said.

"All right, sure. Take a few minutes. Catch your breath a little."

"A few minutes is what I need," she said. "Yes, a few minutes, and everything will be fine." When Malcolm returned with the coffee, she continued. "He's got some kind of string on Cortelyou, and I bet those people at the store down at the corner have those dogs walking in and out of there all the time. He's got us. We're locked up."

"Now, wait," Malcolm said, "there's the whole state of New Jersey out there, and he can't—"

"Yes, he can. If he thinks he can get away with it, and he's got good reasons for thinking he can. Take it on faith. There's no bluff in *him*."

"Well, look," he said, "just what can he do to us?"

"Any damn thing he pleases."

"That can't be right." Malcolm frowned. "He's got us pretty well scared right now, but we ought to be able to work out some way of—"

Virginia said tightly, "The dog's still there, right?" Malcolm nodded. "Okay," she said. "What did it feel like when he hit you? It looked awful. It looked like he was going to drive you clear onto your back. Did it feel that way? What did you *think*?"

"Well, he's a pretty strong animal," Malcolm said. "But, to tell you the truth, I didn't have time to believe it. You know, a man just saying 'kill'' like that is a pretty hard thing to believe. Especially just after tea and cookies.''

"He's very shrewd," Virginia said. "I can see why he had the camp guards running around in circles. He deserved to have a book written about him."

"All right, and then they should have thrown him into a padded cell."

"Tried to throw," Virginia amended.

"Oh, come on. This is his territory, and he dealt the cards before we even knew we were playing. But all he is is a crazy old cripple. If he wants to buffalo some people in a store and twist a two-bit real-estate salesman around his finger, fine—if he can get away with it. But he doesn't own us. We're not in his army."

"We're inside his prison camp," Virginia said.

"Now, look," Malcolm said. "When we walk in Cortelyou's door and tell him we know all about the colonel, there's not going to be any trouble about getting the rent back. We'll find someplace else, or we'll go back to the city. But whatever we do to get out of this, it's going to work out a lot smoother if the two of us think about it. It's not like you to be sitting there and spending a lot of time on how we can't win."

"Well, Malcolm. Being a prisoner certainly brings out your initiative. Here you are, making noises just like a senior officer. Proposing escape committees and everything."

Malcolm shook his head. Now of all times, when they needed each other so much, she wouldn't let up. The thing to do was to move too fast for her.

"All right," he said, "let's get in the car." There was just the littlest bit of sweat on his upper lip.

"What?" He had her sitting up straight in the chair, at least. "Do you imagine that that dog will let us get anywhere near the car?"

"You want to stay here? All right. Just keep the door locked. I'm going to try it, and once I'm out I'm going to come back here with a nice healthy state cop carrying a nice healthy riot gun. And we're either going to do something about the colonel and those two dogs, or we're at least going to move you and our stuff out of here."

He picked up the car keys, stepped through the front door very quickly, and began to walk straight for the car. The dog barked sharply, once. The front door of Ritchey's house opened immediately, and Ritchey called out, "Max! Hold!" The dog on the lawn was over the fence and had its teeth thrust carefully around Malcolm's wrist before he could take another eight steps, even though he had broken into a run. Both the dog and Malcolm stood very still. The dog was breathing shallowly and quietly, its eyes shining. Ritchey and Moritz walked as far as the front fence. "Now, Mr. Lawrence," Ritchey said, "in a moment I am going to call to Max, and he is to bring you with him. Do not attempt to hold back, or you will lacerate your wrist. Max! Bring here!"

Malcolm walked steadily toward the colonel. By some smooth trick of his neck, Max was able to trot alongside him without shifting his grip. "Very good, Max," Ritchey said soothingly when they had reached the fence. "Loose now," and the dog let go of Malcolm's wrist. Malcolm and Ritchey looked into each other's eyes across the fence, in the darkening evening.

"Now Mr. Lawrence," Ritchey said, "I want you to give me your car keys." Malcolm held out the keys, and Ritchey put them into his pocket. "Thank you." He seemed to reflect on what he was going to say next, as a teacher might reflect on his reply to a child who has asked why the sky is blue. "Mr. Lawrence, I want you to understand the situation. As it happens, I also want a three-pound can of Crisco. If you will please give me all the money in your pocket, this will simplify matters."

"I don't have any money on me," Malcolm said. "Do you want me to go in the house and get some?"

"No, Mr. Lawrence, I'm not a thief. I'm simply restricting your radius of action in one of the several ways I'm going to do so. Please turn out your pockets."

Malcolm turned out his pockets.

"All right, Mr. Lawrence, if you will hand me your wallet and your address book and the thirty-seven cents, they will all be returned to you whenever you have a legitimate use for them." Ritchey put the items away in the pockets of his jacket. "Now, a three-pound can of Crisco is ninety-eight cents. Here is a dollar bill. Max will walk with you to the corner grocery store, and you will buy the Crisco for me and bring it back. It is too much for a dog to carry in a bag, and it is three days until my next monthly delivery of staples. At the store you will please tell them that it will not be necessary for them to come here with monthly deliveries any longer—that you will be in to do my shopping for me from now on. I expect you to take a minimum amount of time to accomplish all this and to come back with my purchase, Mr. Lawrence. Max!'' The colonel nodded toward Malcolm. "Guard. Store.'' The dog trembled and whined. "Don't stand still, Mr. Lawrence. Those commands are incompatible until you start toward the store. If you fail to move, he will grow increasingly tense. Please go now. Moritz and I will keep Mrs. Lawrence good company until you return."

The store consisted of one small room in the front of a drab house. On unpainted pine shelves were brands of goods that Malcolm had never heard of. "Oh! You're with one of those nice dogs,'' the tired, plump woman behind the counter said, leaning down to pat Max, who had approached her for that purpose. It seemed to Malcolm that the dog was quite mechanical about it and was pretending to itself that nothing caressed it at all. He looked around the place, but he couldn't see anything or anyone that offered any prospect of alliance with him.

"Colonel Ritchey wants a three-pound can of Crisco,'' he said, bringing the name out to check the reaction.

"Oh, you're helping him?"

"You could say that."

"Isn't he brave?" the woman said in low and confidential tones, as if concerned that the dog would overhear. "You know, there are some people who would think you should feel sorry for a man like that, but I say it would be a sin to do so. Why, he gets along just fine, and he's got more pride and spunk than any whole man I've ever seen. Makes a person proud to know him. You know, I think it's just wonderful the way these dogs come and fetch little things for him. But I'm glad he's got somebody to look out for him now. 'Cept for us, I don't think he sees anybody from one year to the next—'cept summers, of course."

She studied Malcolm closely. "You're summer people too, aren't you? Well, glad to have you, if you're doin' some good for the colonel. Those people last year were a shame. Just moved out one night in September, and neither the colonel nor me or my husband seen hide nor hair of them since. Owed the colonel a month's rent, he said when we was out there."

"Is he the landloard?" Malcolm asked.

"Oh, sure, yes. He owns a lot of land around here. Bought it from the original company after it went bust."

"Does he own this store, too?"

"Well, we lease it from him now. Used to own it, but we sold it to the company and leased it from them. Oh, we was all gonna be rich. My husband took the money from the land and bought a lot across the street and was gonna set up a real big gas station there—figured to be real shrewd—but you just can't get people to live out here. I mean, it isn't as if this was *ocean*-front property. But the colonel now, he's got a head on his shoulders. Value's got to go up someday, and he's just gonna hold on until it does."

The dog was getting restless, and Malcolm was worried about Virginia. He paid for the can of Crisco, and he and Max went back up the sand road in the dark. There really, honestly, didn't seem to be much else to do.

At his front door, he stopped, sensing that he should knock. When Virginia let him in, he saw that she had changed to shorts and a halter. "Hello," she said, and then stood aside quietly for him and Max. The colonel, sitting pertly forward on one of the chairs, looked up. "Ah, Mr. Lawrence, you're a trifle tardy, but the company has been delightful, and the moments seemed to fly."

Malcolm looked at Virginia. In the past couple of years, a little fat had accumulated above her knees, but she still had long, good legs. Colonel Ritchey smiled at Malcolm. "It's a rather close evening. I simply suggested to Mrs. Lawrence that I certainly wouldn't be offended if she left me for a moment and changed into something more comfortable."

It seemed to Malcolm that she could have handled that. But apparently she hadn't.

"Here's your Crisco," Malcolm said. "The change is in the bag."

"Thank you very much," the colonel said. "Did you tell them about the grocery deliveries?"

Malcolm shook his head. "I don't remember. I don't think so.

I was busy getting an earful about how you owned them, lock, stock, and barrel."

"Well, no harm. You can tell them tomorrow."

"Is there going to be some set time for me to run your errands every day, Colonel? Or are you just going to whistle whenever something comes up?"

"Ah, yes. You're concerned about interruptions in your mood. Mrs. Lawrence told me you were some sort of artist. I'd wondered at your not shaving this morning." The colonel paused and then went on crisply. "I'm sure we'll shake down into whatever routine suits best. It always takes a few days for individuals to hit their stride as a group. After that, it's quite easy—regular functions, established duties, that sort of thing. A time to rise and wash, a time to work, a time to sleep. Everything and everyone in his proper niche. Don't worry, Mr. Lawrence, you'll be surprised how comfortable it becomes. Most people find it a revelation." The colonel's gaze grew distant for a moment. "Some do not. Some are as if born on another planet, innocent of human nature. Dealing with that sort, there comes a point when one must cease to try; at the camp, I found that the energy for over-all success depended on my admitting the existence of the individual failure. No, some do not respond. But we needn't dwell on what time will tell us."

Ritchey's eyes twinkled. "I have dealt previously with creative people. Most of them need to work with their hands; do stupid, dull, boring work that leaves their minds free to soar in spirals and yet forces them to stay away from their craft until the tension is nearly unbearable." The colonel waved in the direction of the unbuilt houses. "There's plenty to do. If you don't know how to use a hammer and saw as yet, I know how to teach that. And when from time to time I see you've reached the proper pitch of creative frustration, then you shall have what time off I judge will best serve you artistically. I think you'll be surprised how pleasingly you'll take to your studio. From what I gather from your wife, this may well be a very good experience for you."

Malcolm looked at Virginia. "Yes. Well, that's been bugging her for a long time. I'm glad she's found a sympathetic ear."

"Don't quarrel with your wife, Mr. Lawrence. That sort of

thing wastes energy and creates serious morale problems." The colonel got to his feet and went to the door. "One thing no one could ever learn to tolerate in a fellow *Kriegie* was pettiness. That sort of thing was always weeded out. Come, Max. Come, Moritz. Good night!" He left.

Malcolm went over to the door and put the chain on. "Well?" he said.

"All right, now, look—"

Malcolm held up one finger. "Hold it. Nobody likes a quarrelsome *Kriegie*. We're not going to fight. We're going to talk, and we're going to think." He found himself looking at her halter and took his glance away. Virginia blushed.

"I just want you to know it was exactly the way he described it," she said. "He said he wouldn't think it impolite if I left him alone in the living room while I went to change. And I wasn't telling him our troubles. We were talking about what you did for a living, and it didn't take much for him to figure out—"

"I don't want you explaining," Malcolm said. "I want you to help me tackle this thing and get it solved."

"How are you going to solve it? This is a man who always uses everything he's got! He never quits! How is somebody like *you* going to solve that?"

All these years, it occurred to Malcolm, at a time like this, now, she finally had to say the thing you couldn't make go away.

When Malcolm did not say anything at all for a while but only walked around frowning and thinking, Virginia said she was going to sleep. In a sense, he was relieved; a whole plan of action was forming in his mind, and he did not want her there to badger him.

After she had closed the bedroom door, he went into the studio. In a corner was a carton of his painting stuff, which he now approached, detached but thinking. From this room he could see the floodlights on around the colonel's house. The colonel had made his circuit of the yard, and one of the dogs stood at attention, looking across the way. The setting hadn't altered at all from the night before. Setting, no, Malcolm thought, bouncing a jar of brown tempera in his hand; mood, *si*. His arm felt good all the way down from his shoulder, into the forearm, wrist, and fingers.

When Ritchey had been in his house a full five minutes, Malcolm said to himself aloud, "Do first, analyze later." Whipping open the front door, he took two steps forward on the bare earth to gather momentum and pitched the jar of paint in a shallow arc calculated to end against the aluminum fence.

It was going to fall short, Malcolm thought, and it did, smashing with a loud impact against one of the whitewashed stones and throwing out a fan of gluey, brown spray over the adjacent stones, the fence, and the dog, which jumped back but, lacking orders to charge, stood its ground, whimpering. Malcolm stepped back into his open doorway and leaned in it. When the front door of Ritchey's house opened he put his thumbs to his ears and waggled his fingers, *"Gute Nacht, Herr Kommandant,"* he called, then stepped back inside and slammed and locked the door, throwing the spring-bolt latch. The dog was already on its way. It loped across the yard and scraped its front paws against the other side of the door. Its breath sounded like giggling.

Malcolm moved over to the window. The dog sprang away from the door with a scratching of toenails and leaped upward, glancing off the glass. It turned, trotted away for a better angle, and tried again. Malcolm watched it; this was the part he'd bet on.

The dog didn't make it. Its jaws flattened against the pane, and the whole sheet quivered, but there was too much going against success. The window was pretty high above the yard, and the dog couldn't get a proper combination of momentum and angle of impact. If he did manage to break it, he'd never have enough momentum left to clear the break; he'd fall on the sharp edges of glass in the frame while other chunks fell and cut his neck, and then the colonel would be down to one dog. One dog wouldn't be enough; the system would break down somewhere.

The dog dropped down, leaving nothing on the glass but a wet brown smear.

It seemed to Malcolm equally impossible for the colonel to break the window himself. He couldn't stride forward to throw a small stone hard enough to shatter the pane, and he couldn't balance well enough to heft a heavy one from nearby. The lock and chain would prevent him from entering through the front door. No, it wasn't efficient for the colonel any way you looked at it. He would rather take a few days to think of something shrewd and economical. In fact, he was calling the dog back now. When the dog reached him, he shifted one crutch and did his best to kneel while rubbing the dog's head. There was something rather like affection in the scene. Then the colonel straightened up and called again. The other dog came out of the house and took up its station at the corner of the yard. The colonel and the dirty dog went back into the colonel's house.

Malcolm smiled, then turned out the lights, double-checked the locks, and went back through the hall to the bedroom. Virginia was sitting up in bed, staring in the direction from which the noise had come.

"What did you do?" she asked.

"Oh, changed the situation a little," Malcolm said, grinning. "Asserted my independence. Shook up the colonel. Smirched his neatness a little bit. Spoiled his night's sleep for him, I hope. Standard *Kriegie* tactics. I hope he likes them."

Virginia was incredulous. "Do you know what he could do to you with those dogs if you step outside this house?"

"I'm not going to step outside. Neither are you. We're just going to wait a few days."

"What do you mean?" Virginia said, looking at him as if he were the maniac.

"Day after tomorrow, maybe the day after that," Malcolm explained, "he's due for a grocery delivery I didn't turn off. Somebody's going to be here with a car then, lugging all kinds of things. I don't care how beholden those storekeepers are to him; when we come out the door, he's not going to have those dogs tear us to pieces right on the front lawn in broad daylight and with a witness. We're going to get into the grocery car, and sooner or later we're going to drive out in it, because *that* car and driver have to turn up in the outside world again."

Virginia sighed. "Look," she said with obvious control, "all he has to do is send a note with the dogs. He can stop the delivery that way."

Malcolm nodded. "Uh-huh. And so the groceries don't come. Then what? He starts trying to freight flour and eggs in here by dog back? By remote control? What's he going to do? All right, so it doesn't work out so neatly in two or three days.

But we've got a fresh supply of food, and he's almost out. Unless he's planning to live on Crisco, he's in a bad way. And even so, he's only got three pounds of that." Malcolm got out of his clothes and lay down on the bed. "Tomorrow's another day, but I'll be damned if I'm going to worry any more about it tonight. I've got a good head start on frustrating the legless wonder, and tomorrow I'm going to have a nice clear mind, and I'm going to see what other holes I can pick in his defense. I learned a lot of snide little tricks from watching jolly movies about clever prisoners and dumb guards." He reached up and turned out the bed light. "Good night, love," he said. Virginia rolled away from him in the dark. "Oh, my God," she said in a voice with a brittle edge around it.

It was a sad thing for Malcolm to lie there thinking that she had that kind of limitation in her, that she didn't really understand what had to be done. On the other hand, he thought sleepily, feeling more relaxed than he had in years, he had his own limitations. And she had put up with them for years. He fell asleep wondering pleasantly what tomorrow would bring.

He woke to a sound of rumbling and crunching under the earth, as if there were teeth at the foundations of the house. Still sleeping in large portions of his brain, he cried out silently to himself with a madman's lucidity, "Ah, of course, he's been tunneling!" And his mind gave him all the details—the careful transfer of supporting timber from falling houses, the disposal of the excavated clay in the piles beside the other foundations, too, for when the colonel had more people. . . .

Now one corner of the room showed a jagged line of yellow, and Malcolm's hands sprang to the light switch. Virginia jumped from sleep. In the corner was a trap door, its uneven joints concealed by boards of different angles. The trap door crashed back, releasing a stench of body odor and soot.

A dog popped up through the opening and scrambled into the bedroom. Its face and body were streaked, and it shook itself to get the sand from its coat. Behind it, the colonel dragged himself up, naked, and braced himself on his arms, half out of the tunnel mouth. His hair was matted down with perspiration over his narrow-boned skull. He was mottled yellow-red with dirt, and half in the shadows. Virginia buried her face in her hands, one eye glinting out between spread fingers, and cried to Malcolm, "Oh my God, what have you done to us?"

"Don't worry, my dear," the colonel said crisply to her. Then he screamed at Malcolm, "I will not be abused!" Trembling with strain as he braced on one muscle-corded arm, he pointed at Malcolm. He said to the dog at command pitch: "Kiss!"

I would love to be a pilot. Someday, everything willing, I shall be. When my sister, who is French, tired of reading to me from Robinson Crusoe *in an accent which rendered "parrot" as "pirate," and thus charmingly confused me, she read to me from* Night Flight *and the other aviation volumes of Sainte-Exupery. I think* Only Angels Have Wings *is the greatest junk motion picture ever made, with the possible exception of* Star Wars. *One of my favorite books is Richard Bach's* Stranger to the Ground, *which I found long before anyone had heard of* Jonathan Livingston Seagull, *and another is* Nothing by Chance. *When I was a lad on a chicken farm, I built, on a porch, a contraption with control surfaces connected to a working stick and rudder-bar. I sat in it for hours, aviating.*

The aviation books in my attic, guest room, living room, cellar, and office would startle Martin Caidin by their number. There was no greater fan than I, once, of G-8 and His Battle Aces, *though I could not obtain very many copies, and my first fan letter to an editor went not to* Planet Stories *but to an air war pulp. I find the rarely seen opening sequence of* Breaking the Sound Barrier *is some of the most exciting black-and-white film footage ever shot. Once in a while, my friend Frank Stankovich, the chopper motorsickel fork king who also chromed the three-bearing crankshaft of my Rapier, used to take me for a ride in his Luscombe tail-dragger. But it didn't have a stick. And once I wrote scripts for industrial films. Another time, I worked for girlie magazines. And by the time I wrote this story, I had finished* Michaelmas. *But I remember—oh, I remember—the Saturday my father would not let me go to the Beacon and see not only Episode Four of* Flash Gordon Conquers the Universe *but, also, ah,* Dawn Patrol. *Hello, Mr. Flynn. Happy landings. Happy landings, Frank.*

The Nuptial Flight
of Warbirds

THE WOMAN GASPED slightly as he began to see her. Dusty Haverman smiled comfortably, extending his lean arm in its brocaded scarlet sleeve, white lace frothing at his wrist. He tilted the decanter over the crystal stem glass shimmering in the stainless air of the afternoon, and rosy clarity swirled within the fragile bell. "You'll enjoy that," he said to her. "It doesn't ordinarily travel well."

She was very pale, with dark, made-up eyes and lips drawn a startling red. A lavender print scarf was bound around her neck-length smoke-black hair, and she wore a lavender voile dress with a full calf-length skirt and a bellboy collar. Below the collar, the front of the dress was open to the waist in a loose slit.

She sat straight in her chair. Her plum-colored nails gripped the ends of the decoratively carved wooden arms. The breeze, whispering over the coarse grass that grew in odd-shaped meadows between the lengths of sandy concrete, stirred her hair. She looked around her at the sideboard, the silver chafing dishes of hot hors d'oeuvres, the Fragonard and the large Boucher hung on ornate wooden racks, the distant structures and the marker lights thrusting up here and there from the edges of the grass. She watched Haverman carefully as he sank back into his own chair, crossed his knees, and raised his own glass. "To our close acquaintanceship," he was saying in his slightly husky voice, a distinguished-looking man with slightly waving silver hair worn a little long over the tops of the ears, and a thin-ish, carefully trimmed silver moustache hovering at the rim of the rose cordial. He wore a white silk ascot.

The woman, who had only a very few signs of latter twenty-

Copyright © 1978, Conde Nast Publications, Inc.

ishness about the skin of her face and the carriage of her body, raised one sooty eyebrow. "Where are we?" she asked. "Who are you?"

Haverman smiled. "We are at the juncture of runways twenty-eight Left and forty-two Right at O'Hare International Airport. My name is Austin Gelvarry."

The woman looked around again, more quickly. Her silk-clad knee bumped the low mahogany table between them, and Haverman had to reach deftly to save her glass. She settled back slowly. "It certainly isn't Cannes," she agreed. She reached for the wine, keeping one hand spread-fingered over the front of her bosom as she leaned. Her eyes did not leave Haverman's face. "How did you do this?"

Gelvarry smiled. "How could I not do it, Miss Montez? Ah, ah, no, don't do that! Don't press so hard against your mouth. *Sip*, Miss Montez, please! Withdraw the glass a slight distance. Now draw the upper lip together just a suggestion, and *delicately* impress its undercurve upon the swell of the edging. Sip, Miss Montez. As if at a blossom, my dear. As if at a chalice." He smiled. "You will get to like me. I was in the Royal Flying Corps, you know."

Just at first light, the mechanics would have the early patrol craft lined up on the cinders beside the scarred turf of the runway. They would waken Gelvarry with the sound of the propellers being pulled through. He would lie-up in his cot, his eyes very wide in the dim, listening to the *whup, whup, whup*!

The mechanics ran in three-man teams, one team for each of the three planes in the flight. One would be just letting go the lower tip of the wooden airscrew and jumping a little sideward to turn and double back. One would be doubling back, arms pumping for balance, head cocked to watch the third man, who would be just jumping into the air, arms out, hands slightly cupped to catch the tip of the upper blade as it started down.

They ran in perfect rhythm, and they would do this a dozen times before they attempted to start the aircraft. They said it was necessary to do this with the Trompe L'Oiel engine, which was a French design.

Sergeant-Major MacBanion had instituted this drill. If it were not performed precisely, the cylinder walls would not be evenly lubricated when the engines were started. The cylinder walls would score, and very likely seize-up a piston, and all you fine young gentlemen would be dropping your arses, beg pardon (with a wink) all over the perishing map of bleeding Belgium. Then he knocked the dottle out of his pipe, scratched the ribs of the little grey monkey he liked to carry, and turned his shaved neck to shout something to an Other Rank.

Sar'n-Major Mac's speaking voice was sharp and confident, and his manner assertive, in dealing with matters of management. In speaking to Gelvarry and the other flying personnel, however, he was more avuncular, and it seemed to Gelvarry that he saw more than he sometimes let on.

Gelvarry, who was hoping for assignment soon to the high squadron, reckoned that Sergeant-Major MacBanion might have more to do with that than his rank augured for. Nominally, he was only in charge of instruction for transitioning to high squadron aircraft, but since Major Harding never emerged from his hut, it was difficult to believe he was not dependent on Sergeant-Major MacBanion for personnel recommendations.

Gelvarry swung his legs over the side of the cot, taking an involuntary breath of the Nissen hut's interior. Gelvarry's feet had frosted a bit on a long flight the previous week and were quite tender. He limped across the hut, arranging his clothes, and went over to the washstand.

Gelvarry felt there was no better high squadron candidate in the area at the present time. Barton Fisher of XIV Recon Wing had more flight time, but everyone knew Armed Chase flew harder, and Gelvarry had been in Armed Chase for the past year, now being definitely senior man at this aerodrome and senior flying personnel in the entire MC Armed Chase Wing. "I should like very much to apply for assignment to the high squadron, Sir," he rehearsed as he brushed his teeth. But since he had no idea what Major Harding looked like, the face in the mottled fragment of pier glass remained entirely his own.

He spat into the waste bucket and peered at the results. His gums were evidently still bleeding freely. Squinting into the mirror, he lathered his face cold and began shaving with a razor that had been most indifferently honed by Parkins, the batman Gelvarry shared with the remainder of his flight in the low squadron. Parkins had been reduced from Engine Artificer by

Sar'n-Major Mac, and quite right. "Give 'im a drum of oil and a stolen typewriter," Gelvarry grumbled as he scraped at the gingery stubble on his pale cheeks. "He'll jump his bicycle and flog 'em in the village for a litre of Vouvray."

He rubbed his face with a damp gray towel full of threads and bent to stare out the end window. The weather was expectable; mist just rising, still snagged a little in the tops of the poplars; eastern sky giving some promise of rose; and the windsock pointing mendaciously inward. By the time they'd completed their sweep, low on petrol and ready for luncheon and a heartfelt sigh, it would have shifted straight toward Hunland and God help the poor sod who attempted the feat of gliding home on an engine stopped by fuel shortage or, better yet, enemy action also involving injury to flying personnel. All up then, my lad, and into the *Lagerkorps* at the point of some *gefreiter's* bayonet, to spend the remainder of the war laying railroad lines or embanking canals, *Gott Mit Uns* and *Hoch der Fuehrer*! for the Thousand Year Empire, God grant it mischief.

In fact, Gelvarry thought, going out of the hut and running along the duckboards with his shoulders hunched and his hands in his pockets, the only good thing about the day to this point was that his headache was nowhere near as bad as it deserved to be. Perhaps there was truth in the rumor that Issue mess brandy had resumed being shipped from England. It had lately been purchased direct under plausible labels from blue-chinned peasant gentlemen who cut prices in deference to the bravery of their gallant allies.

"Get out of my way, you creature," he puffed to Islingden, John Peter, Flying Officer, otherwise third Duke of Landsdowne, who was standing on the boards with a folded *Gazette* under his arm, studying the sky. "If you're done in there, show some consideration." They danced around each other, arms out for balance, "Nigger Jack" Islingden clutching the *Gazette* like a baton, his large teeth flashing whitely against his olive-hued Landsdowne complexion, introduced via a Spanish countess by the first Duke, neither of them wishing to step off the slats into the spring mud, their boot toes clattering, until Gelvarry at last gained entrance to the officers' latrine.

● ● ●

The dampness rising from the ground was all through his bones. Gelvarry shivered without cease as he sprinted along the cinder track toward his SE-5, beating his arms across his chest. He paused just long enough to scribble a receipt for the aircraft and return the clipboard to the Chief Fitter, found the reinforced plate at the root of the lower plane, stepped up on it and dropped into the cockpit, his hands smearing the droplets of dew on the leather edging of the rim. He felt himself shaking thoroughly now, proceeding with the business of handsignalling the other two pilots—Landsdowne and a sergeant pilot named O'Sullivan—and ensuring they were ready. He signalled Chocks Out, and the ground personnel yanked sharply at the lines, clearing his wheels and dropping flat to let his lower planes pass over.

As soon as he jassed the throttle to smooth his plugs and build takeoff power, a cascade of water blew back into his face from the top of the mainplane, and he stopped shivering. He glanced left and right, raised his arm, flung his hand forward, and advanced the throttle. The trim little Bristol, responsive as a filly, leapt forward. For a few moments, she sprang and rebounded to every inequality of the turf, while her flying wires sang into harmony with the increasing vibration of the engine and airscrew. The droplets on the doped fabric turned instantly into streaks over the smoke-colored oil smears from the engine. Then there was suddenly the smooth buzzing under his feet of the wheels rotating freely on their axles, all weight off, and the SE-5 climbed spiritedly into the dawn, trailing a momentary train of spray that glistened for an instant in the sunlight above the mist. Soon enough, the remaining condensation turned white and opaque, forming little flowers where the panes of his windscreen were jointed into their frames. Gelvarry held the stick between his knees and smoothed his gloves tighter over his hands, which retained little trace of their former trembling.

Up around Paschendaele they were dodging nimbly among some clouds when Gelvarry suddenly plucked his Very pistol from its metal clip in the cockpit and fired a green flare. Nigger and O'Sullivan jerked their courses around into exact conformity with his as they, too, now saw the *staffel* of Albatros falling upon them. They pointed their noses up at a steep angle toward the *Boche*, giving the engines more throttle to prevent stalling, and briefly testing the firing linkages of their twin Vickers guns. Tracer bullets left little spirals of white smoke in the air beyond Gelvarry's engine, to be sucked up immediately as he nibbled in behind them. He glanced at Landsdowne and Paddy, raising one thumb. They clenched their fists and shook them, once, twice, toward the foe who, mottled with garish camouflage, dropped down with flame winking at the muzzles of the Spandau *maschingewehren* behind the gleaming arcs of their propellers.

Gelvarry felt they were firing too soon. Nevertheless, there was an abrupt drumming upon his left upper plane, and then a ripping. He saw a wire suddenly vibrate its middle portion into invisibility as a slug glanced from it. There was no damage of consequence. He held his course and refrained from firing, only thinking of how the entire aircraft had quivered to the drumming, and of how when the fabric split it was as if something swift and hot had seared across the backs of his hands. It was Gelvarry's professional opinion that such moments must be fully met and studied within the mind, so that they lose their power of surprise.

There were eight Albatros in the diving formation, he saw, and therefore there might be as many as four more stooging about in the clouds waiting to follow down stragglers.

The stench of overheated castor oil came back from his engine and coated his lips and tongue. He pushed his goggles up onto his forehead, hunched his face down into the full lee of the windscreen, and now, when it might count, began firing purposeful short bursts.

The Albatros is a difficult aircraft to attack headon because it has a metal propeller fairing and an in-line engine, so that many possible hits are deflected and the target area is not large. On the other hand, the Albatros is not really a good diver, having a tendency to shed its wings at steeper angles. Gelvarry had long ago reasoned out that even an apparently sound Albatros mainplane is under considerable stress in a dive, and so he fired a little above the engine, hoping to damage the struts or even the main spar, but noting that as an inevitable consequence there might also be direct or deflected hits on the windscreen. He did not wish to be known as a deliberate shooter of pilots, but there it was.

The *staffel* passed through the flight of SE-5s with seven survivors, one of which, however, was turning for home with smoke issuing from its oil cooler. The three British aircraft, necessarily throttling back to save their engines, began to mush out of their climbing attitude. Three Albatros which had been waiting their turn now launched a horizontal attack.

His head swivelling while he half-stood in the cockpit, searching, Gelvarry saw the three fresh Albatros emerge from the clouds. Below him, six of the original assault were looping up to rejoin. On his right, Paddy's aircraft displayed miscellaneous splinters and punctures of the empennage, and was trailing a few streamers of fabric, but appeared to be structurally sound. O'Sullivan, however, was beating at the breechblock of one of his guns with a wooden mallet, one hand wrapped around an interplane strut to hold him forward over the windscreen, the other busy with its hammering as it tried to pop out the overexpanded shell casing. His aircraft was wallowing as he inadvertently nudged the stick back and forth with his legs.

On the left, Nigger was nosedown, his airscrew windmilling, ropy smoke and pink fire blowing back over the cockpit. For a moment, the SE-5's ailerons quickly flapped into a new configuration, and the rudder and elevators came over as Landsdowne tried to sideslip the burning. But they were, in any case, at 7000 feet and at this height there was really no point to the maneuver. Landsdowne stood up in the cockpit as the aircraft came level again, saluted Gelvarry, and jumped, his collar and helmet thickly trailing soot.

"So long, Nig," Gelvarry murmured. He glanced up. A mile above them, the silvery flash of sunlight upon the *Ticonderoga*'s flanks dazzled the eye; nevertheless, he thought he could make out the attendant cloud of dark midges who were the high squadron. He looked to his right and saw that O'Sullivan was being hit repeatedly in the torso by gunfire, white phophorus tracer spirals emerging from the plucked leather of his coat.

Gelvarry took in a deep breath. He pushed his aircraft into a falling right bank, kicked right rudder, and passed between two of the oncoming Nazis. He converted the bank into a shallow diving roll, and so went down through the climbing group of Albatros at an angle which made it useless for either side to fire. He had also placed all his enemies in such a relationship to him that they would have had to turn and dive at suicidal inclinations in order to overtake him as he darted homeward.

He flew above the remains of villages that looked like old bones awash in brown soup, and over the lines that were like a river on the moon, its margins festooned with wire to prevent careless Selenites from stumbling in. A high squadron aircraft dropped down and flew beside him for a while, as he had heard they sometimes did lately.

He glanced over at the glossy stagger-wing biplane, its color black except for the white-lettered unit markings, a red-and-white horizontally striped rudder panel, and the American cocardes with the five-pointed white star and orange ball in the center. The pilot was looking at him. He wore a pale yellow helmet, goggles that flashed in the sun, and a very clean white scarf. He raised a hand and waved reservedly, as one might across a tier of boxes at the concert hall. Then he pulled back on his stick and the black aircraft climbed away precipitously, so swiftly that Gelvarry half-expected a crackling of displaced air, but instead heard, very faintly over his own engine, the smooth roar of the other's exhaust. He found that his own right hand was still elevated, and took it down.

He came in over the poplars, and found that he was going to land cross-wind. Ground personnel raised their heads as if they had been grazing at the margins of the runway. He put it down anyhow, swung it about, and taxied toward the hangar, blipping the engine to keep the cylinder heads from sooting up, and finally cut his switch near where Sergeant-Major MacBanion was standing waiting with the little gray monkey perched on his right shoulder. As the engine stopped, the cold once again settled into Gelvarry's bones.

"All right, Sir?" Sar'n-Major Mac asked, looking up at him. The monkey, too, raised its little Capuchin face, the small lobstery eyes peering from under the brim of a miniature *kepi*.

Gelvarry put his hands on the cockpit rim, placed his heels carefully on the transverse brace below the rudder bar, and pushed himself back and up. Then he was able to slip down the side of the fuselage. He stood slapping his hands against his biceps.

Sergeant-Major MacBanion put a hand gently on his shoulder. "And the remainder of the flight, Sir?"

Gelvarry shrugged. He pulled off his helmet and goggles and stuffed them into a pocket of his coat. He stamped his feet, despite the hurt. Then as the cold began to leave him, he merely stood running his hands up and down his arms, and hunching his back.

"Never mind, Sir," Sar'n-Major Mac said softly. "I've come to tell you we've had an urgent message. You're posted to high squadron immediately, Sir."

Gelvarry found himself weeping silently.

"Follow me to Major Harding's hut, please, Sir," Sergeant-Major MacBanion said quietly and gravely. "Don't concern yourself about the aircraft—we'll see to it."

"Thank you," Gelvarry whispered. He walked behind the spare, erect figure to the Major's hut, watching the monkey gently waving the swagger stick. Then he waited outside, rubbing his hands over his cheeks, feeling the moisture trapped between his palm and the oil film on his skin. He hated the coating in his nostrils and on the roof of his mouth, and habitually scraped it off his lips between his teeth.

Sergeant-Major MacBanion came out of the dark hut, shut the door positively, said, "That's all right, then, Sir," turned his face slightly and shouted: "Private Parkins on the double if you please!"

Parkins came running up with a thud of boots on damp cinders and saluted energetically. "Yes, Sar'n-Major?"

"Parkins, I want you to list three reserve flying personnel with appropriate aircraft for this afternoon's sweep. Make it the three senior men. What flying personnel will that leave at this station during the afternoon hours?"

"Two, Sar'n-Major, in addition to this officer." Parkins nodded slightly toward Gelvarry without taking his eyes off Sergeant-Major MacBanion's steady gaze.

"Don't concern yourself with this officer, Parkins; Chaplain and I'll be taking care of him."

Parkins brought out the sapient manner he had been withholding. "Right, Sar'n-Major. I'll just have Major Harding send them other two officers over to Wing in the Rolls to sign for some engine spares, and that'll clear the premises nicely. I'll take the time to sort through this officer's kit for shipping home, then, as well, shall I?"

"I think not, Parkins," Sergeant-Major MacBanion said meaningly, and Parkins could be seen to bob his Adam's apple. "That is Major Harding's duty. That's what commanding officers are for." The thick, neatly clipped brows drew into a speculating frown. "You're slipping very badly, aren't you, Parkins? I wonder what a rummage through your duffel might turn up; I can't say I care for the smell of your breath."

"Hit's mouthwash, Sar'n-Major!" Parkins exclaimed. "A bit of a soother for me sore bicuspid, like!"

"I'll give you sore, Private Parkins, I surely will," Sergeant-Major Mac declared. "Pull yourself together long enough to attend to your own tasks. You're to telephone Wing for three replacement flying personnel to join here tonight, correct? And there's the lorry and the working party to organize; I want this officer's aircraft crashed *and* burning, no doubt about it, *in* No Man's Land, *be*fore teatime, and *if* that's all quite sufficiently clear to you, my man, you *will* see to it forth*with*!"

Parkins saluted, about-faced, and trotted off, sweating. The Sergeant-Major smiled thinly after him, then turned to Gelvarry. "This way, then, please, Sir," he said, and stepped onto the footpath worn through the scrub beside Major Harding's hut.

Following him, Gelvarry was startled to note the neatly cultivated domestic vegetable plot behind the rusty corrugated sheet iron of the Major's dwelling. There were seed packets up on little stakes at the ends of rows, and string stretched in a zigzag web for runnerbeans. Lettuce and carrots were poking up tentatively along one side, and most of the rows were showing early evidence of shooting. A spade with an officer's cap dangling over the handle was thrust into a dirt-encrusted pile of industrial furnace clinkers that had apparently been extracted from the soil.

"Padre!" Sergeant-Major MacBanion called ahead. "Here's an officer to see you!"

Father Collins thrust his head around the fly of his dwelling tent, which was situated beyond the shrubs screening Major Harding's hut from this far end of the aerodrome. He was a round-faced man of kindly appearance whom Gelvarry had occasionally seen in the mess, fussing with the Sparklets machine and otherwise making himself useful and approved of. He came and moved a little distance toward them along the path, and then waited for them to come up. He put out his hand to shake Gelvarry's. "Always here to be of help," he said.

Sergeant-Major MacBanion cleared his throat. "This'll be a high squadron posting, Padre."

Father Collins nodded a little crossly. "One gathers these things, Sergeant-Major MacBanion. Well, young fellah, let's get to it, then, shall we?" His expression softened and he studied Gelvarry's face carefully. "No need prolonging matters, then, is there? Not a decision to be taken lightly, but, once made, to be followed expeditiously, eh?" He put an arm around Gelvarry's shoulders. Gelvarry found himself grateful for the animal warmth; the cold had been at his ribs again. He went along up the path with Father Collins and Sar'n-Major Mac, and when they reached the little overgrown rise where Father Collins's tent was situated, he stopped. He found he was looking down at a revettment where the transition aircraft was kept.

He walked around and around, a slight smile on his lips, ducking under the planes and squeezing by the end of the rudder where it was nearly right up against the rear embankment. He ran his fingertips lightly over the impeccably doped fabric and admired the workmanship of the rudder and elevator hinges, the delicately shaped brass standoffs that gave extra purchase to the control cables. Everything was new; the smell of the aircraft had the tang of a fitter's storage locker.

He stopped and faced it from outside the revettment. The slim black aircraft pointed its rounded nose well up over his head; it was much larger than he'd expected from seeing one in the air; he'd thought perhaps the pilot was slightly built.

It rested gracefully upon its two fully spatted tires, with a teardrop-shaped auxiliary fuel tank nestled up between the fully faired landing gear struts. Its rest position on its tailskid set it on an angle such that the purposefully sturdy wings grasped muscularly at the air. A glycol radiator slung at the point of the cowling's jaw promised to sieve with jubilation through the stream hurled backward by the three-bladed metal airscrew.

There were very few wires; the struts appeared to be quite thin frontally, but were faired back for lateral strength. It would, yes it would, burgeon upward through the air with every ounce of power available from that promising engine hidden behind the lovingly shaped panels, and it would stoop like a bird of prey. It would not creak or whip in the air; its fuselage panels would not drum and ripple; the dope of its upper surfaces would not star and flake off under the compression of warping wings in a battle maneuver, and one would not find, after twenty or thirty hours, that the planes and the stabilizer had been permanently shaken out of alignment with each other.

This aircraft had the same markings as the one that had flown down briefly, except for the actual numerals. In addition to the national cocardes, it also bore a unit insigne—a long-barreled flintlock rifle crossed upon a powderhorn.

Gelvarry felt a prickling pass along the short hairs of his forearms as he thought of flying under that banner. A great-greatuncle was reputed in his family to have been among that company vanished in search of Providence Plantations, as others had done in attempting to find Oglethorpe's Colony or the fabled inland cities of Virginia Dare's children. North America was a continent of endless forest and dark rumor. And yet something, it seemed—some seed possessed of patience—had been germinating *Ticonderogas* and aircraft construction works all the while, and within reach of Mr. Churchill's remarkable winnow.

"This is the Curtis P6E 'Hawk,' " Sar'n-Major Mac said at his elbow. "This model is the ultimate development of what will be considered the most versatile armed chase single-place biplane ever designed. The original airframe will be introduced in the mid-1920s. As you see it here, it is fitted with United States Army Air Corps-specified inline liquid-cooled four-stroke engine developing 450 horsepower, and two fixed quick-firing thirty-calibre machineguns geared to shoot through the airscrew. The U.S. Navy version, known as the 'Goshawk,' will use the Wright 'Whirlwind' radial air-cooled engine. Both basic versions are very highly thought of, will remain in service in the U.S. until the mid-1930s, and a few 'Hawk' versions will be used by the Republican air forces in the Spanish Civil War, should that occur."

Father Collins had been up at the cockpit, leaning in to polish the instrument glass with a soft white cloth. He came down now, pausing to wipe the step let into the fuselage and the place on the wing root where he had rested his other foot.

"All quite ready now," he said, carefully folding the cloth and putting it away in his open-mouthed black leather case. He rested his hand on Gelvarry's shoulder. "We've kept her in prime condition for you, lad—no one's ever flown her before; Sar'n-Major and I just ticked her over now and then, kept her clean and taut; the usual drill."

Gelvarry was nodding. As the moment drew near, he found himself breathing with greater difficulty. Tears were gathering in his eyes. He turned his face away awkwardly.

"Now, as for the hooking on," Sergeant-Major MacBanion was saying briskly, "I'm certain you'll manage that part of it quite well, Sir." He was pointing up at the trapeze hook fixed to the center of the mainplane like the hanger of a Christmas tree ball, and Gelvarry perforce had to look at him attentively.

"Pity there's no way to rehearse the necessary maneuver, Sir," Sar'n-Major Mac went on, "but they say it comes to one. Only a matter of matching courses and speeds, after all, and then just easing up in there."

Gelvarry nodded. He still could not speak.

"Well, Sir," the Sergeant-Major concluded. "Care to try a few circuits and bumps around the old place before taking her to your new posting? Get the feel of her? Some prefer that. Many just climb right in and go off. What'll it be, Sir?"

Gelvarry found himself profoundly disturbed. Something was rising in his chest. Father Collins looked at him narrowly and raised his free hand toward MacBanion. "Perhaps we're rushing our fences, Sergeant-Major. Just verify the cockpit appurtenances there and give us a moment meanwhile, will you?" He turned Gelvarry away from the aircraft and sauntered beside him casually, his arm around Gelvarry's shoulders again.

"Troubles you, does it?"

Gelvarry glanced at him.

"But there was no doubt in your mind when you spoke to MacBanion about this, was there?"

Gelvarry blinked, then shook his head slowly.

"It's good sense, you know. You'd be leaving us the other way, shortly, if it weren't for this. Bound to." He dug in his pocket for his pipe and blew through it sharply to clear the stem. "Sergeant-Major's been discussing it for weeks. Thin as a charity widow, he's been calling you, and twice as pale, except for the Hennessey roses in your cheeks, beggin' all flyin' officers' pardon, Sir. He's been wanting to do something about it."

Gelvarry gave a high, short laugh.

Father Collins chuckled tolerantly. "Ah, no, no, Lad, hoping we'd make the choice for you is not the same. We always wait 'til the man requests it. Have to, eh? Suppose a man were posted on *our* say-so; liable to resent it, wouldn't he be, don't you think? Might kick up a fuss. Word of high squadron might reach Home. And we can't have that, now, can we?"

Gelvarry shook his head, walking along with his lips between his teeth, his lustrous eyes on his aimless feet.

"Mothers' marches on Whitehall, questions in Parliament— If they're alive, put 'em back on duty or bring 'em home to the shellshock ward—that sort of thing. Be an unholy row, wouldn't you think? And so much grief renewed among the loved ones, to say nothing of the confusion; it would be cruel. Or what would they say at the Admiralty if officers and gentlemen began discussing another Mr. Churchill, he cruising about the skies like the Angels of Mons, furthermore? For that matter, I imagine *their* Mr. Churchill would have quite a bit to say about it, and none of it pleasant to the tender ear, eh?"

Gelvarry smiled as well as he was able. He had never laid eyes on or heard the young Mr. Churchill; he imagined him a plump, shrill, prematurely balding fellow in loosely tailored clothing, gesturing with a pair of spectacles.

Father Collins gently turned Gelvarry back toward the aircraft. "We'll miss you, too, you know," he said quietly. "But we must move along now. It's best if other flying personnel can't be certain who's in high squadron and who's left us in the old stager's way, don't you agree? Gives everyone a bit of something to look forward to as the string shortens. MacBanion's a genius at clearing the field, but time *is* passing. Don't worry, Boy—Major Harding does a lovely job of seeing to it nothing's sent home as shouldn't be, and of course I'll be conveying the tidings by my own hand." They were back beside the P6E. Sergeant-Major MacBanion was standing stiffly attentive, the monkey in the crook of his arm with one small hand curled around the butt of the swagger stick.

"I believe I'll try taking her straight out, Sergeant-Major," Gelvarry said.

"Right, Sir. That's the way! Just a few things to remember about the controls, Sir, and you'll find she goes along quite nicely."

"And thank you very much, Father. I appreciate your concern."

"Nonsense, my boy. Only natural. Just keep it in mind we're all still hitting the Bavarian Corporal where he hurts; high or low makes little difference. Bit more comfortable up where you'll be, I shouldn't wonder, but I'm sure you've earned it. Tenfold. Easily tenfold."

"Let my family down as easily as you can, will you, Father?" Gelvarry said.

"Ah, yes, yes, of course."

Gelvarry climbed up into the cockpit. He sat getting the feel of how it fit him. He waggled the stick and nudged the rudder—there were pedals for his feet, rather than a pivoted bar, but the principle was the same.

Sar'n-Major Mac got up on the lower plane root and leaned into the cockpit over him. "Here's your magneto switch, and that's your throttle, of course; some of these instruments you can just ignore—can't imagine why a real aviator'd want them, tell the truth—and this is a wireless telegraphy device, but you don't need *that*—can you imagine, from the way the seat's designed when Padre and I take 'em out of the shipping crate, I'd say you were intended to be sitting on a parachute, of all things; get yourself mistaken for a ruddy civilian, next thing—but this, here's, your supercharger cut-in."

"Supercharger?"

"Oh, right, right, yes, Sir, no telling how high you might find *Ticonderoga*; things could be a bit thin. And in that vein, Sir, you'll note this metal bottle with petcock and flexible tubing. That's your oxygen supply; simply place the end of the tube in your mouth, open the petcock as required, and suck on it from time to time at altitudes above 12,000 feet, or lower if feeling a bit winded. Got all that, Sir?"

"Yes, thank you, Sar'n-Major."

"Very good! Well, then, Sir, Padre'll be wanting another brief word with you, and then anytime after that, we'll just get her started, shall we? I understand the Navy type has a crank thing called an inertia starter, but the old familiar way's for us. After that, I'd suggest a little taxiing for the feel of the controls and throttle, and then just head her into the wind, full throttle, and pleasure serving with you, Sir, if I do say so. You'll find she favors her nose a little, so keep throttle open a bit until you bring her nearer to level; I imagine she stalls something ferocious. But there'll be no trouble; never had any trouble yet. Just head west and look about; you'll see your new post up there somewhere. Can't really miss it, after all—large enough. Anything else, Sir?"

"No. No, thank you, Ma—Sergeant-Major MacBanion."

MacBanion's right eyebrow had been rising. It dropped back into place. He patted Gelvarry manfully atop the shoulder. "That's the way, Sir. Have a good trip, and think of us grubbing away down here, once in a while, will you?" He jumped from the lower plane and Father Collins came up, holding the bag. "Might be a longish flight, Son," he said. "You've had nothing to eat or drink since midnight, I believe. So you'll be wanting some of this." He opened the bag and handed Gelvarry a small flask and a piece of bread. "And there's windburn at those altitudes." He put ointment on Gelvarry's forehead and eyelids. "Have a safe flight," he said.

Gelvarry nodded. "Thank you again." When Father Collins jumped down, Gelvarry ducked his head below the level of the cockpit coaming and wiped his face. He put his arm straight up in the air and rotated his hand. Sergeant-Major MacBanion and he began the starting procedure.

The aircraft handled very well. He did a long figure eight over the aerodrome at low altitude after he'd gotten the feel of it. The ground personnel of course were busy at their various tasks. An unfamiliar figure leaning with one foot on a garden spade waved up casually from behind Major Harding's hut. The monkey was perched on a new pineboard crate Father Collins and Sergeant-Major MacBanion were manhandling down into the revettment from the back of an open lorry. As Gelvarry flew over, the little creature scrambled up to the apex of the tilting box, grinned at him, and raised its kepi.

Past the field, Gelvarry did a creditable Immelmann turn, gained altitude, settled himself a little more comfortably on the cushion made from a gunneysack stuffed with rags, and flew toward the afternoon sun, looking upward.

The aircraft *was* a joy, he gradually realized. He probed tentatively at the pedals and stick, at first, hardly recognizing he was doing so because he was under the impression his mind was full of confusions and sorrows. But as he held steadily west, his back and his arse heavy in the seat, his mind began to develop a certain wire-hard incised detachment which he recognized from his evenings with the brandy. In fact, as he gained more and more altitude, and began to rock the wings jauntily and even to give it a little rudder so that he set up a slight fishtail, he could almost hear the messroom piano, as it was every day after nightfall, all snug around the stove, grinning at each other if they could, and roaring out: "Warbirds, Warbirds, ripping through the air/Warbirds, Warbirds, fighting everywhere/Any age, any place, any foreign clime/Warbirds of Time!"

Catching himself, Haverman slipped the oxygen tube into his mouth and opened the valve on the bottle. As the dry gas slid palpably into his mouth and down his throat, the squadron theme faded from the forefront of his mind, and he began to fly the aircraft rather than play with it. He reached out, his bared wrist numbingly exposed for a moment between glove and cuff, and cut in the supercharger. There was a thump up forward of the firewall, and the engine note steadied. There was a faint, somewhat reassuring new whine in its note.

He began to feel quite himself again, encased within the indurate fuselage, his dark wings spread stiffly over the crystal-clear air below, the gleaming fabric inviolate as it hissed almost hotly through the wind of its passage. He took another pull on the oxygen. He gazed over the side of the cockpit. Down there, little aircraft were dodging and tumbling, their mainplanes reflecting sunlight in a sort of passionate Morse. He knew that message, and he drew his head back inside the cockpit. He resumed searching the deepened blue of the sky above him. And in a little bit, he saw a silver glint northwest of the sun. He turned slightly to aim straight for it, and flew steadily.

After a while, Gelvarry noticed that his throat was being dessicated by the steady flow of the oxygen. He shut the valve and spat out the tube. Pulling the Padre's chased silver flask from the bosom of his tunic, he drank from it. He also ate the cold dry bread. He did not feel particularly sustained by the snack, but the flask was quite nice as a present.

As he went, the distant speck took on breadth as well as length, and then details, size, and a gradual dulling down as the silvered cloth covering began to reveal some panels fresher than others, and the effect of varying hands at the brushwork of the doping. It now looked much as it did on those occasions when it hovered above the aerodrome and Mr. Churchill came down in his wicker car at the end of a cable, as he had done in addressing the squadron several times during Gelvarry's posting.

Ticonderoga in flight upon the same levels as the tropopausal winds, however, was even larger, somehow, and the light fell altogether differently upon it, now that he looked at it again. Boring purposefully onward, its great airscrews turning invisibly but for cyclic reflections, it filled the very world with a monster throbbing that Gelvarry could not hear as sound over the catlike snarlings of his own engine, but to which every surface of his aircraft, and in fact of his mouth and of the faceted goggles over his eyes, vibrated as if being struck by driving wet snow.

Ticonderoga suspended a dozen double-banked radial engines in teardrop pods abaft its main gondola; they seemed to float just below its belly like subsidiary craft of its own kind. Gelvarry, who had seen one or two Zeppelin warcraft, was struck by the major differences—*Ticonderoga*'s smoothly tapered rather than bluntly rounded tail and bow; its almost fishlike control surfaces, with ventral and dorsal vertical stabilizers, and matching symmetrical horizontal planes, rather than the kitelike box-sections of the Fuehrer's designs; the many glassed compartments and blisters along the hull, and the smoothly faired main and after gondolas, rather than a single rope-slung control car. But the main thing was the size, of course. He resumed taking oxygen.

As he drew nearer, tucking himself into its shadow as if under a great living cloud, *Ticonderoga* began blinking a red light at him from a ventral turret just abaft the great open bay in its belly amidships. Then three aircraft launched from that yawning hangar, dropping one, two, three like a stick of bombs but immediately gaining flying speed and wheeling into formation around him. He saw their unit numbers were in sequence with his. He waved, and their three pilots waved back.

Gelvarry watched them, fascinated. They flew with mesmerizing precision, carving smooth arcs in the air as if on wires, showing no reaction at all to the turbulence back along *Ticonderoga*'s hull. They circled him effortlessly; they in fact created the effect of turning about him while really flying flat spirals along the dirigible's flight path. Gelvarry waved again to show his appreciation of their skill, barely remembering to breathe. His gauntleted hands touched lightly at his own stick and throttle, not so much to make changes as to remind himself that he was flying, too.

One of the P6Es had a commander's broad bright stripe belting its fuselage. As soon as it was clear Gelvarry understood enough to hold while they maneuvered, the flight leader could be seen bringing his wireless microphone to his lips and speaking to *Ticonderoga*. The landing trapeze came lowering steadily down out of the bay, and hung motionless, a horizontal bar streaming along across the line of flight at the end of its complicated-looking latching tether.

The leader looked across at Gelvarry, light shining on his goggles, and pointed to one of the other Hawks, which immediately moved out of formation and approached the trapeze. Gelvarry nodded so the leader could see it; they were teaching him. Then he watched the landing aircraft intently.

The hook rising out of the center of the mainplane was designed very much like a standard snap-hook. Once it had been pushed hard against the trapeze bar, it would open to hook around it, and then would snap shut. The trick, Gelvarry thought as he watched his squadronmate sway from side to side, was to center the hook on the bar at exactly the right height. Otherwise, the P6E's nose would be forced to one side or the other of the ideal flight line, and there might be embarrassing consequences.

But the pilot brought it off nicely, apparently unconcerned about tipping his airscrew into the tether or slashing his mainplane fabric with the trapeze. He sideslipped once to bring himself into perfect alignment, and put the hook around the bar with a slight throttle-blip that put one little puff of blue smoke out the end of his exhaust pipe. Then he cut throttle, the trapeze folded around the hook to make assurance doubly sure, and he was drawn up into the hangar bay, *allez-oop*! in one almost continuous movement.

In a moment, the trapeze came down again, and the second pilot did essentially the same thing. The other half of the trick was not to create significant differences between the forward speeds of the dirigible and the aircraft along their identical flight lines, and Gelvarry lightly touched his throttle again, without moving it just yet. But when he glanced across at the leader, he was being gestured forward and up, and the trapeze was once more waiting. The leader drifted down and to the side, where he could watch.

Gelvarry took in a good breath from the bottle and came up into the turbulence, well back of the trapeze but at about the right height. He took another breath, and his mind crisped. He touched the throttle with delicate purposefulness, and came inching up on the bar, which was rocking rhythmically from side to side until he put his knees to either side of the stick and rocked his body from side to side. Thus rocking the ailerons to compensate, thus revealing that the bar had been quite steady all along, and that he was now reasonably steady with it. He was coming in an inch or two off center. He gulped again at the tube. What can happen? he thought dispassionately, and twitched the throttle between thumb and forefinger, a left-handed pinball player's move. With a clash and a bang, the hook snapped over and the trapeze folded. He closed throttle and cut the magneto instantaneously, *slip-slap*, and he was already inside the shadow of the hangar, swaying sickeningly at the end of the tether, but already being swung over toward the landing stage, with a whine of gears from the tether crane, whose spidery latticework arm overhead blended into the shadowy, endlessly repeated lattice girders that formed frame after identical frame, a gaunt cathedral whose groins and mullions retreated into diminishing distances fore and aft, housing the great bulks of the helium bags, interlaced by crew catwalks and ladders, spotted here and there by worklights but illuminated in the main by the featureless old-ivory glow through the translucent hull material.

Suddenly there was no sound immediately upon his ears, except for the pinging of his exhaust pipes and cylinder heads. The great roaring of passage pierced into the air was gone. What was left instead was a distant buzz, and the sighing rush of air rubbing over the great fabric.

The P6E's tailskid, and then its tires, touched down on the landing stage. A coveralled man wearing a hood over his mouth and a bottle on his back stepped up on the lower plane, then reached to the mainplane and disengaged the hook from the trapeze, which was swung away instantly. Other aircraft handlers stood looking impatiently at Gelvarry, who lifted himself up out of the cockpit and down to the jouncy perforated-aluminum deck. Down past his feet, he could see the structures of the lower hull, and the countryside idling backward below the open bay before the leader's Hawk nosed blackly forward toward the trapeze.

He could see almost everywhere within the dirigible. Here and there, there were housed structures behind solid dural sheets or stretched canvas screens. Machinery—winches, generators, pumps—and stores of various kinds might interrupt a line of sight to some extent, but not significantly. Even the helium bags were not totally opaque. (Nor rigid, either; he could see them breathing, pale, and creased at the tops and bottoms, and he could hear their casings and their tethers creaking). He felt he could shout from one end of *Ticonderoga* to the other; might also spring into the air toward that stanchion, swing to that brace, go hand over hand along the rail of that catwalk, scramble up that ladder, swing by that cable to that inspection platform, slip down that catenary, rebound from the side of that bag, land lightly over there on the other side of the bay and present himself, grinning, to his fellow pilots standing there watching him now, all standing at ease, their booted feet spread exactly the same distance part, their hands clasped behind their backs, their cavalry breeches identically spotless, their dark tunics and Sam Browne belts all in a row above beltlines all at essentially the same height, their helmets on and their goggles down over their eyes.

He licked his lips. He glanced up guiltily toward the catwalk higher up in the structure, where a row of naked gray monkeys the size of large children was standing, paws along the railing, motionless, studying things. Gelvarry glanced aside.

The flight leader's plane was swung in and then rolled back to join the dozen others lashed down along the hangar deck. The man had jumped down out of the cockpit; he strode toward Gelvarry now. As he approached, Gelvarry saw his features were nondescript.

"You're to report to Mr. Churchill's cabin for a conference at once," he said to Gelvarry. He pointed. "Follow that walkway. You'll find a hatch forward of the main helium cells, there. It opens on the midships gondola. Mr. Churchill is waiting."

Gelvarry stopped himself in midsalute. "Aren't you going to take me there?"

The flight leader shook his head. "No. I can't stand the place. Full of the monkeys."

"Ah."

"Good luck," the officer said. "We shan't be seeing more of each other, I'm afraid. Pity. I'd been looking forward to serving with you."

Gelvarry shrugged uncomfortably. "So it goes," he said for lack of something precise to say, and turned away.

He followed directions toward the gondola. As he moved along, the monkeys flowed limb-over-limb above him among the higher levels of the structural bracing, keeping pace. As they traveled, they conducted incidental business, chattering, gesticulating, knotting up momentarily in clumps of two and three individuals in the grip of passion or anger that left one or two scurrying away cowed or indignant, the level of their cries rising or falling. The whole group, however, maintained the general movement with Gelvarry.

He was fairly certain he remembered what they were, and he did what he could to ignore them.

He came to the gondola hatch, which was an engine-turned duraluminum panel opening on a ladder leading down into a long, windowed corridor lined with crank-operated chest-high machines, at each of which crouched and cranked a monkey somewhat smaller than Gelvarry. As he set foot on the ladder, several of the larger monkeys from the hull spaces suddenly shoved past him, all bristles and smell, forcing their way into the corridor. They were met with immediate, shrieking violence from the nearest machine monkeys, and Gelvarry swung himself partway off the ladder, his eyes wide, maintaining his purchase with one boot toe and one gloved hand while he peered back over his shoulder at the screams and wrestlings within the confined space.

Bloodied intruder monkeys with their pelts torn began to flee back toward safety past him, voiceless and panting, their expressions desperate. The attempted invasion was becoming a fiasco at the deft hands of the machine monkeys, who fought with ear-ripping indignation, uttering howls of outrage while viciously handling the much more naive newcomers. Out of the corner of his eye, Gelvarry saw exactly one of the intruders—who had shrewdly chosen a graying and instinctively diffident machine monkey several positions away from the hatch—pay no heed to the tumult and close its teeth undramatically and inflexibly in its target's throat. In a moment, the object of the maneuver was a limp and yielding bundle on the deck. While all its fellows streamed up past Gelvarry and took, dripping, to the safety of the hull braces the one victorious new monkey bent over the dispossessed machine and began turning the crank. No attention was paid to it as things within the gondola corridor returned to normal.

Gelvarry closed and secured the hatch while monkeys returned to their machines. The wounded ones ignored their hurts cleverly. Neither neighbor of the successful invader paid any overt attention to matters as they now stood, but Gelvarry noticed that as they bobbed and weaved at their machines, with the new monkey between them and with the dead cranker supine at his feet, they unobtrusively extended their limbs and tails to nudge lightly at the body, until they had almost inadvertently kicked it out of sight behind the machines.

Each of the machines displayed a three-dimensional scene within a small circular platform atop the device. Aircraft could be seen moving in combat among miniature clouds over distant background landscapes. Doped wings glistened in the sunlight, turning, turning, reflecting flashes. Dot dot dot. Dash dash dash. Dot. Dot. Dot. Gelvarry brushed forward between the busy animals and moved toward the farther hatch at the other end of the corridor. Atop the nearest machine, he saw a Fokker *dreidekker* painted red, whipping through three fast barrel rolls before resuming level flight above the floundering remains of a broken Nieuport. Dot dot dot dash.

The monkey at that machine frowned and cranked the handle backwards. The Baron's triplane suddenly reversed its actions. Dash dot dot dot. The Nieuport reassembled. Stork insignia could be seen painted on its fuselage. The crank turned forward again. The swastika-marked red wings corkscrewed into their victory roll again above the disintegrating Frenchman.

The monkey at the machine was crooning and bouncing on the balls of its feet, rubbing its free hand over its lips. It moved several knobs at the front of the viewing machine, and the angle changed, so that the point of view was directly from the cockpit of the Fokker, and pieces of the Nieuport flew past the wing struts to either side. The monkey jabbed its neighbors with its elbows and nodded toward the action. It searched the face on either side for reaction. One of them, turning away from a scene of Messerschmitt 262 tactical jet fighters rocketing a column of red-starred T-34 tanks on the ice of Lake Ladoga, glanced over impatiently and pushed back at the Fokker monkey's shoulder, resuming its attention to its own concerns. But the other neighboring monkey was kinder. Despite the fact that its flight of three Boeing P-26s was closing fast on a terrified Kawanishi flying boat over the Golden Gate Bridge, it paused long enough to glance at the Baron's victory, pat its neighbor reassuringly on the back, and utter a chirp of approbation. Pleased, the first monkey was immediately rapt in rerunning the new version of the scene. The kind monkey stole a glance over again, shrugged, and resumed cranking its own machine.

Gelvarry continued pushing between the monkeys to either side. The flooring was solid, but springy underfoot. The ceiling was convex, and wider than the floor, so that the duraluminum walls tapered inward. They were pierced for skylights above the long banks of machines, but *Ticonderoga* was apparently passing through clouds. There were rapid alterations of light at the ports, but only slight suggestions of any detail. Over the spasmodic grinding of the cranks, and the constant slight vocalizations of the monkeys, the sound of air washing over the walls and floor could be made out if one paused and listened ruminatively.

Gelvarry reached Mr. Churchill's compartment door. He knocked, and the reassuring voice replied: "Come!" He quickly entered and closed the sheetmetal panel securely behind him.

The compartment was large for his expectations. Its deck was parqueted and dressed in oriental carpets. Armchairs and taborets were placed here and there, with many low reading lamps, and opaque drapes swayed over the portholes. Mr. Churchill sat heavily in a Turkish upholstered chair at the other end of the room, facing him, wearing his pinstriped blue suit with the heavy watchchain across the rounded vest. He gripped a freshly lighted Uppman cigar between his knuckles. The famous face was drawn up into its wet baby scowl, and Gelvarry at once felt the impact of the man's presence.

"Ah," Mr. Churchill said. "None too soon. Come and sit by me. We have only a moment or two, and then they shall all be here." His mouth quirked sideward. "Rabble," he growled. "Counterjumpers."

Gelvarry moved forward toward the chair facing the Prime Minister. "Am I a unique case, Sir?" he said, sitting down with a trace of uneasiness. "I was told high squadron posting was voluntary only."

Mr. Churchill raised his eyebrows and turned to the taboret beside him. He punched a bronze pushbell screwed to the top. "Unique? Of course you're unique, man! You're the principal, after all." A doorway somewhere behind him opened, and a young woman with soot-black hair and bee-stung lips entered wearing a French maid's costume. She brought a silver tray on which rested two crystal tumblers and a bottle of the familiar Hennessey *Rx Official*. "Very good! Very good!" Mr. Churchill said, pouring. "Mr. Dunstan Haverman, I'm introducing Giselle Montez," he said, giving her name the Gallic pronunciation. "It is very possible that you shall—" He shrugged. "meet again." Gelvarry tried not to appear much out of countenance as Miss Montez brought the salver and stood gracefully silent, her eyes downcast, while he took his tumbler. "Charmed." he said softly.

"Thank you," she murmured, turned, and retreated through her doorway. She had left the bottle with Mr. Churchill.

Gelvarry sipped. Mr. Churchill raised his glass. "Here's to reality."

Haverman shuddered. "No," he said, drinking more deeply anyway, "I was beginning to depend on it too much. Sam, what's going wrong?"

Sam grunted as the amber liquid hit his own esophagus. He was normally a self-contained, always pleasant-spoken individual—the typical golf or tennis pro at the best club in the county—who in Haverman's long experience of him had once frowned when a drunk at a business luncheon had pawed a waitress. And then calmly tipped a glass of icewater into the man's lap, costing himself a thirty-nine-week deal.

"Sam?" Haverman peered through the Hennessey effect at his grimacing old acquaintance.

"Take a look." The leaner, longer-legged, short-haired man sitting in the chrome-and-leather captain's chair turned toward the hard-edged cabinet standing beside him. The pushbell atop it seemed incongruous. Sam flipped up a panel and punched a number on the keyboard behind it. He closed the panel and nodded toward a cleared area of the panelled, indirectly lighted room. Haverman immediately recognized it as a holo focus, of course, even before he remembered what an inlaid circle in the flooring signified. It was a large one—half again the size of normally sold commercial receivers—as befitted the offices of a major industry figure.

Laurent Michaelmas appeared; urbane, dark-suited, scarlet flower in his lapel. "Good day," he said. "I have the news." He paused, one eyebrow cocked, hands slightly spread, waiting for feedback.

Sam raised his voice slightly above normal conversational level. "Just give us the broadcast industry top story, please," he said, and the Michaelmas projection flicked almost imperceptibly into a slightly new stance, then bowed and said:

"The top broadcast story is also still the top general story, sir. Now here it is:" He relaxed and stepped aside so that he was at the exact edge of the circle, visually related to the room floor level, while the remainder of the holo sphere went to an angled overhead view of Lower Manhattan.

"Well, today is October 25, 1992, in New York City, where the impact of the latest FCC ruling is still being assessed by programming departments for all major media." The scene-camera point of view became a circling pan around Wall Street Alley, picking up the corporate logos atop the various buildings: RCA, CBS, ABC, GTV, Blair, Neilsen. In a nice touch, the POV zoomed smoothly on an upper-storey window, showing what appeared to be a conference room with three or four gesticulating figures somewhat visible through the sun-repelling glass. It was excellent piloting, too—the camera copter was being handled smoothly enough in the notorious off-bay cross-currents so that the holo scanner's limited compensatory circuits were able to take all the jiggle and drift out of the shot. Here was a flyer, Haverman thought, who wouldn't be a disgrace at the trapeze. Then he winced and took another nibble at the Hennessey.

"While viewers reaped an unexpected bonanza," Michaelmas said, and the background cut to an interior of a typical dwelling and a young man and woman watching Laurent Michaelmas with expressions of pleasant surprise, "industry spokesmen publicly lauded the FCC's Reception Release Order." The cut this time was to a pleasant-looking fellow in a casual suit, leaning against a holo cabinet. He smiled and said: "Folks, it's got to be the greatest thing since free tickets to the circus." He patted the cabinet. "Imagine! From now on, you can receive *every* and *any* channel right where you are, no matter *what* type of receiver you own! Yes, it's true—for only a few pennies, we'll bring you and install one of the new Rutledge-Karmann adapter units, with the best coherer circuit possible, that'll transform any receiver into an *all-channel* receiver! Now, how about that? Remember, the government says we have to use top-quality components, and we have to sell to you at *our cost*! So—" He grinned boyishly. "Even if we wanted to screw you, we can't."

"Others, however," Michaelmas said, "were not so sanguine. Even in public."

The holo went to Fingers Smart in the elevator lobby of what was recognizably the New York FCC building. He was striding out red-faced, followed by several figures Haverman could recognize as GTV attorneys and GTV's favorite consulting lawyer. "When interviewed, GTV Board Chairman Ancel B. Smart had this to say at 1:15 P.M. today:"

Now it was a two-shot of Smart being faced by an interested, smiling Laurent Michaelmas, while the lawyers milled around and tried to get a word in edgewise. Nobody ever effectively got between that friendly-uncle manner of Michaelmas's and whoever he was after.

"That's exactly right, Larry," Smart was saying. "We built the holovision industry the way it is because the FCC wanted it that way then. Now it wants it another way, and that's it. Public interest. Well, damn it, we're part of the public, too!" Smart's other industry nickname was Notso.

"Are you going to continue fighting the ruling?"

A belated widening of Smart's eyes now occurred. "Who says we're fighting it? We were here getting clarification of a few minor points. You know GTV operates in the public interest."

Sam chuckled, unamused, while Haverman peered and thought. GTV controlled eighty-seven entertainment channels that operated twenty-four hours a day. There were six GTV-owned channels leased to religious and political lobbies. There was also, of course, GTV's ten percent share of the public network subsidy. Paid off in programs given to PTV from the summer Student Creative internship plan.

That was how the dice had fallen when the Congress legislated cheap 3-D TV. The existing broadcast companies were trapped in their old established images with heavy emphasis on sports or news, women's daytime, musical variety, feature documentary anthologies, and the like. That had left an obvious vacuum which GTV had filled promptly.

All-channel receivers at an affordable price had been out of the question. As usual, Congress had been straining technology to its practical limits, and compromises had had to be made in the end. A good half of the receivers sold, Haverman remembered, were entertainment only. Now, apparently, because of something very cheap called the Harmon-Cutlass or something, he wouldn't have to remember it any longer.

"Oh!" he said, raising his eyes to Sam's nod.

Michaelmas cocked his head at Smart. "Just one or two more questions, please. Are you saying you haven't already cut your ratings guarantees to your advertisers? I believe your loss this quarter has just been projected at nearly twenty percent of last year's profits."

Smart glanced aside to his legal staff. But he was impaled on Michaelmas's smile. He tried one of his own; it worked beautifully at the annual entertainment programming awards dinner. "Come on, Larry—you know I'm no bean-counter. GTV's going to continue to offer the same top-drawer—"

"Well, one would assume that," Michaelmas said urbanely. "You have most of the season's product still on the shelf, unshown. No one would expect you to just dump a capital investment of that scope. What is your plan for after that? Or don't you expect to be the responsible executive six months from now?"

"Ouch!" Haverman said.

"I don't think I have to answer that here," Smart said quickly. He frowned at Michaelmas as he moved to step around him. "Come to think of it, you're in competition with us now, aren't you?" He actually laid a hand on Michaelmas's arm and pushed him a little aside, or would have, if Michaelmas didn't have a dancer's grace. "No further comment," Smart said, and strode off.

Michaelmas turned toward the point of view, while the background faded out behind him and left him free-standing. He shrugged expressively. "These little tiffs sometimes occur within the fellowship of broadcasting," he said with a smile. "But most observers would agree that competition is always in the public interest." There was the faintest of flicks to a stock tape; computer editing was instantaneous in real time, smooth, and due to become smoother. Even now, only an eye expecting it could detect it. "And that's how it is today," flick, "in broadcasting," flick, "and in the top story at this hour." He bowed and was gone.

Haverman rolled his eyes. "What happened?" he said. "I thought Hans Smart had a lock on Congress."

Sam grinned crookedly and grimly. "He's dead, poor chap. His liver gave out two weeks ago, and there went Notso's brains."

"Physiology got to the wrong brother."

"Yeah. It wouldn't have been as bad as it was, but three days before he went, NBC sprang a prime-time documentary. It was about this new little engineering company in Palo Alto that could pick up all channels on your $87.50 Sony portable. He wasn't cold in the ground before a dozen senators were on the all-channel bandwagon. The House delegation from California began lobbying as a bloc, New York City, and then Nassau and Dutchess counties jumped in, and the next you know Calart-Hummer or whatever it is, is the law of the land. Hans Smart could handle legislators with the best of 'em, but I don't think it was the booze that killed him; it was that friggin' feature."

Sam grinned more genuinely. "It was a beaut. NBC sent out engraved invitations, on paper, messenger-delivered to every member of Congress and anybody else they figured could swing a little. About six months ago, they had bought excerpt rights to about a dozen old *Warbirds* things. Newsfeature use only; you know how that goes, I guess. Well, it all turned up in that show. Michaelmas walking around narrating over it. Only they scaled it down behind him, so he was just stepping around over the battlefields and the planes were buzzing around him while he just smiled and talked. King damned Kong in a pinstripe suit. You wouldn't have believed it. Show it to you sometime; everybody in the business must have made a copy of it. Scare hell out of you. Even if you weren't personally involved, I mean."

Haverman sucked a little more Hennessey carefully between his lips and across the edges of his tongue. "What's been happening to the *Warbirds* ratings, Sam?"

Ticonderoga Studios produced other things besides *Warbirds*, but *Warbirds* was what it was known for in the industry, and *Warbirds* was GTV's top-rated show. GTV's contract was what kept Ticonderoga flying.

"Well, Dusty, we're having to be ingenious." Sam looked down at the stick between his fingers, then broke it open and inhaled in a controlled manner. "These things are pretty good," he remarked. "I think they'll catch on."

Haverman settled himself carefully in his chair. "Isn't this thing bound to settle out? I mean, it's a new toy. Notso may flail around for a while—"

Sam nodded, but not encouragingly. "He's gone. He knows it. But he's telling himself he can make it unhappen if he just yells and shits loud enough. Flailing around isn't the phrase you need. But he's gone. I've got some GTV stock; want it?"

"It'll work its way back up again, Sam," Haverman said carefully. "Especially if Smart gets kicked out by the Board and they hire a new president." Haverman suddenly sat up straighter. "Hey, Sam, why couldn't that be you?"

"I've thought about that."

"Right! It's perfect for them—a top gun from outside, but not too far outside. An experienced new broom. The PR is made for it, friend!"

"I don't want it."

Haverman looked at him watchfully. "Oh?"

Sam shook his head. "Too soon. I'm staying right where I am and building a record. Some other poor son of a bitch can have the next couple of years to get ulcerated in."

Haverman pursed his lips thoughtfully. "It's going to be that bad." He had one hundred percent respect for Sam's judgment. "I guess I'm being a little slow. If our audience can switch away to other channels, can't their people switch to GTV?"

"All of them can and some of them will. But they're hardcore generalists; they'll take a little of us, and a little of CBS, and a little of NBC, and a little of Funkbeobachter, and a little Shimbun, and some ABC, and God knows what else when the new relay sets go in. No, these are the kind of people that're used to a little of everything, no matter what network they're from. Any of 'em that hankered for a little side action from GTV or anyplace else could afford additional sets long ago. But *our* viewers, you know—" He held his hand out, palm up, and slowly turned it over.

Haverman said reluctantly: "That's not how we talk at the awards dinners."

"I don't see any chicken and peas around here right now," Sam said. "There's no way I would have pulled you out of your milieu if I didn't think we were in trouble."

"We can counterprogram," Haverman said emphatically. "We've got the skills and the facilities."

"Yes, I have."

"O.K. We can do news and sports stuff like the other people. That's the way it's going to go anyhow—back to the way it was in flat-V time, when everybody had a little of everything."

"Yeah, but not now," Sam said. "Later. Meanwhile, how do we get the National League to break its contract with ABC? Where do you think CBS's legal department would be if we started talking option-breakers to Mandy Carolina? Two years from now, Michaelmas's contract is up for renewal at NBC. There's talk he's thinking of going freelance. *That*'ll start a trend. Give me enough bucks, and I'll build you the top-rated action news show. *Then.* Then, Dusty," he said gently. "Not now. And now is when Fingers Smart and old Sam the Ticonderoga are fighting for their lives, you know?" He inhaled deeply on the stick and threw the exhausted pieces to the floor.

"I can't start another league to compete with what ABC can show my people. There aren't that many big jocks in the world. And I can't find another talk show hostess; only God can make a mouth. I can't get Michaelmas, I can't get Melvin Watson. I *can* get the guy who's sick of being Skip Jacobson's Sunday-night backup, and so what. What I've got is actors. I can get actors. I can get enough actors to fill eighty times twenty-four hours of programming every week, if I have to." Sam sighed. "I can make actors. So can anybody else; it's no secret how you do almost two thousand different shows a week, thirty-nine weeks a year. So you know what I've got left?" Sam leaned forward.

"Me," Sam said. "I've got me, and what's in me here." He tapped his head and patted his crotch. "And we're gonna find out how many years it's good for."

The silence had persisted palpably. "And me, Sam," Haverman said finally.

"Uh-huh," Sam said. He poured another shot into Haverman's glass. "Here," he said, and sipped his own to knock off the stick effect. "Have a snort. Now, listen. You're my guy, and don't forget it. You were one of the first people to sign on with me, and you've been the principal of *Warbirds* ever since almost the beginning."

Haverman nodded emphatically. There had been a Rex something or other. But that was long ago. "I have a following," he said confirmingly, as if that was what he thought mattered to Sam about him. And of course it was one of the things that did matter. It must. Sam was not a creative for his health.

"That's right," Sam said gently. "And I'm going to protect you, and you're going to help me."

"I'm not going back into *Warbirds*."

"Something like *Warbirds*. Something recognizably like it, and you're going to have the same character name."

Haverman cocked his head. "But there *are* going to be changes."

"Oh, yes. Got to have those, so it can be new and different. But not too many, really—got to save something so they can identify with the familiar. It'll have airplanes and things."

"Ah," Haverman said warily.

"A new show. All your own. Name over the title. We're going to promo hell out of it—'Haverman Moves!' Maybe 'Dusty Moves!' I don't know. Hell with it. Think of something better. Not the point. We'll get every one of the *Warbirds* audience, and with that kind of promo, we'll get plenty of new lookers. Once they've looked, we'll have 'em. Guarantee it."

"Well, certainly, if it's one of your ideas—"

"Hell, yes, it's one of mine. More important, it's the one whose time has come. What the hell—eighty-odd channels of our own for a looker to choose from, and God knows how many more coming from all kinds of places. It's got to happen; I can hit the FCC with First Amendment and Right of Free Choice at the same time. It'll be years before they beat me. And you know something, Duster?" he said in a suddenly calm voice, "I don't think they're ever going to beat me. I think we really can make it stick."

"Oh?" Haverman felt the skin prickle sharply at the backs of his hands. He had never seen Sam like this; only heard of such moments, when the conviction of having thought and done exactly right transformed his good friend's face. The triumphant force of having created a truth came blazing from his eyes. And when he said "I think we can make it stick," his voice reharmonized itself so that though it never rose in volume, it might have been played by solo viola. Haverman could only say again: "Oh."

Sam was grinning. Grinning. "It's beautiful, Duster," he said. "Once we've beaten the test case, we can do another thing—open up a whole channel to the genre. Maybe more than one. And you shoot the whole thing on one set, with a couple of pieces of furniture and just a handful of props, and a holoprojected background. There's no long shot, and damned little tracking, so you do it with two cameras. One, if you're willing to settle. But I wouldn't. Or at least I'd want a damn good optical reflector to back me up. A whole new show, and then a whole channel full of new shows, for a third—maybe a fourth—of what anything else costs."

"And I'm going to do the first one," Haverman said. "Smart'll go for it. He has to. What kind of show is it, exactly, Sam?"

When Sam explained it to him further, he sat shaking his head. "Oh, no, Sam, no, I'm not sure I could do that."

But Sam said: "Sure you can."

Haverman sat uncertainly through the beginning of the conference. First the door to the office corridor was opened, and the senior technical staff came in; Hal, the most senior, carried a model of an aircraft carrier and a model of a silvery biplane, both of which he set down on Sam's white table. Sam turned them over in his hands, and nodded and winked at Hal, who smiled and sat down in the nearest of the informally grouped chairs. Dusty sat back along the wall, in a comfortable alcove next to Miss Montez's door, waiting.

Sam looked around at his people. "Everybody ready? O.K., let's give the great man a call," he said, and apparently punched up Ancel Smart's phone number, because Smart, after a little work with a secretary, appeared in the holo circle. He sat in a chair with his own people around him, and said heavily: "Shoot."

"Right," Sam said. "Anse, you know Hal and the rest of the boys, here. Now, we're proposing as follows—"

And it continued from there, with Smart nodding from time to time, or interposing a question, and changing his POV to watch whoever on the Ticonderoga staff was giving him the data. Then he'd turn back to Sam. Occasionally, one of Smart's people would address Sam. But it was Smart and Sam one-on-one, as it ought to be, Dusty saw, beginning to feel better as his friend clearly established dominance over the meeting. Smart was inclined to cough and play with his chin. Sam sat slim and upright, his hands, spread-fingered, molding premises in the air above the white tabletop where the models waited. Dusty began to feel better as Sam grew.

"All right, I promise you this new show'll grab 'em and won't let go. I've taken a closer look at the tentative figures we discussed earlier, and I'll stand behind 'em." Sam named an in-the-can cost half of what it might have been. "And no concept fee, absolutely nothing in front. I get it back on reruns; we go to full rate on those, but, what the hell, if we ever *see* reruns, you're golden and you don't care, right? O.K., so that's Part One of what Ticonderoga's prepared to do. What do you do, Anse?"

Smart nodded. "Like I said. If it packages up the way you described, GTV'll help with the Feds. We've still got an office in Washington, after all, and my brother left a well-trained staff."

"Specifically, you're agreeing to hold Ticonderoga harmless in the event of criminal penalties or monetary losses caused by legal or regulatory action. Is that correct?"

One of Smart's legal staff suddenly leaned forward and began to whisper urgently in his ear. Smart waved him off impatiently. "That's right. I haven't changed my mind."

"On the record, and on behalf of GTV?" Sam pointed toward his own lawyer, who held up a sealed recorder.

"If we buy the program at all, GTV defends," Smart confirmed.

"O.K.," Sam said. "Now I'm gonna tell you who's in it."

"Ah."

"According to the formula we discussed," Sam said, turning to his holo box, talking aside, "we're going for a total ego-spectrum across four archetypical blocs. Now, each bloc embodies several potent identification features. We go young woman, young but experienced man, older and ego-stable woman, fully sophisticated man at the top end of middle age. We go soft, wiry, tight, sinewy; dark, reddish, blondy, silver. Sometimes we vary a little; there's room to do it; you get different overlaps, but you still cover it all the way across your maximized consumer ideals. We anchor at each end with an identifiable regular, but we can vary in the middle. Right so far?"

Smart nodded. "Acceptable." His and Sam's lawyers nodded.

"All right." Sam was still turned toward the control cabinet and speaking along his shoulder at Smart. He began to slowly raise one arm toward the top of the box. It was a good move; Haverman could see the tension building in Smart, and the distraction that was mirrored in the flickering of his eyes. More and more, Haverman felt the welling of admiration for Sam, and the comfort of being one of his people. "Now, you buy the concept of guest celebrities?"

"As long as they fit the formula."

"As long as they fit the formula defined above," Sam corroborated. "Are you worried about our being able to create authenticity?"

"With your makeup and research departments? Never. You guarantee audience believability, and I'll take your word for it right now."

"So guaranteed. Done." Sam nodded. "All right, we work from now on the assumption that the celebrity pair on each show will cover the two middle blocs, and Ticonderoga has discretion there as long as the portrayals remain convincing. To whom? Do you want to designate an audience-reaction service, Ancel?" His hand was poised above the holo controls now.

Smart shrugged. "We've been using TeleWinner all along. Let's give 'em this, too. Split the cost, right?" He chuckled. "What the hell, you know the reason GTV buys *Warbirds* is because I'm hooked on it. I'm my own symbol-bloc survey; they just make it official."

Sam smiled faintly. Audience size was what made it official.

"And, what the hell," Smart said, "you're keeping the alternate time tracks premise for the new show, aren't you? So if somebody says Rocky Marciano wasn't lefthanded or Sonja Henie didn't rollerskate, well, hell that was *then* but this is *elsewhen*, right? But it has to *look* right; that we've got to have."

"Absolutely." Even if there'd been no other public source of visual data, there was GTV's own Channel '29, steadily programming out reprocessed old movie and newsreel footage for all the WW II warbabies who'd just missed it. The reprocessing was done by TStudiolab, Inc., one of Sam's subsidiaries.

"Okay, so we've got all that out of the way," Smart said. "Now let's see the goods."

"Of course." Sam smiled. His hand moved unexpectedly, and rang the little pushbell. "Let me introduce our talented newcomer. The next big word in viewer households, known to you and me as the young bloc archetype and all that implies, but professionally known as Giselle Montez—"

On her cue, Miss Montez came through her door in a high squadron pilot's uniform, the leather of her boots and Sam Browne belt glistening. She swept off her aluminized goggles and her helmet with one deft swirl of the hand that released her cloud of hair, and stood holding them on her hip, while her other hand rested its fingertips at the first button in the vee of her tunic. Ancel Smart leaned forward sharply in his chair. His mouth formed a loose o.

"Thank you, Miss Montez," Sam said, and she about-faced and walked out quickly; the door closed behind her with one darting flip of her fingertips. "And at the other end of the spectrum, the fine silver of sophisticated experience." Sam touched the cabinet controls. A sketch materialized in the air, facing Smart. It was a deceptively loose artist's rendering, life size, of a whipcordy-slim man with delicate limbs and waving, glossy white hair struck with contrasting pewter-colored lowlights. The expression of the aristocratic face suggested certain things.

Smart nodded reservedly. "Yes. All right. Looks all right. Who's going to play it? Something familiar about him. Who was your artist using for a model? Dusty Haverman?" Smart grinned.

Sam did not. He simply kept looking steadily at Smart, whose eyes first narrowed, then enlarged. "You're kidding! You're— How do we do *Warbirds* without him?—Jesus—" He slapped his thigh. "Perfect! It's perfect! It's a stroke, Sam, a fuckin' stroke!"

"Sure," Sam said.

The back of the meeting was broken. It was all a big long happy glide thereafter. Sar'n-Major Mac would come to the fore as the real manager of low squadron, and Private Parkins would play up raffishly. Major Harding's part would be padded a little, and Father Collins would listen to his troubles as he thrashed about trying to assert himself and spoil MacBanion's schemes. At its own expense, as an additional contribution to the relief of the crisis, Ticonderoga Studios would go back into the existing unshown episodes and re-edit to the new slant, so the Gelvarry character would be free to Go West, grow up, and change shows immediately. Sam had some experimental footage, it seemed, which might fit some of that.

In return, GTV would guarantee renewal next year. About next year—Sam's latest idea was to move on to dirigible-launched P6E's against Fiat CR32 biplanes; he held up the glittering model of the 220-mph Italian fighter, which had not gone out of use until 1938. They would be launched from the *Graf Zeppelin*, which had been Nazi Germany's sole aircraft carrier. Named for the man who pioneered practical lighter-than-air flight.

Smart considered the possibilities and the twists. "Cute," he admitted. "I like it." He shook his head. "I don't know where you get your ideas, Sam. Christ. Planes that sound like cars comin' off a ship that sounds like a dirigible, and what do they run up against? Damn! Yeah—let me see some footage pretty soon, will you?"

Sam had some, it seemed, which would fit some of that. They'd be able to show a rough cut in about a week.

"How about the new show? How soon can I have that?"

Well, it took a little while to get the actors into the milieu. Smart could understand that.

Yes, he could. But—

Oh, they'd push it. Tell you what; how about a progress report in ten days?

Well, if that meant they were close to delivery on the pilot episode.

Right. The *pilot* episode.

Everybody suddenly laughed, and Sam promised to send the little models over to Smart's office right away, for the shelves over the bar.

Smart punched off, and everybody in Sam's conference room began to grin and make enthusiastic quips. They were a high-morale outfit. It almost reminded Haverman of— Well, it should, shouldn't it? Art mirrors life.

Haverman got up from his inconspicuous seat and went over to Sam. "I thought it went very well."

Hal raised an eyebrow. "Well, hello!" he said.

Sam smiled reassuringly. "You heard the man, Duster," he said. "GTV's buying it, and they'll protect us. So it's all right." His eyes said: *I told you I'd take care of you.*

"I'm sure of that," Haverman said with conviction. "It's a Ticonderoga production," and everyone within earshot smiled.

"Why don't we get started?" Sam said and, putting an arm around his shoulders, walked with him out through the door to the technical spaces, which in this area were half-partitioned workrooms and offices grouped-up to either side of the long central aisle that ran back toward the sound stages. Overhead were the whitewashed skylights and the zigzag trusses of the broad, arching roof, and to either side of them were the sounds of word-processing machines and footage splicers. They walked along to a side aisle, and there Sam had to leave him, after opening and holding open for him the heavy wood-grained door marked ACTORS AND MEDICAL PERSONNEL ONLY.

A bright-looking young medical person leafed through his printout. "Dusty Haverman," he said wonderingly. "I never knew you'd been an accounting student."

"Isn't Doctor Virag going to do me? Doctor Virag and I know each other very well," he said, sitting stiffly in his chair.

The medical person did his best to smile disarmingly. "Doctor Virag is no longer with us, I'm afraid. Time passes, you know. I'm Doctor Harcourt; I think you'll find me competent. Sam personally asked me to take you."

"Oh. Well, I didn't mean to imply—"

"That's all right, Mr. Haverman. Now, if you'll just relax, Miss Tauchnitz will begin removing that hairpiece and so forth." Harcourt's fingers danced over keys, and he peered at the screen beside his chair. "Let me just refresh myself on this— yes, well, I think you may find it a relief to wear your own hair, for one thing; we'll just bleach it up a little bit. And we'll tan you. That'll be better than that tarty pinky-cheeks tinting, don't you think? Other than that, there's just a *tiny* bit of incising to do . . . a touch of a lift to one eyebrow, and that'll have the desired effect, I'm sure. Oh, yes, the cosmetology here is minimal, minimal. Which is just as well, since we do have a rather thick book of response-adjustments to perform, but, then, none of us is perfect for our role in life, really. Or is it 'are perfect'? Would you happen to know which it is, Miss Tauchnitz?"

When they had that done, they walked him down the corridors, past the rows of costume mannequins, and to the processing room, which was hung in soft black nonreflecting fabric, and where they had symphonic control of the lighting. They put him in the chair with the trick armrests and the neck brace.

"This is wine, Mr. Haverman," and he peered aside at the rollaway table with the clear decanter of rosy clarity, and the goblet. As long as he moved his arm smoothly and no more quickly than was gracious he could reach out and take it, and sip. "That's right. Have some more," the pleasant voice behind him said, and when he had had some more, they showed him a holo of Miss Montez and stimulated an electrode.

"Ah! Ah-ah-ah!"

"A little more wine, Mr. Haverman." And again the Montez and the incredible sensation beside which all past experience paled.

To see her come fully lighted out of the featureless soft warm darkness, and to feel what he could feel when she did that, he had only to reach out and take more wine. There was no thought in him of a spastic attempt to pluck something from his skull.

"Shouldn't you be feeding me oysters or Vitamin E? Perhaps some Tiger's Milk?" he jested once after they had stopped the wine and given him some Hennessey to refresh him. The pleasant voice murmured a throaty chuckle behind him.

When there was no further response to his gambit, he said: "Ah, well, I've really always been a steak and potatoes man, actually," and carelessly reached around to circle his hand into the unknown space behind him, but the pleasant voice said: "More wine, Mr. Gelvarry," and an unnoticeable hand put the goblet into his fingers. "Good enough," Gelvarry said. "Ah! Yes, yes, good enough, I say."

• • •

They showed him a slim, freckled woman with prominent front teeth, dressed in a calf-length skirt and a cardigan sweater over a cotton blouse. She wore soft leather street boots over dark lisle stockings, and moved like something wary in a strange part of the forest. They wiped, and went to a reprocessed, tinted, computer-animated photo of the famous person this was supposed to represent, and when he sipped the wine, they gave him the pleasure effect. Soon enough in the process he found it difficult to distinguish between the photo and the actress in her costume, no matter how the costume changed per reveal, for they always had a fresh photo after each wipe-and-switch, and the costume had clearly been cued by something in the photo, as much as chiffon can be patterned to remind one of gingham. In truth, in a while, he could not distinguish at all, and he found that although after a while they didn't wipe the actress, he had to concentrate very hard to make her out behind the features he now saw for her. So they gave him more wine, and the idea of concentrating was, to his relief, lost.

They did roughly the same thing with the identity of the purposeful young man with the angelic eyes.

And it was done.

"It's good, Sam," Haverman said, sitting in the office with the Hennessey.

"Sure," Sam said.

"I feel it. I feel absolutely certain." He ran a hand along the silvery waves at the side of his head, and touched one finger to his pencil moustache. His hand was lean and browned by the suns of expensive resorts. A chased gold ring set with a ruby glittered on his little finger. "The way you can make me see the guests, instead of the actors playing them—"

"Yeah, well, they aren't actually playing them, you know. We've got this computer tied into the cameras, and when those people move around, the image data gets put through and modified by this fancy program I had the fellows work up. It's pretty good; probably get better. As long as the players don't do anything grossly out of character, the computer can edit the image to fit the model character. That's what goes on the air."

"But how do I see it, playing with them?"

"Well, you can't, Duster, that's why we do that hocus-pocus in the dark room. One of the hocus-pocuses." Sam patted him lightly at the neck. "Saves you having to act, you know, old Duster." He was sitting beside him on the couch, and leaned forward to cap the Hennessey.

"I think I could act it," Haverman said very softly.

Sam sighed. "Well, perhaps you could. But you see, this way it all goes smoothly and very naturally, don't you see? No lines to remember, no breaks for lunch—But those are all technical details, Dus, and there's absolutely no need for you to learn them."

"Still and all," Haverman said. "Still and all." Sam was uncapping the wine now. "I think you're very inventive," Haverman hastened. "That was always true of you. Do you know what I think? I think your next computer program will make it completely unnecessary to have anyone walking around for the cameras to focus on. Sam, that's true, isn't it? That's what you'd really, really like, isn't it?"

"Why, that's not true at all," Sam almost said; Haverman strained to hear him say that, and it seemed to him he was saying it, just outside the range of human hearing. He peered, and he craned his neck. But Sam was saying: "It's almost studio time, Dus. Have some wine," in his pleasant voice.

Haverman sighed. "Oh, all right, if that's the best you can do."

"My name is Austin Gelvarry," he repeated to Miss Montez, who was probably staring over his shoulder at the glistening, intricately decorated brass bed. "I have the power to call up whatever pleases me." He sipped from his glass, as she was doing. A nice light was developing in her eyes.

"I—seem to remember something different—"

"Have some more wine. It does no harm. It's strong drink that is raging," Gelvarry said, preoccupied, watching the little monkey plucking fruit from the bowl on the sideboard. The monkey caught his eye and winked.

"Listen," Miss Montez said, "It's just you can't find a secretary job anywhere anymore," but she was sipping.

Gelvarry smiled. Beyond her a Lockheed Electra was just touching down, crabbing a little in the wind as one might very well expect of so small an aircraft, even if it were an all-metal cabin twin. She settled in nicely, with just a spurt of blue smoke at the tires, and began to run out. He watched the pilot swing the Electra around deftly, and begin taxiing toward them.

"Do I please you, Austin?" Miss Montez said over the rim of her glass, looking at him through her lashes. She seemed quite nicely settled in now.

"Ah," Gelvarry said. "Ah." The Electra came to a halt and the cabin door popped open. A slim figure jumped down and waved, and began running toward them. "Here's Amelia!" Gelvarry exclaimed gladly.

A Ryan high-wing monoplane, lacking the reflection of sun on windscreen glass, came over low, light glittering at its engine-turned cowling. A figure waved down from a side window, and then the *Spirit of St. Louis* banked away to line up upwind, flaring out for its landing, its prominent wheels seeming to reach down for the ground against the red outline of the evening sun. Gelvarry and Miss Montez both half-rose with pleasure. "And here's Lucky Lindy now!"

SCIENCE FICTION BESTSELLERS FROM BERKLEY

Frank Herbert

DUNE	(03698-7—$2.25)
DUNE MESSIAH	(03930-7—$1.95)
CHILDREN OF DUNE	(03931-5—$2.25)

Philip José Farmer

THE FABULOUS RIVERBOAT	(03793-2—$1.75)
TO YOUR SCATTERED BODIES GO	(03744-4—$1.75)
NIGHT OF LIGHT	(03933-1—$1.75)

Robert A. Heinlein

STRANGER IN A STRANGE LAND	(03782-7—$2.25)
THE MOON IS A HARSH MISTRESS	(03850-5—$1.95)
TIME ENOUGH FOR LOVE	(03471-2—$2.25)
STARSHIP TROOPERS	(03787-8—$1.75)

Send for a list of all our books in print.

These books are available at your local bookstore, or send price indicated plus 30¢ for postage and handling. If more than four books are ordered, only $1.00 is necessary for postage. Allow three weeks for delivery. Send orders to:

Berkley Book Mailing Service
P.O. Box 690
Rockville Centre, New York 11570

FANTASY FROM BERKLEY

Robert E. Howard

CONAN: THE HOUR OF THE DRAGON	(03608-1—$1.95)
CONAN: THE PEOPLE OF THE BLACK CIRCLE	(03609-X—$1.95)
CONAN: RED NAILS	(03610-3—$1.95)
MARCHERS OF VALHALLA	(03702-9—$1.95)
ALMURIC	(03483-6—$1.95)
SKULL-FACE	(03708-8—$1.95)
SON OF THE WHITE WOLF	(03710-X—$1.95)

* * * * * * *

THE SWORDS TRILOGY (03468-2—$1.95)
  by Michael Moorcock

THONGOR AND (03435-6—$1.25)
THE WIZARD OF LEMURIA
  by Lin Carter

Send for a list of all our books in print.

These books are available at your local bookstore, or send price indicated plus 30¢ for postage and handling. If more than four books are ordered, only $1.00 is necessary for postage. Allow three weeks for delivery. Send orders to:
  Berkley Book Mailing Service
  P.O. Box 690
  Rockville Centre, New York 11570